PRAISE FOR VANESSA MILLER

THE LADIES HALL

"*The Ladies Hall* is a beautifully envisioned novel that invites readers into a richly drawn world that's too rarely seen in fiction. Through the stories of Mary Church Terrell, Anna Julia Cooper, and Ida Gibbs, author Vanessa Miller deftly captures the triumphs, defeats, compromises, and breakthroughs that marked Black women's experiences at integrated Oberlin College during a period of profound social change. Miller's words convey her heroines' courage and grit alongside their deeply human desires—for friendship, for love, for belonging, for purpose. *The Ladies Hall* gifts us a layered, unflinching portrait of three American heroines and their determination to reshape the world for the better."

—Ashton Lattimore, award-winning author of *All We Were Promised*

"In the 1880s, three Black women move into Ladies Hall residence at Oberlin College. The progressive college accepts Black students but for Mary, Anna, and Ida every day is a struggle to excel and prove themselves to their white classmates. Based on true characters, it's not an easy story to tell, but Vanessa Miller skillfully balances the women's friendships and genteel life on campus against the cruel realities of the era's pervasive—and sometimes deadly—racism. This inspiring and informative novel is a must-read."

—Janie Chang, bestselling author of historical fiction

"An important story of resilience and belonging. *The Ladies Hall* brings a vital chapter of history to life while reminding us that true progress means lifting others as we rise."

—Meagan Church, *New York Times* bestselling author of *The Mad Wife*

AF798037

"*The Ladies Hall* is a vivid and deeply moving portrait of Mary Church Terrell, Anna Julia Cooper, and Ida Gibbs Hunt as young women forging their identities at Oberlin College. Vanessa Miller captures both the barriers they faced and the brilliance they cultivated despite them. For those who honor the legacy of the NACWC, this novel resonates profoundly, revealing the early roots of 'Lifting as We Climb.' Miller offers not just history, but a celebration of Black women's resilience, sisterhood, and rising power."

—Denise E. Williams, 32nd National President, The National Association of Colored Women's Clubs, Inc.

"*The Ladies Hall*, the fictionalized account of Mary Church Terrell, Ida Gibbs Hunt, and Anna Julia Cooper's time at Oberlin, flung me, headlong, into reminiscences of my girlhood: crisp Easter clothes, the careful memorization of a monologue, a full-pewed church of elders, expectant that you will be great . . . and the trembly bravery of thinking you might be. Miller, in efficient, tender, and resonant manner, conjures how these women, just years removed from slavery, managed not only to graduate from this rigorous program but excel in the face of adversity, and this work made me feel immensely proud."

—Addie E. Citchens, author of *Dominion*

THE FILLING STATION

"The 1921 Tulsa Race Massacre is, shockingly, little more than a footnote in history—because history has always been written by white men. Miller's book, thankfully, reverses that egregious oversight. By making us live through the eyes of two sisters who suffered catastrophic loss, we viscerally learn how this vibrant Black community fought devastation with resilience, faith, and grit."

—Jodi Picoult, #1 *New York Times* bestselling author

In a novel that should be required reading, Miller (*The American Queen*) movingly explores the aftermath of racial trauma and how resilient people can open their hearts again."

—***Library Journal***

"Miller (*The American Queen*) doesn't shy away from the hardships the Justices face—racism, unscrupulous developers, sickness-inducing conditions in the rebuilding Greenwood—and Margaret's faith journey is hard-won and convincing. The Tulsa Race Massacre is rarely covered in historical fiction, and this story is an absolutely worthy addition to the genre.

—***Booklist***

"*The Filling Station* is a compelling contribution to the understanding of Black Wall Street and the 1921 Tulsa Race Massacre. The depth of research, coupled with Vanessa Miller's ability to bring these historical events to life, ensures that these stories are not only remembered but resonate with readers. So many of the names and places come to life in a way that makes me have to stop reading and process the fact that this event actually happened, and it happened in my community to people I have known."

—Michelle Burdex, program coordinator for Greenwood Cultural Center

THE AMERICAN QUEEN

"Readers are mesmerized by the incredible blend of hope, heartbreak, and determination in Louella's journey. *The American Queen* is about more than survival—it's about redefining what freedom truly means."

—Best Historical Fiction of 2024 from the She Reads editorial team

"Vanessa Miller's *The American Queen* is a rare untold novel showcasing a hidden gem of factual history about North Carolina's Queen Louella of the Kingdom of the Happy Land—the only queen that ruled on American soil. Inspirational and unforgettable, Miller weaves a fascinating story set in rugged Appalachia in a community built by emancipated formerly enslaved men and women."

—Kim Michele Richardson, *New York Times* bestselling author of The Book Woman of Troublesome Creek series

"The struggles in *The American Queen* resonate with contemporary issues, making the story not just a journey into the past but a reflection of our present and a hopeful vision for the future."

—Rhonda McKnight, author of *The Thing About Home*

"Vanessa Miller's page-turner *The American Queen* takes readers on a winding journey through the horrors and triumphs of the post–Civil War / Reconstruction era to show how a broken formerly enslaved woman transforms into an actual queen over her people. Louella Bobo Montgomery emerges from a Mississippi plantation with a vision of a 'happy land' where her people will live together in peace and with dignity. Turning that vision into a reality, however, tests the very foundations of her faith. *The American Queen* is a moving, heartwarming story that reminds us that all things are possible with faith, hope, love, and forgiveness."

—Kaia Alderson, author of *Sisters in Arms*

"Some books just feel inspired. You feel blessed for having read them. They feel like a gift. This is one of those books. *The American Queen* is definitely a story everyone should know, and a year from now, I have a feeling they will. Put it at the top of your bookstagram reading list."

—Jamie Ford, *New York Times* bestselling author of *The Many Daughters of Afong Moy*

"Miller (*The Light on Halsey Street*) captivates with a propulsive historical based on the true story of a group of formerly enslaved people who founded a utopian society in the Appalachian mountains in the 1860s . . . Readers will be won over by Louella's gumption, optimism, and tenacity. Miller brings to enthralling life a hidden gem in American history."

—*Publishers Weekly*

"*The American Queen* by Vanessa Miller is a rich, multilayered saga of a little-known true story that completely captivated me with one of the strongest and most compelling protagonists I've ever read. The dreams of Louella Montgomery were strong enough to infuse an entire community and carry them on the wings of hope off the plantation. I had to blink several times to come back to the present after finishing the last page of this wonderful novel. Everyone should read this book!"

—Colleen Coble, *USA TODAY* bestselling author

"Regal, self-possessed with inner strength and dignity—that's the portrayal of Louella Bobo Montgomery in Vanessa Miller's *The American Queen*. Miller crafts a stellar image of resilience, giving life to a little-known story of American royalty. There's something special, soul-stirring to read of a woman, a wife, a queen building a space with her husband and found family that makes a community's hope of freedom come true. Everyone should read *The American Queen* and be inspired."

—Vanessa Riley, award-winning author
of *Island Queen* and *Queen of Exiles*

"Queen Louella, the American Queen, is a character so richly drawn, she writes the story of American history. Born into slavery, robbed of her mother and family, Louella has no reason to love or be loved. However, the superb Vanessa Miller has created a new world of possibility and the story takes flight. The impossible path to forgiveness is as arduous as the road to freedom is for the enslaved. When Louella decides it's her world, one that she will make her own in emancipation, the sky opens up and rains hope. This novel is a triumph."

—Adriana Trigiani, bestselling author of *The Good Left Undone*

"*The American Queen* is beautifully told, a story rife with struggle, intrigue, and the indomitable spirit of a woman strong enough to carry the weight of a community, bold enough to dream the impossible, and determined enough to fashion dreams into reality. Louella Montgomery is a woman for the ages. I loved traveling alongside her and meeting the people of The Happy Land."

—Lisa Wingate, #1 *New York Times* bestselling author of *The Book of Lost Friends*

"*The American Queen* brings to light another hidden triumph in Black American history. Queen Louella is frankly a woman that everyone should know. Filled with bravery and cultural beauty, this marvel of a novel transported me while educating me on the sheer determination of an emancipated community to not only survive but also to thrive."

—Sadeqa Johnson, *New York Times* bestselling author of *The House of Eve*

THE LIGHT ON HALSEY STREET

"Dana Jones is just trying to survive in 1985 Brooklyn, which is a tough task while having a cocaine-addicted mother and a boyfriend who's a petty thief. Her best friend Lisa Whitaker lives just around the block but has a fairy-tale life and dreams of making a difference in her predominately African American Bedford-Stuyvesant neighborhood. One fateful night sets both young women on a path that seems unchangeable—one to prison, the other to college. Jumping ahead in time, Miller (*Something Good*) explores how one bad decision can change a life forever, but she also brings the main characters plenty of chances for redemption. Bedford-Stuyvesant, at once tight-knit and fractured, is practically a main character in this women's fiction offering, and many will recognize similar ebbs and flows in their own cities. VERDICT: Friendship and the power of community are the shining stars of this novel, which doesn't shy away from tough issues but also offers a hefty dose of hope and humor. Read-alikes include *Lean on Me* by Pat Simmons and *No One Ever Asked* by Katie Ganshert."

—Library Journal

"*The Light on Halsey Street* is an emotional story that takes you on an up close and personal journey across the decades with two friends. The plot is woven with friendship, forgiveness, and faith. An unforgettable read from cover to cover by Vanessa Miller."

—Tia McCollors, bestselling author

"Vanessa Miller's *The Light on Halsey Street* is women's fiction at its finest. Riveting and redemptive, *The Light on Halsey Street* vividly transports us back to 1980s Brooklyn with an unforgettable cast of characters and leaves you with the firm belief that light can truly never be extinguished by darkness."

—Joy Callaway, international bestselling author of *All the Pretty Places*

"Vanessa Miller set *The Light on Halsey Street* in Bedford-Stuyvesant, New York, but she takes readers on a decades-long exploration of the heart. In her coming-of-age story, two women learn about the impact of bitterness and resentment and the power of love to heal and restore what was lost. Readers will find it hard to put this novel down, and they'll hold on to these life lessons long after they turn the last page. Well done!"

—Robin W. Pearson, Christy Award–winning author

"Vanessa Miller delivers a poignant story of friendship and betrayal, bringing Lisa and Dana full circle, with an uplifting ending that proves there is power in prayer."

—Lacey Baker, *USA TODAY* bestselling author

"Vanessa Miller's latest, *The Light on Halsey Street*, reawakened memories of my own growing up in the neighborhood of Bedford-Stuyvesant in Brooklyn, which is a testament to her skill as a weaver of words. *The Light on Halsey Street* is not only a story of times gone by but the resiliency of friendship, family, and faith. This redemptive story of two friends, Lisa and Dana, poignantly demonstrates that we need not be a product of our circumstances and that the power to change is within all of us. Miller has created a timeless tale that will resonate long after the last word is read."

—Donna Hill, author of *Confessions in B-Flat* and *I Am Ayah: The Way Home*

"Vanessa Miller serves a heartfelt and fulfilling, Brooklyn, New York, literary buffet in this 1980s coming-of-age journey through friendships and hardships, all nourished by 'the Light on Halsey Street.'"

—Pat G'Orge-Walker, *Essence* and national bestselling author and creator of the Sister Betty Christian comedy series

WHAT WE FOUND IN HALLELUJAH

"Two sisters reunite with their mother in Hallelujah, S.C., in the satisfying latest from Miller (*Something Good*) . . . The result is a potent testament to the power of faith and family in the face of tragedy."

—*Publishers Weekly*

"Three strong women, family drama, secrets, and a setting that works masterfully with the plot—Vanessa Miller is at her best in this book! The complex, nuanced relationships between mothers and daughters captured my attention and drew me in from the very first chapters. This book is a heartwarming treat that will leave readers hopeful and singing their own Hallelujah praise!"

—Michelle Stimpson, author of *Sisters with a Side of Greens*

"In *What We Found in Hallelujah*, Vanessa Miller so brilliantly tells a heartwarming, page-turning, beautiful story about family secrets, mother-daughter relationships, forgiveness, and restored faith, and I thoroughly enjoyed this saga from beginning to end! So well done, Vanessa!"

—Kimberla Lawson Roby, *New York Times* bestselling author

"Vanessa Miller has created a soul-searching story in *What We Found in Hallelujah*. Her ability to weed through the hard topics with grace, humor, and family makes her stories like no other. I was invested in the characters and felt like praising with them in the end."

—Toni Shiloh, author of *In Search of a Prince*

"Vanessa lays a solid foundation for the fictional town of Hallelujah. Her characters are rich in diverse personalities. She layers the plot with an artistic flair that readers race to the finish line for the big 'reveal.' Redemption and reconciliation are sweet in Hallelujah."

—Pat Simmons, award-winning and national bestselling Christian author of the Jamieson Legacy series

SOMETHING GOOD

"The enjoyable if familiar latest from Miller (*Once Upon a Dream*) follows three women who are connected by a car accident . . . prayer for 'something good' brings together the three women in an unlikely friendship, changing hearts and restoring marriages . . . triumph of faith over tragedy will resonate with inspirational fans."

—Publishers Weekly

"*Something Good* by Vanessa Miller is a literary treat that captivated me from the first page. This story of three women drawn together by the unlikeliest of circumstances had me sitting back and realizing that no matter our backgrounds, no matter our struggles, when it's for God's purpose, we can come together. With characters that I could relate to and women who I wanted to win, I enjoyed *Something Good* from the beginning to the end."

—Victoria Christopher Murray, *New York Times* bestselling author of *The Personal Librarian*

"Vanessa Miller's thoughtful and anointed approach to crafting *Something Good* made for a beautiful page-turner full of depth and hope."

—Rhonda McKnight, award-winning author of *Unbreak My Heart*

"Vanessa Miller's latest novel is a relevant and heartwarming reminder that beauty for ashes is possible. This page-turning read inspires understanding, connection, and hope."

—Stacy Hawkins Adams, bestselling author

"This real-to-life story doesn't shy away from some hard issues of the modern world, but Miller is a master storyteller, who brings healing and redemption to her characters, and thus the reader, through the power of love and faith. I thoroughly enjoyed this book."

—Rachel Hauck, *New York Times* bestselling author

"Vanessa Miller's *Something Good* warms the heart with a vivacious tale of faith, redemption, and renewal. She masterly creates a sisterhood of unlikely friends who realize that there is something good, absolutely wonderful in accepting people as they are and believing they can be better."

—Vanessa Riley, bestselling author of *Island Queen*

"With bright threads of faith, resilience, and finding a way forward where there seems to be no way, Vanessa Miller weaves together the lives of three women in a beautiful tapestry of redemption and hope, friendship and found family. A story that shows, even when we think we've bolted all the doors, something good can find a way in."

—Lisa Wingate, #1 *New York Times* bestselling author of *Before We Were Yours*

"*Something Good* is much better than good. It's great! Vanessa Miller always delivers, and you know you will get unforgettable characters and a redemptive, heartwarming story that readers will find unputdownable. Get ready to laugh and to feel all the feels."

—Michelle Lindo-Rice, Harlequin Special Edition author

"Vanesa Miller's *Something Good* unveils the reality of living with guilt, shame, and the weight of unforgiveness through the lives of three women. This story will offer readers a beautiful perspective of redemptive healing and the measure of peace which comes with a forgiving heart."

—Jacquelin Thomas, national bestselling author of the Jezebel series and *Phoenix*

THE LADIES HALL

ALSO BY VANESSA MILLER

The Filling Station

The American Queen

The Light on Halsey Street

What We Found in Hallelujah

Something Good

THE LADIES HALL

A Novel

VANESSA MILLER

THOMAS NELSON
Since 1798

The Ladies Hall

Copyright © 2026 by Vanessa Miller

All rights reserved. No portion of this book may be reproduced, stored in a retrieval system, or transmitted in any form or by any means—electronic, mechanical, photocopy, recording, scanning, or other—except for brief quotations in critical reviews or articles, without the prior written permission of the publisher.

Published by Thomas Nelson, 501 Nelson Place, Nashville, TN 37214, USA. Thomas Nelson is a registered trademark of HarperCollins Christian Publishing, Inc.

Thomas Nelson titles may be purchased in bulk for educational, business, fundraising, or sales promotional use. For information, please email SpecialMarkets@ThomasNelson.com.

Publisher's Note: This novel is a work of fiction. Names, characters, places, and incidents are either products of the author's imagination or used fictitiously. All characters are fictional, and any similarity to people living or dead is purely coincidental.

Any internet addresses (websites, blogs, etc.) in this book are offered as a resource. They are not intended in any way to be or imply an endorsement by Thomas Nelson, nor does Thomas Nelson vouch for the content of these sites for the life of this book.

Without limiting the exclusive rights of any author, contributor or the publisher of this publication, any unauthorized use of this publication to train generative artificial intelligence (AI) technologies is expressly prohibited. HarperCollins also exercise their rights under Article 4(3) of the Digital Single Market Directive 2019/790 and expressly reserve this publication from the text and data mining exception.

HarperCollins Publishers, Macken House, 39/40 Mayor Street Upper, Dublin 1, D01 C9W8, Ireland (https://www.harpercollins.com)

Library of Congress Cataloging-in-Publication Data

Names: Miller, Vanessa author
Title: The ladies hall : a novel / Vanessa Miller.
Description: Nashville : Thomas Nelson, 2026. | Summary: "Based on the real lives of Mary Church Terrell, Anna Julia Cooper, and Ida Gibbs Hunt, The Ladies Hall is a mirror into times of great change--where progress and new possibilities are met with violence and resistance . . . but hope always rises. And it rises still"—Provided by publisher.
Identifiers: LCCN 2026012488 (print) | LCCN 2026012489 (ebook) | ISBN 9781400351107 paperback | ISBN 9781400351114 hardcover | ISBN 9781400351138 | ISBN 9781400351121 epub
Subjects: LCSH: Terrell, Mary Church, 1863-1954 | Cooper, Anna J. (Anna Julia), 1858-1964 | Hunt, Ida Gibbs, 1862-1957 | African American women civil rights workers | African American women suffragists | African American women—History—19th century | African American women—History—20th century | LCGFT: Fiction | Autobiographical fiction | Historical fiction
Classification: LCC PS3613.I5623 L33 2026 (print) | LCC PS3613.I5623 (ebook)
LC record available at https://lccn.loc.gov/2026012488
LC ebook record available at https://lccn.loc.gov/2026012489

Cover Design: James W. Hall
Interior Design: Tai Blanche

Printed in the United States of America

26 27 28 29 30 LBC 5 4 3 2 1

MAP OF OBERLIN COLLEGE

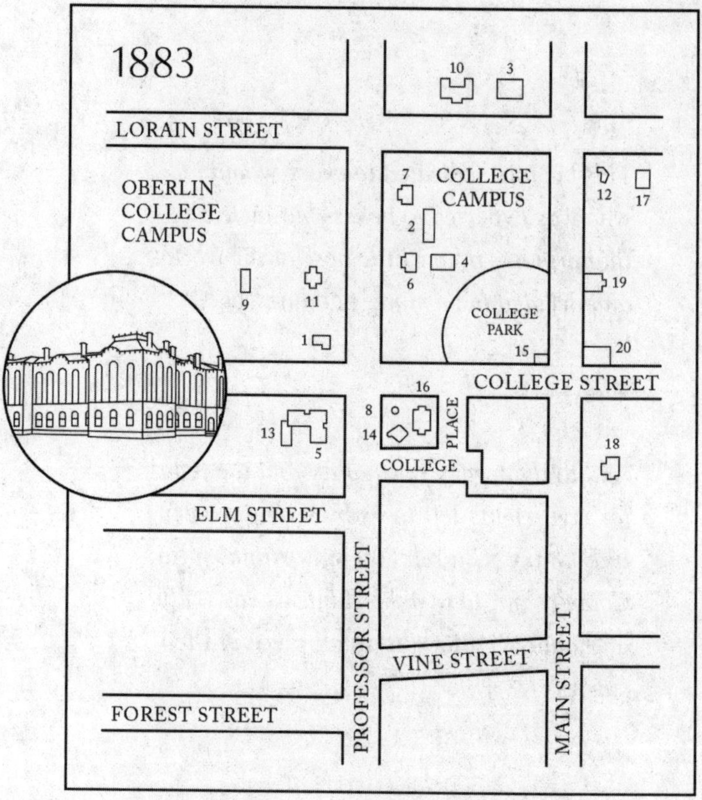

1. Mahan-Morgan House
2. Tappan Hall
3. First Congregational Church
4. College Chapel
5. Ladies Hall
6. French Hall
7. Society Hall
8. Solders' Monument
9. Men's Gymnasium
10. Council Hall
11. Cabinet Hall
12. Stewart Hall
13. Women's Gymnasium
14. Sturges Hall
15. Historic Elm
16. Second Congregational Church
17. Baptist Church
18. Central School Building
19. Town Hall
20. Hotel

This book is dedicated to every woman who was expected to be less but instead thumbed her pretty little nose at the world and decided to be more. I admire you!

And to the legacy of equality and the fight for civil rights left to us by strong women like Mary Church Terrell, Anna Julia Cooper, and Ida Gibbs Hunt. It was truly an honor writing this small piece of their stories.

A NOTE TO THE READER

Dear Reader,

When I first decided to write this novel, I had no clue that as the book would be released into the world, equality would be under attack again, nor did I know that over three hundred thousand Black women would be pushed out of their jobs, many of them career positions, to make way for White men, most of whom were not as qualified as the educated Black women they replaced . . . But here we are.

Mary Church Terrell and Anna Julia Cooper boldly fought for equality for women during a time when women could not vote or own property and had no say in "manly" decisions. Mary Church Terrell served as president of the National Association of Colored Women's Club, whose motto was "Lifting as We Climb."

Today, it appears that powerful men have decided that women have too much say in this country. If they can take away our job opportunities and limit our earning ability, they think we will behave. But I fear these men have missed the plot. Throughout history there have always been women who refused to be silent. I wrote this book because I want readers to see what standing up for equality looked like over a hundred years ago.

Equality then, equality now, equality forever—this will be our battle cry. And if we all join together, we will win this fight . . . again.

The Ladies Hall is for every woman who had a man tell her she couldn't but stood on business and did it anyway. For every Black woman who has stepped out in her excellence but has been told time and time again that she didn't earn the position but only received it due to some diversity initiative, when the fact remains that diversity initiatives wouldn't be necessary if racism didn't run rampant in this beautiful America.

Life hasn't been easy for Black folks in the United States, but we haven't given up. We're still shining like diamonds in a world that refuses to see our true value.

In this book I've used words such as *mulatto* and a few others that would not be acceptable in contemporary novels, but this is a historical novel and I believe I should use the language of the time period. You will also note that Mary Church Terrell uses the phrase "the dominant group" to describe White people in this novel. Based on research, this is a phrase she actually used in reference to the White race. Therefore, I introduce this theory in the novel to be true to her character. Mary once walked this earth in an excellent manner. I hope she and Anna come alive to you and that you begin to understand their struggles and triumphs and even the things that brought them sorrow. Those are the things that fueled them to change the mindset of a nation.

I pray you will enjoy this story that I sweated and pulled my hair out over. Once you close the book, I pray you understand equality in a more personal way than you've ever grasped it before. But most of all, I pray that you truly begin to see truth. And remember, the battle isn't over when one person succeeds, as Mary Church Terrell believed. We win when we lift as we climb, so let's all remember to lend a helping hand.

Thank you for reading,

Vanessa

If I could talk with all my white fellow-countrymen on the subject [of race], I would say to them, in the language of Scripture: "Come and let us reason together."

—Frederick Douglass, "The Color Line," 1881

PROLOGUE

Yellow Springs, Ohio
1874

Was it the color of skin or was it the fire in hate-filled eyes that stilled the march toward equality? Mary Church had never thought—never dreamed—that she was seen negatively through a stranger's eyes until the day she discovered a world where color defined.

"Mary, it's your turn to recite our history lesson," her teacher called out to her.

She was seated in her primary school classroom that held twenty students. She was the only student of color, though that was of no consequence to Mary, as she was a bright and bubbly standout in her class.

She walked to the front. Her teacher handed her a piece of paper and said, "God rest his soul, President Lincoln freed the slaves. And it is all documented in the Emancipation Proclamation." She nudged Mary forward. "Please read it in our hearing."

In all her eleven years of life, Mary had never studied the Emancipation Proclamation. She knew that Lincoln had freed the enslaved many, many years ago but had learned nothing further of the incident. She read the Southern states affected by the proclamation, including Arkansas, Texas, Louisiana, Mississippi, Alabama, Florida, and Georgia, and then continued:

"'And by virtue of the power, and for the purpose aforesaid, I do order and declare that all persons held as slaves within said designated States, and parts of States, are, and henceforward shall be free; and that the Executive government of the United States, including the military and naval authorities thereof, will recognize and maintain the freedom of said persons.'"

When Mary finished reading, her teacher said, "So, class, you see, Mary and her parents and grandparents were recipients of this great gift from President Lincoln."

At her teacher's words, Mary's head dipped back to the proclamation. She searched for the date. When? The year of her birth, 1863. Her father was born in Mississippi. If the emancipation didn't occur until 1863, then . . .

The truth swept over her in a dizzying wave as she stood in front of kids who laughed and learned beside her, kids who had many of the same likes and dislikes she had. Only one thing separated them.

They weren't descendants of enslaved humans . . . but she was.

Heat crept up Mary's neck. She could feel every eye on her, staring, waiting. White faces with green eyes and blue eyes.

Her hand trembled as she held on to that proclamation. Her parents never told her they had been enslaved. But for this piece of paper she held, she, too, would have toiled on a plantation as a slave. Shame burned not only for what her family had endured but for her own ignorance. How could she not have known?

Tears rushed down her olive-toned face. What must they think about the circumstances of her birth? Why was she in Yellow Springs instead of Memphis with people who were like her . . . people who looked like her . . . people who carried the shame of slavery . . . as she did.

Her eyes blurred with the pain of what everyone else had already known about her. She let the paper fall to the floor and then ran out of the room. Opening the door of the schoolhouse, she went to the home where her father had procured her a room.

Mr. and Mrs. Vaughan were upstanding members of the community. Her father would only allow her to stay with quality people. But they were in their forties and Colored, so they must have been enslaved, as her parents had been.

"Mary, are you okay?" Mrs. Vaughan asked as she entered the home.

"I'm fine." Mary ran up the stairs and slammed the door behind her. Once she stepped into her room, she flopped on the bed, brought her knees up to her chest, and let the tears flow again. How could she go back to that school with overwhelming humiliation clinging to her like a second skin she couldn't peel away, no matter how hard she tried?

She stayed in that spot until the sun set. Her tears had dried and she'd calmed enough to go downstairs to eat her supper. All the while thinking of the White kids she went to school with, kids who were never owned by anyone. Kids who weren't descendants of slaves.

Mrs. Vaughan glanced across the table at her. "Your father placed you under our care, and I consider it my personal duty to help with whatever ails you."

Mr. Vaughan cut in, saying, "We can't do that if you won't talk to us."

Mary put her fork on the plate, placed her hands in her lap, and cleared her throat. "My father never told me that he had once been enslaved. Or that I'm the descendant of former slaves. I discovered that in school today, and . . . and it left me stunned and disgraced before my classmates."

Mr. and Mrs. Vaughan's heads swiveled toward each other. Mrs. Vaughan's mouth parted as if to speak, but no sound came. Mr. Vaughan frowned, his brows knitting. A beat passed between them, thick with uncertainty. Then Mrs. Vaughan asked in the gentlest fashion, "You didn't know?"

Lump forming in her throat, Mary shook her head. She gulped back the weight of it all. "I don't know how I'll ever be able to face my classmates after this."

"You'll face them with your head held high," Mr. Vaughan told her. "Your father is one of the richest Black men in this country. He has done well for himself, and no one can take that away from you. He is respected, and you will be respected as well."

Hearing those words helped Mary regain her composure. She went back to her bedroom with the resolve that even as a descendant of slaves, she would show her White classmates that she was their equal. Never again would she bow her head low to any of them.

Part 1

CROSSING THE COLOR LINE

Few evils are less accessible to the force of reason, or more tenacious of life and power, than a long-standing prejudice. It is a moral disorder, which creates the conditions necessary to its own existence, and fortifies itself by refusing all contradiction.

—Frederick Douglass, "The Color Line," 1881

CHAPTER 1

Raleigh, North Carolina
July 1880

Clouds drifted over Raleigh, gliding across the sky like memories gone by, swallowing joy and any semblance of resolve Anna Julia Cooper's heart could hold. Would she ever hear back from Oberlin College? Would there ever be distance from this misery?

"George, oh George," she whispered through trembling lips, her voice barely rising above the ache in her chest. She pressed a handkerchief to her cheek, but the tears refused to cease. Her body bent under the weight of longing and loneliness too heavy for one heart to carry.

Her beloved had died a year ago. The wound remained fresh, raw and gaping. Each morning she awoke to silence where his voice once lived, and each night she clutched his memory as grief soaked through her pillow, seeping into her soul. She was untethered, unmoored. Drifting through a world that no longer made sense without him.

Two years of marriage and nothing to hold on to but a hollow ache and fading memories. No child to cradle in her arms, only a grave site to visit.

Her husband, her George, was gone.

The silence he left behind screamed louder than any cry. Most mornings, she had to will her body to rise . . . to dress . . . to move.

The only thing that gave her purpose now was her work with the children at St. Augustine's Normal School. They were the only light in her otherwise shadowed days. Still, the tears came hot, bitter, and unrelenting. The saltiness clung to her lips like a cruel reminder. Her love, her one and only, her future, now lay beneath the earth, his casket swallowed by the dust that had no mercy.

Her husband had no headstone to mark his grave. Anna was left to remember her steps to find the correct spot where her dear George lay. Grass grew on the mound of dirt they'd placed over his casket. Soon she would have trouble finding the burial site. The sheer poverty that was her lot in life was also her shame.

Being paid a hundred dollars a year to tutor the Colored children in her community, along with her small salary from St. Augustine's, would hardly afford her the Paris trip she'd been dreaming about ever since she received the top scores in her history and language classes.

The books she read opened her eyes to other countries besides America. Places where no one knew her name or the circumstances of her birth. Anna let out a huff. Dreaming would get her nowhere.

Blowing her nose, she fixed her eyes on the dirt and grass

that covered her husband. "I'm sorry for thinking on such things when I can't even afford a proper headstone."

Placing a hand over her stomach, she turned away from the love she'd thought would last a lifetime and made her way back to St. Augustine's to work on her lesson plan. Work was good. Work was children who needed her. Work was days with something to do.

The children of the formerly enslaved came to St. Augustine's to receive instruction in reading, writing, and mathematics. It was her pleasure to teach in whatever capacity they allowed. She herself had become a student here when she was nine years old.

If Reverend Brinton hadn't offered her a scholarship for St. Augustine's, she wouldn't have been able to attend school at all. Her mama needed help with the washing she did for the rich White folks, but she didn't want to stand in Anna's way.

"I've never seen a child as smart as you," her mama said while wiping worn hands on her apron. "Where you get that brain?"

At nine Anna wondered about all sorts of things. Her mother couldn't read as well as Anna could. But no one had taught her. Anna's mother was smart in other ways, like cooking and managing the house and handling them White folks that came around, trying to get free services. Her mama had a way of saying no with sprinkles of sugar on top.

But maybe reading had come easy to her daddy. Maybe he was book smart like her. "Do you think I get my brain from my daddy?"

Her mama, Hannah Haywood, placed the iron she'd been using to take the wrinkles out of the sheets she'd recently washed and dried for Mr. George Haywood down on the board. She put her hands in the pockets of her apron and sucked air through her teeth. "You know better than that. As far as things go 'round here, you don't have no daddy. It's you, me, and your brother, and that's all it's ever gon' be."

"Yes, Mama." Anna lowered her head. She didn't know why her mama kept such secrets from her. Most days when she played with the kids in the yard, they teased her about not knowing who her daddy was. They guessed it was either Mr. George, the man who'd enslaved her mother, or his brother, Mr. Fabius.

Anna had stayed in the house reading books rather than go outside and watch other kids walk down the street with their daddies . . . play catch with their daddies . . . or get a whupping for back-talking from their daddies. It had been easier to stay inside and read rather than see so many daddies when she had none. Maybe that was how she got so smart.

Leaving St. Augustine's for the day, Anna chided herself for thinking on past troubles. She headed to the post office as she'd been doing for the last two months, praying that each day would bring the correspondence she'd been waiting for. Her mind was jumbled with thoughts that complicated life here in Raleigh. She loved teaching children and was thankful she'd been allowed to do so, even while married.

Most women were forced to quit working after marriage. George, who had been a man of the cloth, didn't mind that she continued teaching. The money was useful and she had needed something to fill her days while he handled his ministry duties. Now she needed something to fill her nights. Again, she chose books.

Crossing the street, she had almost made it to the post

office when the door to the bank opened and out walked Dr. Fabius Haywood Sr. with his son.

She froze. She should say something. Should demand he tell the truth her mother never could. But something molasses-like once again glued her mouth shut as it did whenever she came within inches of the Haywood clan. The two men walked past her as if she were something to be sidestepped.

Anna's heart constricted. She exhaled and went inside the post office, preparing herself for the usual "No mail today." She was fourth in line, then third. The postal clerk told the woman, "Sorry, nothing from your husband in over a month." Tears rolled down the woman's cheeks as she walked away with knowing in her eyes.

Get out of the line. You're asking for disappointment. The clerk handed a stack of mail to another customer. Anna shuffled her feet, trying to determine whether she should walk away or take her chances with the clerk.

As Anna stood between *always*, *maybe*, and *this time will be different*, the clerk glanced over at her. "Anna, I've got something for you today." He held up a finger, then rushed into the back, reappearing with a white envelope from Oberlin College.

Anna's hands hesitated. The weight of her future delivered in such a small package. She wanted to rip it open and let the contents spill forth. What if they rejected her? What if twenty-three was too old for a woman to begin college? What if they simply said no, essentially telling her she wasn't good enough for a college that accepted both White and Black students? Better to open it at home where she could cry without alerting outsiders of her failings.

Her heart was aflutter with fear and anticipation when she arrived home. She sat down on her bed and opened the envelope, hands still trembling as she slid out the single sheet of paper. Pushing aside heartbreak and letdowns, she unfolded the letter. The correspondence that would determine so much.

Her eyes trailed across "Congratulations, you have been accepted . . ." She screamed.

"Girl, what's wrong with you?" her mother called from the kitchen.

Anna jumped up from the bed, heart pounding like a drum. She burst into the kitchen, clutching the letter in her hands. "Mama!" she cried, her voice catching with disbelief and joy. "Mama, look!"

She thrust the letter forward, barely able to contain herself. Her mother, who'd allowed Anna to teach her to read years ago, gently pulled the letter from Anna and scanned the words with wide, watering eyes.

"I've been accepted into Oberlin," Anna whispered, as if saying it too loud might make it vanish. "They want me, Mama. Me. Can you believe it?"

Tears spilled down her cheeks. After the struggles, the silence, the sacrifices . . . this. Her name on that letter was like a doorway cracking open. Her mother's lips quivered into a proud, tearful smile, and Anna fell into her arms. The two of them wrapped in the moment, wrapped in history, wrapped in hope.

"I had no doubt you'd be accepted." Mama pursed her lips as her old argument rose up, and she handed the letter back. "I don't understand why you have to go so far away from home."

"It's a respected college. The fact that their doors are

open to Black students as well as Whites is the challenge I've dreamed of." She needed this, needed to prove to herself that she was as good as the people who wouldn't even speak when they passed her on the street.

"But why can't you continue your studies at St. Augustine's? You already teach the younger students. Why not attend their college? They done good by you."

"Oberlin has a music department. I love music as much as languages." Competing with White students was almost as important as the music and language classes, but she wouldn't tell her mother that.

Her mother continued, "If you're tired of them folks at St. Augustine's, what about Shaw University? Colored folks in Raleigh are proud of that school. And you're thumbing your nose at it, in favor of that White school hundreds of miles away. Don't seem right, is all."

Anna's heart ached every morning she woke up in the place that had caused her so much pain. Instead of telling her mother all the secrets her heart held, she said, "Being here hurts too much."

Mama patted Anna's hand. "It's a right shame that man died on you like that. But this still your home."

Anna stepped back. "If I stay here, I'll suffocate and die. I'm miserable." She flung her hands in the air. "And this isn't about my dead husband. It's everything in and about this town."

"What's gon' be different at Oberlin? Why you have to go up north for your education?"

Anna was tired of the South and its order and way of doing things. Her chest heaved as little-girl pain trampled her heart. "I passed Dr. Fabius while he walked down the street with his son. Neither of them gave me a smile or even the slightest greeting. I'm invisible to the Haywoods. And I hate them for that."

Mama put a hand over her mouth and her belly. She seemed to shrink an inch. Sighing deeply, she shifted her tear-stained face from her daughter. "Then you must hate me too."

Anna gulped a sharp intake of breath. "No! Don't think that. I could never hate you." She rushed to her mother and wrapped her arms around the woman who had raised her the best she could. There were days when she thought her mother cold and unyielding. But her mother had allowed her to be educated. She hadn't wanted Anna to only have ambitions of being a washerwoman.

"I live with such shame . . ." Mama began.

But Anna shook her head. "We carry too much shame that doesn't belong to us. Let it go, Mama. It's not yours."

Her mother wiped her eyes and held on to Anna real tight. When she let her go, Mama opened a cabinet above the kitchen counter. She pulled down one of the tin cans they normally collected bacon grease in, opened it, and grabbed a fistful of dollars and coins.

She turned Anna's hand palm up and placed the money there. "I been saving this. It's seven dollars. All I have in this world. Take it with you up north."

Anna glanced around the kitchen. A bucket sat on the floor to collect water when the roof leaked. The floorboards in the living room were squeaky, and the sofa had tears on the armrest. "I can't take this money. Too many things need fixing in this house that the landlord isn't taking care of."

Her mother pressed the money into Anna's hands and stepped back. "No need for you to concern yourself about this house. You go on to that school and come back here and take over as principal of St. Augustine's. Wouldn't that be something? A former slave girl running a schoolhouse."

Pride filled her mother's eyes, and for that reason Anna held her tongue. But she didn't want to be in this place where she would forever be a fatherless child. She wanted to fly far away from here and experience life as Anna Julia Cooper. Not the former slave girl. Not the girl whose dead husband resided six feet under with no headstone to mark his grave. Not someone to ignore.

Anna needed to be seen for who she was.

CHAPTER 2

Oberlin, Ohio
September 1880

Mary Elza Church stood motionless outside Ladies Hall at Oberlin College, her breath caught between awe and disbelief. The golden light of early evening bathed her skin, now burnished two shades deeper than its usual olive hue, a proud mark of her summer spent under an unrelenting sun that had kissed her face like a grandmother's love. No one could mistake her for anything other than what she was, a Negro woman with high standards and a brilliant mind.

She raised a hand to shield her eyes, gazing up at the imposing redbrick giant before her. Ladies Hall rose three stories high, solid and immovable like the promise of a future within reach. Its imposing structure anchored the corner of Professor and College Streets like a sentinel of learning, standing watch over all who dared to dream inside its walls.

Across the street, College Park stretched out in full autumn glory, its canopy of trees swaying gently in the breeze like a choir in praise. Students drifted along the winding paths with books under their arms and ideas in their eyes. The grass was manicured to perfection, soft, green, almost too perfect. As Mary took a slow, deliberate step forward, it struck her: She was here. She had arrived. Not as an exception. Not as a shadow. But as a force.

Inhaling the aroma of freshly cut grass, Mary glanced to the left of Ladies Hall and spotted the women's gymnasium. Everything she needed was right here on campus. Her freshman year was beginning and she was delighted to conquer new territory.

While taking her preparatory classes, Mary lived at a boardinghouse in Oberlin. She would've happily stayed with her boarders and walked through town to get to her classes, but her father wanted her to experience college life, connect with more students. They might be useful contacts later in life, he'd told her. Mary had wanted to object. She didn't care about contacts for some future purpose she didn't know about. She liked being at the Vaughans' boardinghouse and was thankful they had moved from Yellow Springs to Oberlin when she transitioned from primary to preparatory school. But saying no to Robert Reed Church simply wasn't done.

When she wasn't in Oberlin, she loved being in Memphis, Tennessee, with her family and loved being called Mollie, a nickname given to her by her father. Robert Church had climbed his way out of poverty by working several odd jobs; then when yellow fever struck Memphis, killing thousands of its residents, he purchased homes and land for pennies on the dollar. Reselling those homes after the plague brought him great fortune. Her mother, Louisa, owned a hair salon.

Due to their parents' wealth, Mary and her brother, Thomas, wanted for nothing. So if her father thought living at Ladies Hall was best, Mary would do that. But sometimes she wondered how useful connecting with educated women was in a world that had little use for women outside of the home.

"Why are you standing out here staring at the building when the movers are here?" her roommate asked.

With a spark of joy, Mary told her, "Thinking about writing a poem about our first day on campus."

Ida grabbed Mary's arm and pulled her forward. "Let's unpack and then you can write as many poems as your heart desires."

Ida Gibbs's father was wealthy like Mary's. Judge Mifflin Wistar Gibbs made his money through his law practice and real estate. He also served as a politician, becoming the first Black judge ever appointed to the position in the United States. The fact that they were only seventeen years from the Emancipation Proclamation and there were numerous well-off Black families in America spoke volumes as to what could be accomplished through hard work and God's blessings.

A few White students ran up to Ladies Hall as Ida pulled Mary toward the door. They were full of laughs and giggles. Mary recognized one them from the summer program, and she waved. "Hey, Katherine."

Katherine was tall with long blonde hair she wore in a bun atop her head. "Hey, Mary . . . Ida." She waved and kept running into the house and up the stairs.

This was Mary's and Ida's first year of studies for the four-year Classical Gentlemen's Course. While Oberlin was a coeducational college, most of the women were enrolled in the less academically rigorous two-year Ladies' Course. Those taking the Ladies' Course would only receive a certificate at the end of studies, while a bachelor of arts degree was awarded to those in the Classical Gentlemen's Course.

In fact, the freshman class at Oberlin consisted of sixty-five men and only fifteen women who dared to take the Gentlemen's Course.

Chaos ensued all around as girls ran in and out of the building, bringing furniture and clothes. The men Mary's and Ida's fathers had hired to move their dressers and other furniture into their dorm room headed up to the second floor.

"Don't drop that armoire. It was made special for me, and I plan to pass it down to my children," Ida said as the heavy piece of furniture almost slipped from a mover's grasp. She followed the men up the stairs and directed them to the room.

Mrs. Johnston, the principal of the Ladies' Department and housemother of Ladies Hall, stood tall and lean in the middle of the gathering room, waving her hands and shouting, "Ladies! Ladies! Let me have your attention." The gathering room was the first area students came to as they entered the Ladies Hall. It held three full-sized sofas. One faced the fireplace, while the other two were on opposite sides of the room, facing each other.

In the midst of situating belongings and greeting old friends, everyone glanced in Mrs. Johnston's direction. Once the room quieted, she said, "Welcome back to Ladies Hall to our returning students. For many of you this is your first year living amongst so many other women. It will be an adjustment, but we will all work together to make you feel right at home." She glanced around the room, daring anyone to disagree.

About a hundred students lived in Ladies Hall. The majority of the girls were White; six were Black. Of those six only two were enrolled in the Classical Gentlemen's Course: Mary and Ida.

Mary had attended school with White students since she was eight years old. Along the way she had developed friendships with some of the students in her primary and preparatory classes. The residents of Oberlin, Ohio, were welcoming, friendly, and warm. But this was the first time she would be living among so many people who were of a different race than she and from different places around the country.

One of the new girls eyed her curiously. Mary gulped down a bit of nerves while silently praying that the ladies in this massive dormitory would be like the residents of Oberlin.

"As you all can see, our home is large enough to house a hundred women. The second and third floors are where you will find the dormitories. There is to be no male visitation in those rooms."

A few girls giggled at that.

Mrs. Johnston continued, "My office is on the first floor"—she pointed to the left—"down that hallway. If you need anything, I'm available unless I'm meeting with another student. Please be considerate."

One of the girls lifted her hand. Mrs. Johnston acknowledged her. "Do we need to make an appointment, or can we knock on your door?"

"Great question." Mrs. Johnston tucked a wayward strand of brown hair back into the bun atop her head. "You can do both."

Ida came back down the stairs. She walked over to Mary with a lifted brow. "What's going on?"

"Mrs. Johnston is giving us the lay of the land." Mary looped an arm around Ida's so the girl wouldn't follow the movers back up to their room when they brought in the next piece of furniture. She rather liked the fact that she was no longer the only Colored girl in the room.

"The dining room is to the right." Mrs. Johnston gestured in that direction. "We also have the society room on the first floor. That room is used for our women's literary societies' teas and debates. We have an assembly room and a reading room on this floor as well. If I should request to meet with all of you at once, please meet me in the assembly room."

Mrs. Johnston provided a few other instructions and then said, "You will have fun this year, ladies. The opening social for the school will be held in Ladies Hall. President Fairchild will also host a community reception here. And the faculty will take tea here as well. You all will have plenty of opportunities to become acquainted with your teachers and community leaders."

"Maybe we can talk them out of giving hard tests," one of the students said, and several girls around her laughed.

Mrs. Johnston grinned at that. "You can try. I'm not sure if that plan will work for you, though."

When the impromptu meeting was over, everyone went back to gathering their items and taking them to their rooms. Mary took a suitcase in her hand as she told Ida, "Sounds like we made the right decision to live here. We'll definitely be able to curry favor with some of our professors."

"Don't know if I can trust favor with some of these professors. I'd rather study and make my grades."

"Of course I'm going to study. But it's always nice to have an edge over the other students."

"Come on." Ida waved her toward the stairs. "Let's get our room in order."

Privilege and proximity were being laid before them like a feast before kings. Mary was beginning to see why her father wanted her here rather than at the Vaughans'. "Yes, let's get organized."

She walked up the stairs and entered her new room. There was a woodburning stove toward the back, which would come in handy during the cold winter months. Two beds, one on the left side and the other on the right. Both Mary and Ida had their own dressers and desks.

The movers had thrown things in the room without thought to proper placement. Clothes and shoes were strewn across their beds, and knickknacks were scattered on the floor. "We have class tomorrow. There's no way this room will be put together in time."

If only she could borrow her housekeeper from home, this room would be organized in a flash. Mary would have to speak with her father about the manner in which her move was handled. But for now, she would fold her clothes the way she was taught and put them away in her dresser. One thing at a time.

CHAPTER 3

"Test? But this is only the second day of class. How can he possibly schedule a test this week?" Seated in the front row of her philosophy class, Mary bit down on her bottom lip and scratched her earlobe.

"I didn't expect this either." Ida closed her book and stood.

As they walked out of the lecture hall, Mary confided, "I have a mathematics quiz tomorrow and two chapters to outline for science." How on earth was she supposed to get all of this done?

Ida chewed on her fingernail. "We need a study group or something."

As they passed by the men's gymnasium, the door swung open and a burst of laughter spilled out, along with the smell of sweat and soap. A few men jogged past in white shorts and gray shirts, but two stopped right in front of them.

The dark-skinned one, with a cleft chin and brown eyes that glowed at the edges of his pupils as if they could read secrets, smiled and held out a hand to Mary. "Didn't I see you at chapel the other day?"

Mary's pulse jumped, but she tilted her chin, pretending not to care. "I don't remember you." Of course she remembered him. Those eyes were impossible to forget.

The other man introduced himself to Ida. She gave a polite "Nice to meet you" and clutched her books tighter.

"I'm Mason," the one in front of Mary said. "Would the two of you like to take a walk with us?"

Ida's hand shot out and hooked Mary's arm. "Our parents didn't send us to college to go on walks with boys when we have studying to do."

Mary let herself be pulled, though every step away from him felt like defiance in the wrong direction. She glanced back. Mason was still standing there, watching her. When he waved, she let a smile flicker, quick and teasing.

"Hey!" he called. "You didn't give me your name!"

"Mary!" she called back, heat rising in her cheeks.

"Don't be so fresh," Ida scolded. "You don't even know that boy."

Mary pressed her lips together to hide a grin. Not knowing him had nothing to do with a lack of wanting. "Did you see his eyes?" she whispered. "Like something out of Greek mythology. Zeus, maybe."

"Would you please focus?" Ida sighed. "If I get a low mark, I'll never hear the end of it from my father."

Mary adjusted the strap of her satchel. "We can handle our studies and have a little fun. College isn't supposed to be a convent."

Mary had been the smartest girl in her primary and preparatory classes. She understood the necessity of studying, and she wouldn't let Ida down. They opened the door to

Ladies Hall. Girls gathered in small clusters, books open or gossip in full swing. Mary sighed, glancing around. Maybe she could balance both worlds—the sensible and the thrilling. "We might find a few girls to study with in here," she said, as much to convince herself as Ida.

Ida motioned toward the back of the room. "I recognize her. She's in our philosophy class."

With her books in one hand, Mary used the other to pull Ida forward. In her haste to get to the other side of the room, she bumped into Suzie McFarland.

"Watch where you're going." Suzie jabbed a finger toward the floor where her bread, ham, tomatoes, and pickles were sprawled.

"I'm so sorry. I didn't see you," Mary said.

"I told Mrs. Johnston that you people would dirty up this place, and look at you." Suzie glared at her. "Pick it up!"

You people. Mary crossed her arms and leaned back, studying the girl. Her behavior was as familiar as the sting of cold splashing water on winter mornings. Suzie's cheeks were blotched red from the heat of self-importance. The scent of vinegar from the pickles mixed with the sharp tang of sawdust on the floor, biting at Mary's nose.

She didn't move. Murmurs from the students drifted around the room, while silence stretched taut like a rope between Mary and Suzie. Suzie shifted her weight, her shoes creaking against the wood planks.

Mary's eyes dropped to the sandwich, its contents bleeding into the wood, then rose again, filled with determination. The pulse in her throat steadied. "No," she said, her voice low and unbothered.

Suzie's thin lips snarled. The tick of the wall clock filled the room, loud and hollow. Mary bent, not to gather the food, but to retrieve a small scrap of notepaper that had fallen from her book. She brushed it clean and walked away, leaving Suzie standing in the middle of the room, green eyes bulging, with the mess at her feet.

After that incident in the gathering room, Mary and Ida chose not to seek out a study group. They went to their room and dug into their books. Later that week, Mary received an A on her math quiz and an A on the philosophy test. She then presented a poem to her literature professor. It was not as flowery as she had first imagined her "Ode to Oberlin" poem would be.

"Beautiful prose. The first four stanzas are glowing, but as we come to the end of your verses, it seems as if you're trying to convince yourself of your original thought."

"I'm a mood writer," she told her professor.

On the walk back to her dorm, her steps slowed. The whole scene with that awful girl played again in her head—the sharp words, the hate on Suzie's face. Maybe it wasn't as bad as she'd made it. Maybe she had let it cling to her longer than it deserved.

With a sigh she made her way to the parlor. The week's tests were behind her, and the hum of voices inside sounded almost like permission to let it go.

About five White students were on one side of the room in deep discussion. Another group of students were on the right. Mary took a seat in the center. She spotted Katherine in the entryway and waved her over. A few other students arrived as well, full of laughs and good cheer. Mary was the only

Colored student present, but that didn't dissuade her from taking a respite from her studies.

"Tell us about Strasbourg," Katherine said as the group settled in.

"Strasbourg?" Mary grinned. "Where to begin?"

One by one other students appeared and found their way to the group of their choice. A few others joined Mary and Katherine, and their group closed up until they were a compact island in the middle of the room.

One of the girls snapped her fingers. "You went with your parents, right? That's the last thing I remember you saying during our summer program."

"With my parents and my wits," Mary said, theatrical and unapologetic. "I got lost, I danced with strangers, I nearly ruined a wedding cake—"

A chorus of groans and delighted protests followed. Katherine clapped her hands together while another girl pretended to faint.

"She's impossible," another student said, smiling. "But I can't not listen."

Mary leaned forward, hands painting the air; the group leaned with her as she continued her story. When she paused for effect, many in the group laughed at her antics. Attention was the currency; Mary spent it lavishly and left everyone richer for it.

"You're a card," one of the newcomers said to Mary with an extended hand. "I'm Janet Huntington McKelvey. I hope you don't mind that I joined the group."

"Janet's the president of the Aeolian Literary Society," Katherine told her.

Mary shook Janet's hand. "I don't mind at all, but you must be fun and participate to be a part of this group."

"I don't know if I'm as fun as you, but I'll try."

The group continued with their jovial discussions until 7:30 p.m. rolled around and it was time to vacate the room so students could study. As they rushed out, Janet hung back and walked with Mary.

"You're engaging, Mary. I enjoyed listening to your stories."

"I enjoyed your stories as well." The two continued down the hall as naturally as if the world had never drawn lines between them.

Had her father been right about Ladies Hall? Was this the place she would make connections that could last a lifetime? Were most of the girls in her dormitory like Janet, or were they like that nasty Suzie McFarland? Only time would tell, but Mary would rise to the occasion; she always had.

CHAPTER 4

As Anna packed her bag, a smile tugged at her lips. Her mother had sewn three new dresses from scraps of cotton, leftovers from patching up the gowns of society ladies. Tucked neatly beside them were two freshly laundered chemises and two petticoats: one plain and narrow for everyday wear, the other full and billowing, meant to lend grace and fullness to her Sunday best. Anna touched the soft fabric, marveling at how much care her mother had stitched into the seams.

Anna had always dreamed of wearing a white dress to Sunday service, something soft yet crisp, like the fine ladies wore. But the only white fabric her mother had left was set aside for her undergarments. Only plain brown cotton remained for her dresses. That morning, she wore a pleated skirt and a button-down bodice of the same coarse cloth. The sleeves were long and serviceable, without a puff, frill, or stitch of embroidery. Nothing that hinted at finery, only what was necessary.

Stepping back from her bag, Anna clasped her hands together. "That's that. I'm ready, I think."

Her brother, Rufus, took her bags and put them in the wagon he'd borrowed from Dr. Fabius. If Anna had any other way of getting to her new school, she would have told Rufus to take that wagon right back where he got it from.

Mama pulled her into an embrace, then quickly backed away. "You go on now." Putting a hand to her mouth, eyes watering, her mother rushed back into the house.

Rufus rolled his eyes heavenward as he helped Anna into the wagon. "She acts like you're never coming back."

As they rode away from the rented house, Anna wished she could turn her back on Raleigh forever. "I'm sure I'll be back. But I'm not so sure I'll want to see this place again."

Rufus nodded. "You get all the book learning you can. Might not have to come back with all them doors opening for Colored folks in the North."

"I'm surprised to hear you talk like that. You're always so spirited about this so-called new South, which doesn't seem much different from the old South in my estimation."

The scent of pine hung thick in the autumn air. Rows of tobacco stretched across the fields like patchwork quilts. A pair of hawks circled overhead as the tall, swaying longleaf pines whispered in the breeze.

Holding on to the reins while the horse-drawn buggy moved them farther and farther from their hometown, Rufus told her, "I only talk like that so the folks in these parts don't get jittery around me . . . start wondering if I'm going to do to them what they done to us."

Anna shoved her brother's arm. "Hush with that kind of talk. You're not a violent man. They have no fear of retribution from you."

Rufus took one hand off the reins and lifted it heavenward. "God's truth, some days I wish I was."

Ann shifted in her seat. "I'm glad you're not. Hate seeing what these White men do to our Colored men when they feel they've gotten beside themselves."

"No need to worry about me. Sooner or later, I'm getting out of here too." He flicked the reins as the buggy rattled along the red clay road. "Getting my plans together now, but you wait and see. Your brother's gon' start a musical band, and we're going to tour all over this country."

She had no doubt he would succeed. Rufus was a musical genius. "Send me a ticket. I want to be in the front row for your first concert."

Rufus grinned like a kid receiving a compliment from his teacher on penmanship. "You'll get that ticket. I promise you that."

Since they had to stop along the way to rest the horses and water and feed them, they expected the journey to take between fifteen and twenty days as they made their way through North Carolina, Virginia, and West Virginia on their way to Ohio.

Anna didn't mind the beat of the sun during the day, her bonnet providing some protection. Nor did she mind nights spent sleeping on the wooden bed of the wagon. She bore it all good-naturedly.

But on the tenth day of their journey, passing through

Virginia, Anna asked Rufus to stop at the general store so she could get them both a treat with some of the money her mother had given her.

"I don't know; we're not from around these parts. Might be best to keep moving."

Their mother had made a basket of fried chicken for their journey. But they'd eaten all of that several days ago. Now Rufus was catching critters or going fishing when they stopped. They'd set a fire at night and cook whatever he caught, fill their bellies, and then go to sleep. "Don't be silly. You deserve something special for all the trouble you're enduring."

Rufus loved peppermint sticks and taffy. Candy was a luxury they simply couldn't afford often. But Anna wanted to spend a few cents on something that would bring him enjoyment.

As Anna stepped out of the general store, the paper bag warmed her palm, its crinkle a small, secret song. The smell of sugar and spice trailed after her, sweet as the smile tugging at her lips. She was already thinking of sharing the treats with Rufus when her gaze caught on a figure by the wagon.

A White man.

His arm sliced the air, finger stabbing toward Rufus like an accusation. The sound around her dimmed—the creak of wagon wheels, the chatter from the porch—all of it swallowed by the fear tick-tick-ticking in her head. Her throat tightened, as if the air itself had turned to clay. The bag sagged in her hand.

No. Please no.

Her heartbeat thudded in her ears, too loud, too fast. All thoughts of sweetness gone.

As she drew closer, she caught the man's words. "You stole this wagon. I know you did."

She searched Rufus's face, but he was still, his jaw tight. Anna climbed into the wagon beside him, the boards rough beneath her trembling hands. "No, sir . . ." she began, voice barely above a whisper. Rufus lifted a hand to stop her, his eyes warning her of what she already knew. Words could make things worse.

She swallowed hard, kept her gaze low, the taste of fear dry as dust in her mouth.

Rufus told the man, "I was given permission by Mr. Fabius Haywood of Raleigh, North Carolina." Rufus took a piece of paper out of his pocket and handed it to the man.

The thing that puzzled Anna was that this man didn't seem to be any sort of authority. He didn't wear the badge of law enforcement, so why was he asking about the wagon?

The man snarled as he handed the paper back to Rufus. "Why you have so much free time, escorting this girl all the way to Ohio? You must not be employed."

Rufus didn't say anything.

The man cackled like he'd reeled in a big fish. "You know what we do with unemployed Coloreds 'round these parts, don't you?"

"Yes, sir, I sure do." Rufus's lips were tight as he reached into his pocket and pulled out another piece of paper. "You'll find that my employment papers are in order."

After glaring at the papers, the White man flung them

at Rufus. Anna grabbed one of the pages and Rufus grabbed the other before they fell to the ground. Lord knew what would happen if the papers ended up on the ground and then got torn.

"Thought of everything, didn't you, boy?"

Rufus stared at the man without responding.

Anna held her breath.

The White man tipped his hat to Rufus. "Let me give you a bit of friendly advice. Don't show your face in these parts again or I'll run you straight to the judge and let him sort out whether or not them papers are forgeries."

Rufus nodded. "Good day to you." He slapped the reins on the horse and hightailed it out of there as fast as the horse would go.

When they were miles away from trouble, Rufus glared at Anna with fire in his eyes. "The next time I tell you it's not safe, don't question me, you hear?"

"Yes, of course." Anna's hands were still trembling. She glanced over her shoulder to make sure they weren't being followed. Her brother could have been lost to them simply for pieces of candy.

"That judge he spoke of would have put me in jail and forced me to work on a plantation."

Free labor one way or another. A tear rolled down her face. "I'm so sorry. I should've listened." She lifted the bag. "I feel like throwing this candy away."

He grabbed the bag from her. "Don't be so hasty. I deserve a peppermint stick after what I endured."

They continued on their journey with minimal stops as they kept watchful eyes on the trail. Anna didn't eat one piece of the candy. Instead she let Rufus have it all. The smile on his face as he sucked on a peppermint stick or pulled on some taffy was a balm to her soul.

Ladies Hall was all aflutter with activity as Mary entered the reception hall. Windows were opened, floors scrubbed, rugs beaten to remove unwanted dust. Some of the furniture from the first Ladies Hall, built back in 1835, had been brought over to the current Ladies Hall. The tables, chairs, and curtains in the reception hall were from that long-gone-by era.

The second Ladies Hall was less than twenty years old, but the furnishings in some of the rooms and the lack of detail in construction dated it. The reception room and other areas in their dormitory were in disrepair. Paint and plaster peeled from the walls, the chairs were wobbly, and the reception room was generally gloomy and dark.

The faculty at Oberlin College would be arriving within hours for the scheduled reception with President Fairchild. The best they could do was a thorough cleaning. Mrs. Johnston had said, "Make the room sparkle."

It was a great honor for Ladies Hall to be selected to host such a prime event. Mary grabbed a rag and bucket of water and began wiping down the old and worn tables while Ida washed the window seals. Mrs. Johnston sat behind the piano and played.

Lifting her hands, Mary let her hips sway from one side to the other, losing herself for a fleeting moment in the rhythm pulsing through the room.

"Oh look." Suzie's voice cut through the music like a shard of glass. "The monkey can dance."

A ripple of laughter followed: sharp, cruel, echoing louder than the piano keys. The sound crawled up Mary's spine. Her stomach dropped, twisting itself into knots. Of course. Why did she think they'd let her have this one moment?

Her eyes snapped toward Suzie and her little circle of minions. For half a breath Mary imagined walking over there, saying something—anything—that would shut them up. But the words died in her throat. What good would it do? They'd only laugh harder.

Mary's jaw tightened. The rag in her hand met the next table harder than necessary. Wipe, circle, repeat. The motion steadied her, gave her somewhere to put the anger. Her shoulder rolled back, as if she could shake off Suzie's insult. *Let it go, Mary. Let it go.*

But beneath the surface, the heat stayed, a slow, silent burn she couldn't scrub away. One day she would make Suzie and others like her eat their insulting words. Wipe . . . circle . . . repeat. One day they would recognize her for who she was and not simply for the color of her skin. Wipe . . . circle . . . done.

She dropped the rag into the bucket, the water clouding gray around it. She straightened, smoothed her skirt, and walked away from them. Head high, steps steady. Let them laugh. Dirt washed off easily enough. Someday their scorn would too.

Mary and Ida didn't finish with responsibilities until an hour before the reception was due to start. By the time they reached the bathroom, there was a line so long, Mary grumbled to Ida, "We're going to be late to the reception."

Ida loudly said for all to hear, "If these girls would

expeditiously take care of their needs, we could all get to the reception on time."

A few of the girls glared at Ida; others shrugged and ignored her . . . and the line lingered. Fifteen minutes behind the hour, Mary and Ida swept into the reception hall, their silk skirts rustling like whispers in the candlelit corridor. The scent of lavender water and beeswax polish lingered in the air, mingling with the soft hum of conversation.

Mary's heart lifted as she caught sight of herself in the tall looking glass. Her cornflower-blue evening gown shimmered beneath the glow of gaslight, the delicate lace trim at the high neckline framing her face like a fine cameo. Most days she wore modest calico or wool, her attire dictated by the rigors of campus life, but tonight she could indulge in elegance.

The room was alive with movement and voices, polished shoes clicking against the floor, hand fans fluttering, and laughter rising in delicate waves. President Fairchild stood near the mantel, engaged in an animated discussion with several faculty members. As Mary drew closer, she caught the name "Garfield" spoken with a thread of hope. The newly nominated political candidate was on everyone's lips.

"The convention made the right choice," one professor said, adjusting his spectacles. "Garfield's vision aligns with the soul of the nation."

Mary's ears perked up. Her father had written to her a few days ago, the ink still fresh with hope. *"This man, this Garfield, might finally mean real progress for our people,"* he had said. *"His presidency could bring true change for the Negro race, with his support for Black suffrage and government-sponsored education."*

As the chandelier sparkled like a constellation of stars, a

thrill stirred inside Mary. It wasn't the lace at her collar or the excitement of polite society; it was more a sense that the river of history was shifting, and somehow she was standing right in the current of it.

Ida nudged Mary as she indicated a table at the front of the room. "There's the chemistry professor. I struggled with the assignment he gave us last week. I'm going to see if he can give me some pointers." The professor's chemistry lessons were sometimes hard to grasp, but he was a good teacher.

As Ida went off, Mary spotted Professor Churchill. She was in his mathematics and philosophy classes this semester and hoped to make a good impression. She walked over to him. "Professor, are you enjoying yourself this evening?"

"I am. You young ladies always do a marvelous job of hosting this event."

She stuck her hand out to him. "I'm Mary Church. I don't know if you remember, but I'm in two of your classes this semester."

He shook her hand. "Of course I remember you, my dear. You're Robert Church's daughter, correct?"

"Yes, sir, I am." She answered with a mix of pride and a slight tinge of regret that she wasn't remembered on her own merits.

Mary made her way around the room, holding conversations with the Greek language professor and the nice young man who'd taken over the penmanship class after the last professor was stricken with writer's cramp.

When she finished speaking with them, her favorite professor from the English Department caught her attention. As she moved closer to him, one of the other professors lifted a finger in the direction of the window. "I don't remember those drapes being torn at the reception last year."

"Fairchild doesn't throw money out on frills," another one of their guests said.

Those heavy drapes, a gift to the college from some long-forgotten benefactor, hung limp and faded by years of sun and dust. Mary's eyes swept across the room, taking in the hairline crack that ran like a crooked vein up the plaster wall and the wallpaper curling at the corners, yellowed and flaking like old parchment. The once-elegant rugs, now threadbare and dull, were a pitiful reminder of better days, when perhaps this parlor had held a certain charm. Now it whispered of neglect. Despite all the work they had put in to spruce up the reception hall, the disrepair still showed.

If her father had been invited to the reception room, he would swear that Mary was living in squalor. She had been horrified by her father's demand at the first boardinghouse she'd stayed in while in primary school in Yellow Springs. He'd told them that her bedroom was not up to his standards and demanded that it be fitted properly. He then sent money to change out the furniture.

Could she help Mrs. Johnston improve the appearance and feel of the reception room? There was no way they could continue hosting such elaborate events in this space without complete mortification.

CHAPTER 5

After weeks of traveling dust-ridden roads, Rufus pulled up to 33 East Vine Street. It was a two-story brick structure with a covered hip roof porch that extended across the front of the house. The roof was held up by square brick pillars, with white siding on the bottom and sides of the porch.

This boardinghouse would be her home away from home. Although Mr. Wilson Bruce Evans and his wife, Sarah, could easily be mistaken for White, they were Colored. Born free in North Carolina, they refused to pass and lived their lives without apology or lies that might have made things easier for them.

The Evanses and some of their family members had moved to Oberlin during the years of slavery. Mr. Wilson's name had grown to hero status after he took part in the Oberlin-Wellington Rescue, in which a group of Colored men had successfully snatched John Price, a runaway slave, from slave catchers. Their efforts began nonviolently, but when negotiations with the slave catchers failed, they physically overpowered them. With the help of other rescuers, Price was able to escape and hide with John and Mary Fairchild, two Oberlin residents, until he was able to travel to Canada safely.

Mr. Wilson and several other men were arrested for their actions. They were put in the Cuyahoga County jail. The men refused bail and stayed in the jailhouse until their trial. They were eventually released, but their rescue efforts became one of the most well-known acts of resistance against slavery in Oberlin's history. However, a quieter aspect of Oberlin's resistance had to do with the Underground Railroad. And Mr. Wilson's home had been one of the stops toward freedom.

Rufus got out of the wagon, walked around to Anna's side, and helped her down. "We're here. Ready for your new life?"

Anna stepped down from the wagon and let her lungs fill up with the light fall breeze on the northern side of the world. This was new . . . This was . . . She closed her eyes and breathed in again. The air was crisp with a fresh, sharp aroma like chlorine. Most likely it would rain later tonight. But that wouldn't dampen her spirit.

The surrounding neighborhood included a mix of Tudor, ranch, and oddly shaped homes. She glanced down the street as far as the eye could see, and not one of the structures was as large as the plantations or manors she knew from North Carolina. Anna liked what she saw. It seemed like a simple, easygoing kind of life.

The door to the boardinghouse opened and a light-complected woman stepped out onto the porch, waving them forward. Anna glanced at the woman. Instead of seeing the smile and the open arms waving them toward the door, Anna fixed on the warmth in the woman's eyes.

"Come on in here and take a load off. You must be Anna?" the woman asked, then added, "I'm Sarah."

"Yes, ma'am." Anna walked up the porch stairs while Rufus gathered her bags. "Thank you so much for allowing me to stay at your home."

"We expected you two weeks ago, when school started. But better late than never." Sarah grinned at Anna.

"We misjudged how long it would take. But like you said, better late than never."

Standing in the living room, Anna took in the beautifully crafted wood on the walls and up the side of the staircase: high-quality woodwork with intricate detail.

Did the wainscoting hide a secret door where Mr. Wilson used to hide runaway slaves? Anna's hand shook ever so slightly as she extended it to Mrs. Sarah. "I'm happy to meet you, ma'am. I've read so much about you and your husband that . . ." She stepped back and lowered her head as nerves got the better of her. "It's an honor to be in your presence."

Through letters before her arrival, Anna and Mrs. Sarah had agreed that she would pay a portion of her boarding fee with housecleaning. The boarding home had four bedrooms, one downstairs where Mr. and Mrs. Evans slept and three upstairs for the boarding students.

But Anna would not be required to clean the other two bedrooms that students were staying in. She was happy to see that the boardinghouse was well kept and clean upon her arrival. She shouldn't have a problem maintaining the home.

Rufus put her bags on the floor in the living room. Mrs. Sarah told him, "You're welcome to stay the night. I can make up the living room sofa for you."

He waved off her suggestion. "I'd best be getting back on the road. It's a long journey."

"All the more reason for you to rest. You'll get a good meal and a good night's sleep before heading back to Raleigh."

Taking off his dusty hat, Rufus smiled his relief. "I thank you for the kindness, ma'am."

While Anna enjoyed the lunch of fried chicken and potato salad with her brother, reality struck like a blow as she watched Rufus gobble down his food as if someone might steal it from him. Was she making a mistake? Could she handle being on her own while her family was hundreds of miles away?

After swallowing the last spoonful of potato salad from her plate, Anna went over to Rufus and hugged him tight enough for him to carry her love all the way back home. "I'm going to miss you. Give Mama a kiss from me."

He gave her a squeeze before he pulled away. "I'll miss you too."

Wiping the wetness from beneath her eyelids, she stepped back. "I need to get over to the college now. I pray my delay won't cost me my greatest desire."

"And what's that, dear?" Mrs. Sarah asked.

Anna told Mrs. Sarah, "I'd like to continue my study of languages."

She leaned back in her seat and studied Anna a moment. "Well, it would seem that you're a determined young lady. If you have any trouble in the admissions office, let me know and I'll send Wilson down there to speak on your behalf."

As Anna was leaving the boardinghouse to head to the admissions office, she noticed a framed photograph on the mantel. The photo showed the twenty men, Mr. Wilson being one of them, who took part in the Oberlin-Wellington Rescue. They were standing outside the jail after being arrested for their actions.

The rescue was a landmark event in the fight against slavery. Anna's eyes glistened with joy as she stared at it. No man deserved to be owned by another or captured like an animal simply for existing in a Black body. She was thankful that the men in that picture saw the world the way she did and had been willing to go to prison for their beliefs.

Stepping out of the house, the grass somehow seemed greener than that of the scorched-earth grass in the South. The leaves were just beginning to stain with color, but the trees were still full, so she experienced several moments of shade with a cool breeze that added beauty to the areas right outside the school's administrative office.

Anna was worn out from the journey. All she wanted to do was fall into bed and sleep for a week. But she needed to get registered for her classes. Rest would come later.

In the registrar's office, Anna examined the registration form, then glanced back up at the administrator. "I did not enroll in the two-year Ladies' Course."

He jutted a finger at the paper. "This form was created based on your requests."

"No, I'm sorry, there must be some mistake. I'm interested in the same courses the men have. I was informed that I would be able to take a test in order to prove my aptitude."

The administrator stood to his full height and peered down his nose at Anna. "It's a fine time to ask for special treatment with school already in session."

"It couldn't be helped, sir. Please, is there anything that can be done about this mix-up?"

He didn't appear to budge as he said, "Most of the women enrolled find the Ladies' Course to be plenty. The curriculum includes mathematics, natural science, philosophy, and general literature."

In that moment Anna pictured herself riding back home if this man would not let her enroll in her desired courses. But she couldn't do that. Her life was no longer in Raleigh. There had to be another way.

She filled her lungs with air, then released it on a long-suffering sigh. "The Ladies' Course doesn't include rhetoric or Greek and Latin. Nor does it include the study of ancient history and literature. And those are the courses I'm most interested in." Music as well, but this was not the time to mention that, since she could take music classes in the Ladies' Course.

Anna planned to resume her position as a teacher when she finished her studies. But she needed to learn much more in the disciplines the Classical Gentlemen's Course provided to be as effective a teacher as she knew she could be.

"Most women aren't interested in the languages or rhetoric," he told her.

Anna handed him her transcript from St. Augustine's. "If you'll read over my paperwork, I think you'll agree that I'm more than qualified for the four-year degree." She held her breath.

He perused her papers. "You've studied Latin *and* Greek?"

"Yes, sir, I have a good understanding of those languages, but I hope to become fluent."

"The letter from St. Augustine's states that you teach and tutor at the school."

"Yes, sir, teaching is a passion of mine." Anna bit down on her bottom lip, silently praying for divine intervention. In her estimation she was probably more qualified than some of the men who'd already been accepted simply on the basis of their manhood.

"Well . . ." He hesitated, but only for a moment. "You'll still have to take the test."

Anna exhaled. "I would expect nothing less." She'd fought to take the so-called men's courses at St. Augustine's. She'd won that battle. Anna prayed she'd win this one as well.

Anna sat for almost three hours, taking the rigorous test. Nerves tried to creep in halfway through the examination. Sweat rained down her forehead as she deciphered Greek and Latin. She needed a chance. She'd catch on to these other words and concepts with a bit more study. She blinked hard, and the room blurred for a second.

You know this stuff. Answer the questions. Forcing her focus back to the paper, she scrawled her last few answers, then handed it to the administrator.

He sat down at his desk and went over the test. Each time he made a mark on her examination, Anna cringed. Had she come in here only to humiliate herself? If she failed this test, what would happen to the next Colored woman who desired to enroll in the men's degree program?

He glanced up from the paper, studying her for a heartbeat as if weighing a question, then bent back over the exam. What did that mean? Had she written something confusing? Would he give her a chance to elaborate?

After several uncomfortable minutes of sitting, waiting, and guessing, Anna watched as the administrator walked back over to the administration desk. "Mrs. Cooper."

Anna jumped out of her seat and rushed over to him. "I can retake the test if there were things that I didn't understand fully," she said before allowing him to speak.

"That won't be necessary. You passed your examination and I'm enrolling you in our four-year degree program. I have no doubt you will excel."

Anna clamped her hand over her mouth, trying not to scream and alert others to her joy. She removed her hands. "Thank you . . . thank you so much for allowing me to take the test."

"No need to thank me. Your work speaks for itself."

A smile crept across her face as she walked back to the boardinghouse. Head tilted heavenward, she silently said, *Guess what, George? I'm an official student at Oberlin College. Can you believe it?*

"I'll be taking the men's courses," she told him and then laughed. George had teased her more than a few times about her inability to follow norms and decorum. The older women in their church would wag their fingers at her when she had to miss the ladies' committee meetings due to schoolwork.

Thinking about her husband's church, the ministry that had so often taken him away from her, and the illness that had finally stolen him for good, Anna bowed her head under the weight of the memories. A tremor passed through her voice as she whispered, "Wish you were here. That's all."

CHAPTER 6

September 27, 1880

"Thank you all. With your help, we pulled off another successful reception. Now let's get this room put back in order," Mrs. Johnston said to the group the morning after the reception.

Mary stood and addressed the principal. "The reception was indeed a success, but a few of the faculty commented on the drabness of the room. Does the school have any plans to remodel our dormitory?"

Mrs. Johnston nodded. "We received new carpet in the common area two years ago and new wallpaper in the hallway. But I must agree. It is most gloomy in our reception room."

"You should feel at home, Mary. Charity cases have no right to ask for more than is given to them," Suzie stated from where she stood on the opposite side of Mrs. Johnston.

Mary's eyebrow rose. "I am not a charity case. Why would you even think such a thing?"

"Colored people are always asking for handouts," Suzie said as if her statement was as true as rain in springtime.

Insult after insult, Mary had held her tongue. Her father had warned that not everyone would accept her with open arms. Even though the authorities at Oberlin had built this college to serve men and women and Colored and White folks as equals, there were those who opposed such good work. But she was done turning the other cheek. "I've seen more poor Whites needing charity than any of the Colored folks I know back in Memphis."

"Mary!" Mrs. Johnston's voice rose as she admonished her. "We don't speak like that in Ladies Hall."

"I'm sorry, Mrs. Johnston, but Suzie said that I'm Oberlin's charity case, and my father has never needed anyone to help with my school expenses."

"Be that as it may, we can't insult our fellow classmates."

Suzie had done nothing but hurl insults at Mary since she'd moved into Ladies Hall, and Mrs. Johnston hadn't corrected the girl. Was this the way it was going to be?

Mrs. Johnston straightened her blouse and cleared her throat. She told Mary, "You're not the only one to mention the condition of the reception hall. Many others have commented on its disrepair. So I suggest we do something about it."

Ida stepped forward. "What can we do? Are you thinking we should ask our parents for the money to repair the room?"

Another student said to Ida, "Doesn't your father use his money for politics and Black causes? Who will help the poor Blacks if your father spends his money on your whims?"

Of course poor Black families were in need of help. You couldn't enslave people for hundreds of years, turn them away with nothing, and think they'd simply rise to the top. Mary was appalled by the way the suffering in Black communities was discussed by those in the dominant group, as Mary had dubbed the White race.

The dominant group had poor people as well. But the way they talked, you'd think that only Colored folks were afflicted by poverty. It was a shame they didn't open their eyes to see that all groups in America needed to rise against an administration that would impoverish its people in order to line the pockets of the robber barons. But as long as the dominant group could look down on another race of people, they would never be able to see the true enemy.

And what did they know of wealth in the Black communities? The way some of these girls spoke to them, it was obvious they couldn't conceive of an America where there were Black millionaires other than Ida's and Mary's families. When William Alexander Leidesdorff Jr. became the first Black American millionaire in 1856, he was a sea captain out of New Orleans until they passed the Negro Seamen Act. Leidesdorff Jr. was also one of the founders of San Francisco. After his death, gold was discovered on his land, which made his estate worth millions of dollars.

In the 1830s James Forten was worth a hundred thousand, and now he, too, was a millionaire. Warren Clay Coleman built the first Black-owned textile mill in the United States. And Colonel John McKee had many land holdings in Philadelphia and was quite wealthy. There might not be hundreds in the Colored aristocracy, but there were others. Mary took pride in knowing that Ida's father and hers were not the only Black men of wealth in this country. It just went to show that with pride and ingenuity, Colored folks could do great things in this country.

"Your parents do enough for the college," Mrs. Johnston told them. "If we're to convince President Fairchild of our plight, we'll need to start a petition. And it wouldn't hurt if we could raise funds for the renovations ourselves."

A great discussion about the matter floated around the room. Janet, the president of the Aeolian Society, said, "I believe this is a matter the Aeolian and the Ladies Literary Societies should champion."

The women's literary societies had been established at Oberlin a few decades before as a space for women students to participate in literary public speaking, debates, and cultural activities.

Shouts of agreement went up, then Janet said, "I don't mind taking the lead, but since Mary brought this issue to our attention, I nominate her to work on the committee."

Mary's heart sped up as a smile broke free. She straightened, unable to hide the delight within. "I hope the work I'm able to do with this committee brings honor to Ladies Hall."

The group dispersed. Mary and Janet walked out of the room together. Mary said, "Thanks, friend."

Janet grabbed hold of Mary's arm and stopped her from continuing down the hall. "Friend? Do you mean that?"

Mary hesitated. Had she made a mistake? Was this girl the kindred spirit she'd assumed after their meeting in the parlor? "Well, you seem friendly, and so I called you friend. But if the term offends, I shall not use it again."

"Oh no, no." Janet waved a hand in the air. "I'm not offended in the least. I never had a Colored woman call me friend before, and I wanted to make sure we were on the same path. I would very much like to be your friend."

Mary hadn't known this girl for long, yet there was an unexpected tug at her heart, a kind of certainty that she had found a lifelong friend. Perhaps it was the warmth in the young woman's eyes or the way her smile came easily, without hesitation or pretense. There was no trace of the guarded politeness Mary had grown used to in mixed company, only genuine curiosity and kindness. For a moment the world outside, with its whispered disapproval and boundaries drawn by custom and color, seemed to fall away.

This was the true beauty of Oberlin College. This was what the founders had dreamed of: a place where Colored and White students could not only study side by side but come to see one another as equals, as friends. Here in this modest reception hall, under the soft glow of lamplight and the murmur of conversation, that vision was taking shape in the most human of ways.

Two women, one Black, one White, discovering connection across the color lines that society had drawn between them. No grand speeches were made, no thunderclaps rang out, just a simple act as natural as a fish slipping through water. It shouldn't have been remarkable, but in a world still learning to see clearly, it was.

Mary and the committee got to work expeditiously. This was her first assignment at Ladies Hall, and she wanted to do her best. Mary fully admitted that as a Colored woman, she valued being on top of things at all times. She was paving the way for other women of color in the future, and she aimed to do it with grace.

In the week since the women's societies at Oberlin decided to collect signatures and donations, Mary had been hard at work, collecting signatures for her petition. With Ida trailing her, Mary ran into Mrs. Johnston in the hallway as she was headed outside. Mary showed her the petition. "Can you believe I have fifty signatures already?"

"That's amazing. Thank you for all your hard work."

"My goal is to get a hundred before the end of the week."

Mrs. Johnston took the writing instrument out of Mary's hand and signed her name to the petition. "There, now you have fifty-one signatures. And you can put me down to donate one hundred dollars."

Ida's eyes widened. "Are you sure? That's generous."

Mrs. Johnston shrugged. "I live here with you girls. I don't pay any sort of rent, so I can afford to contribute." She had been widowed now for almost twenty years. Her marriage hadn't produced any children.

Most people who signed the petition did not donate, but for those who did, Mary was grateful. "Thank you!"

"Can you hold off on the petition a moment?" Mrs. Johnston asked Mary. "I need to speak with you in my office."

Mary handed the petition to Ida. "Can you take this to the music conservatory? I was told that the faculty were interested in donating to our cause."

"I'll take care of it."

Ida headed out the door as Mary asked Mrs. Johnston, "Is there a problem?" Mary was wondering if nasty ol' Suzie had submitted complaints against the Colored students again. When Mary had first moved into the dormitory along with Ida and four other Colored women, Suzie had dared to say that they were dirtying up what had once been beautiful accommodations.

"No problem. Come with me, please." They continued down the hall.

Mrs. Johnston's office was a small box-sized room that barely fit the desk and two chairs in front. Stacks of papers were piled on the floor directly below her window. A Colored woman sat in one of the chairs in front of her desk.

Mary nodded toward the woman whose complexion was a little darker than her own. "Hello."

The other woman nodded in her direction. "Good day to you."

Mrs. Johnston stood in front of her desk. "Mary, I'd like to introduce you to our newest student." With an outstretched hand, Mrs. Johnston said, "This is Anna Julia Cooper."

"Nice to meet you, Miss Cooper." Mary smiled but at the same time noted that Anna's dress was made from fabric in fashion three seasons ago. Which made her wonder at Anna's parentage. Why hadn't they provided clothes that would make the proper impression of a young woman of higher learning?

"Call me Anna."

Mrs. Johnston said, "I think the two of you should become fast friends."

Mary hesitated a moment, then lifted her chin. "That depends on how much we have in common, doesn't it?" She hated when people were lumped together based on the color of their skin or their gender. Mary believed that the content of a person's character should be the defining factor.

"Of course." Mrs. Johnston stretched out her hand toward Anna. "I'm sure you'll find Mrs. Cooper suitable. She passed the administrative test to be admitted into the classical studies as you and Ida did."

Mary's eyes widened with appreciation for Anna's accomplishment. Not many women at Oberlin were brave enough to sit through that rigorous exam.

Mrs. Johnston continued, "I brought you in here to ask that you show Mrs. Cooper around campus to get her acclimated to Oberlin and all its glory."

"I would be delighted to show Anna around." With a slight smile, Mary said, "Come with me, and I will introduce you to Ida Gibbs."

Anna stood and walked out of Mrs. Johnston's office with Mary. "Thank you. I appreciate your kindness."

"It's my honor." Mary headed to the front door. "Will you be staying here at Ladies Hall?"

Anna shook her head. "A family in town has taken me in."

"Who are they? If they attend First Church, I probably know them."

Anna answered, "I'm staying with the Evans family. I believe they attend Second Church."

"Oh." Mary raised an eyebrow. "Are you attending that church?"

"I only recently arrived in town, but I plan to attend. Don't all the Colored people here attend Second Church?"

Mary pressed a hand to her heart. "My word, no. I attend First Church. It's important for the Negroes here on campus to build relationships with our White counterparts. My attendance at First Church is one of the ways I'm bridging the divide."

The polite smile on Anna's face faltered enough for Mary to notice. In that brief silence, Mary determined to show the newcomer how to comport herself so she would benefit from her time at Oberlin.

CHAPTER 7

Anna stood at the corner of Main and College Streets beneath the wide-reaching arms of the old elm tree that shaded a portion of College Park. Anna glanced beside her and still couldn't believe it. Mary Church, elegant, self-assured, and the daughter of one of the wealthiest Black families in the country, walked with her, gesturing toward buildings and smiling warmly as if they'd known each other for years. The moment was dreamlike yet real.

The crisp northern air filled Anna's lungs, cooling the heat of nerves that fluttered in her chest. She closed her eyes for a moment, letting the breeze settle her heart. She was no longer in survival mode. She was beginning again.

Oberlin, this sanctuary carved out of possibility. The brick buildings, tree-lined paths, and clusters of earnest students suggested a new beginning, a place where she could stretch her mind, forge new friendships, and leave behind the labels of her past. Here, no one seemed to stare at her with pity, as if her parentage or widowhood told the whole of her story.

"I've read numerous papers on your father. I'm sure he is proud of you."

Mary shrugged. "My father would rather I find a suitable husband than spend two extra years in college. But after I explained my heart's desire, he finally relented. But I'm still not sure if my choice of degree makes him proud."

"Whatever his feelings, I'm glad he saw the need for higher learning. If we're going to compete for jobs, then we simply must be prepared."

The elm that stood in the middle of the campus caught Mary's attention as Anna talked about being prepared for the workforce. "I brought you to this spot for a reason." Mary's eyes trailed upward as she gazed at the over-fifty-foot elm. "As the legend goes, the year that Oberlin's founders picked the site for the college, they found this elm tree in this spot. It was only about five inches tall and thin." Mary continued, "The tree was surrounded by a forest of sturdier trees. But the men tied their horses to this tree, knelt beside it, and dedicated it to the college. They saved it from the axe, as most all the other trees were cut down to build everything you see here." Mary's hand jutted in the direction of the buildings on each side of the elm tree.

"I wonder what they found so special about this tree. Why'd they let it live and thrive?" Anna asked.

With her head tilted backward, Mary let her gaze trail the height of the tree. Her voice softened. "Maybe they saw its potential."

Looking at the elm before her, Anna felt a spark of hope ignite in her heart. A new understanding of what could come from patience—and the chance to grow.

"Is this your first year of college?" Mary lifted a hand. "Pardon me if I'm prying. You appear older than other freshmen."

Anna laughed. "I'm certainly not eighteen. I spent years teaching and tutoring at St. Augustine's before I decided to apply to this college." Anna couldn't bear to tell Mary all of the reasons her schooling had been delayed. It would only bring tears to her eyes again.

"I'm only seventeen. I don't turn eighteen until next September."

The young girl carried herself in such a mature manner that Anna could hardly believe her age. "Well, that is certainly a surprise."

"You must be smart as a whip." Mary's eyes lit as she nodded her approval. "Passing the test for the men's courses is no easy feat."

"And yet you accomplished the task at seventeen." Anna's voice held admiration as they walked over to Lorain Street and stood in front of the most beautifully constructed Gothic Revival architecture she'd ever seen.

"This is Council Hall. You won't have much need for this building. It's the theological seminary and men's dormitory."

Before leaving Lorain Street, Mary mentioned the building next to Council Hall. "This is First Church. Maybe you'll attend as my guest one Sunday."

Anna wondered at the girl's forceful push. "Is there a reason *you* can't attend church with *me*? I met Reverend Nunon from Second Church, and he seems like a lovely steward of his flock."

Mary lifted her pious nose heavenward. "If we're ever to

make progress with respect to equality in this country, we must be viewed as equal to Whites. That will never happen as long as we keep to ourselves."

"Sometimes the best place for us is amongst our own people." Frustration coiled hot and tight in Anna's chest. Mary's words, though well-meaning, carried that sanctimonious tone she'd heard too many times before. As if proximity to whiteness were the only path to dignity. Anna's jaw clenched. How could she explain the exhaustion of always trying to be "seen," always performing humanity for eyes that refused to recognize it?

She wanted to say more, to ask Mary if she'd ever felt safe among those who smiled too politely, but the words tangled behind her teeth. Instead she jabbed a finger in the direction of Professor Street. "What's down there?"

Her long legs carried her forward before Mary could answer, each stride a release of irritation, a silent vow not to let the conversation trap her in the same old circles. Anna didn't mind attending classes with White students, but her place was with other Colored folk on Sunday mornings. If Mary didn't understand that and continued to push the First Church on her, then she would soon discover that Anna would not be moved in this regard.

"Wait up!" Mary yelled after Anna. "I promised Mrs. Johnston I'd show you around. You can't leave in the middle of my tour."

Anna halted mid-step, her shoes sinking slightly into the dust of the road. The air smelled faintly of coal smoke and garden roses, a strange mingling of progress and autumn. She drew in a slow breath, steadying the tremor in her chest.

She didn't want to be thought of as unwilling to help the cause of equality. But first she had to make something of herself. No one would listen to anything she had to say until then. Mary could spout off all she wanted about being in spaces with White Americans, but Anna knew the truth. Mary's wealth made her tolerable. She had no right to ask Anna to be a part of circles where she would be treated as a nuisance or a charity case.

As Mary caught up, she nodded toward the building Anna was standing in front of. "This is Tappan Hall. The main walk across campus passes through this building."

Mary could speak of equality while surrounded by silk and silver spoons. But for Anna, the word came with calloused hands and polite dismissals and men who fought progress for women at every turn. "Will I have classes here?"

"Doubtful. There are four rooms for recitation purposes on the first floor, but the other floors contain about ninety single sleeping rooms for the men."

"Women aren't allowed to use those recitation rooms?"

"Certain buildings such as Tappan Hall and Ladies Hall were built either for men or for women. Occasionally women use the recitation rooms at Tappan Hall, as the men have been invited to Ladies Hall in the society room. But mostly we are separated by gender."

Anna motioned behind her, at Lorain Street. "Council Hall was a men's dormitory as well. Seems like we're surrounded by things for the men, with little for women."

Mary nodded. "Oberlin has more male students than female, but times are changing."

"Somebody has to show these men what we're about."

Anna's voice lifted with pride. She was as smart as any man, and she would not continue to take a back seat to them.

"The only man I'm trying to show anything to is my father. He seems to think women are only good for marriage."

"Husbands are good. But if you don't find the right one, it can complicate things for a woman with ambition," Anna told her, then lowered her gaze. She wouldn't think on her losses . . . not today when she had so much to be thankful for.

They were standing in front of the men's gymnasium. The door opened and several men stepped out of the building. Mary grabbed Anna's arm and ran with her. "Come with me. I want to show you one last thing."

When they reached their destination, Anna and Mary stopped running and caught their breath.

"Okay, what's so important that we had to run down the street like that?" Anna asked.

Mary glanced down Professor Street. "Mason stepped out of the men's gymnasium. He asked me out and I still haven't decided if I want to go."

"So you needed a diversion?"

Mary gnawed at her bottom lip. "I hope I didn't make you run too fast."

Anna glanced back up the street. Two Colored men stood in front of the building. She wasn't sure which one was Mason, but she was starting to understand that Mary had more on her mind than books. "You'd better hope he doesn't catch you."

Mary waved a hand. "He's harmless." They were now standing in front of a massive structure with several pointy spears at the four corners and a spire directed toward the sky at the top. "This is the Soldiers Monument. Ninety-six names of Oberlin men who were killed during the Civil War are inscribed on it. Fifty-five of the men were enrolled at our school before they gave the ultimate sacrifice."

Anna stared at the fixture, taking in the names of the dead engraved on it. She had so many questions about the sacrifice those men had made. Why did they do it? What was in it for them?

"The people in this city believe it was their abolitionist work that sparked the Civil War, so everyone honors it. You'll see people saluting it from time to time."

Anna pulled her gaze away from the monument. The weightiness of everything she had taken in caused her shoulders to slump. "The War Between the States was so long ago that I rarely think about how many soldiers were killed for the freedom we now enjoy."

"There are times when I want to forget." Mary continued to stare at the monument.

"Most of the White folks in the South blame the Negro for their loved ones who didn't come home." Anna wrapped her arms around herself as if a chill had swept through her. "It's painful to know that war had to break out in order for the South to stop buying and selling Colored folks."

CHAPTER 8

November 6, 1880

Mary and Ida were seated in the third row from the front at First Church on Sunday morning after an eventful week of working on the petition. Mary managed to collect a little over a hundred signatures and hundreds of dollars in donations.

"All rise," Reverend Brand said, then waited until everyone in the congregation was standing. He prayed and thanked God for the newly elected President Garfield.

Mary's father had supported Garfield's campaign and had made sure the Colored men knew who to vote for in this election.

Glancing around the room, Mary spotted only a few Colored faces. She wished there were more people like her in the room to celebrate this grand news. One day . . . one day.

As Reverend Brand opened the Bible and began preaching his sermon, Mary's mind drifted to the paper she had to write on *A Tale of Two Cities* by Charles Dickens. The book was simply a masterpiece. She was thrilled to explore the depth and cunningness of the writing. But thinking on the title as she glanced around the sanctuary caused Mary to ponder the tale of two churches.

There had only been one church in Oberlin originally. Blacks and Whites attended and worshipped together. Then a few Whites who were new to the area opposed the practice of Blacks and Whites sitting next to each other and eating with one another during social functions.

"*We need to put these Coloreds in a section of the church where they can all congregate together*," one of the White men had said.

Back then Reverend Finney was the pastor of First Church. To Reverend Finney's credit, he vehemently objected to any form of segregation.

His stance was appreciated, but it hadn't been enough to halt the revolt of Black parishioners. John Ramsey and the rest of his crew got it in their minds to form their own church. A place where Black people could worship in peace, away from those who hated them without a cause.

It was a shame that Oberlin now had this tale of two churches, when one should have been enough for them all. Especially since the auditorium could seat over a thousand people and many of the seats were now empty.

Ida poked her left arm. "Are you listening or daydreaming about Mason?"

Mason hadn't been on her mind this morning. She hardly knew him. Only the thought of unity and how she could get her Black brothers and sisters over at Second Church to come back where they belonged troubled her mind.

"Gather 'round, girls. I have news." Mrs. Johnston stood at the front of the assembly room as the women entered.

Mary and Ida rushed in and found seats. Many of the ladies whispered to one another as they settled in to hear Mrs. Johnston's announcement. "What's happened?" Mary asked Ida.

Ida shrugged. "I was in philosophy class with you this morning. I have no idea."

"Well, ladies, I received word from President Fairchild. He informed me that with the petitions and the money we've collected, we will be remodeling."

The ladies jumped out of their seats. Shouts went up around the room. Mrs. Johnston stretched out a hand to Mary. "Come stand with me."

Mary glanced around. People were still dancing and shouting. She blinked, using her index finger to poke her chest while questioning eyes stared at her.

Their principal nodded. "Yes, you." She motioned with her hand, encouraging Mary to move quickly.

Mary pushed through the crowd. The shouting diminished as the ladies stared at her. Mary was as clueless as they were. Why would she be needed up front? "What's going on?" she whispered to Mrs. Johnston when she reached her.

"All will be revealed in a moment." Mrs. Johnston turned Mary to face the other students.

Mary couldn't ponder why she had been called to stand in front of her peers, until Mrs. Johnston's next words made it clear.

"President Fairchild was rather impressed with the number of signatures Mary was able to obtain on the petition and the fact that her father donated a good portion of the funds for our building project."

Beaming with pride, Mary was about to thank Mrs. Johnston when Suzie crossed her arms and harrumphed.

Mary faced the girl. Hate flamed through Suzie's green eyes, searing Mary to the core. What had she done to evoke such malice?

"I helped with those petitions. And my father gave fifty dollars for the building fund. Mary didn't do anything special." Each word out of Suzie's mouth spewed fire.

"Many of you worked hard on this project, and I'm thankful for that." Mrs. Johnston tried to defuse the situation.

"Then why do you praise a Colored girl when White women worked as hard as if not harder than she did?"

Janet's eyes flashed with anger as she confronted Suzie. "Why are you being so hateful? You barely had twenty names on your petition and you know it."

Suzie's fists tightened. She set her gaze on Janet. "You can paint your face black and join their race. But don't try to pull the rest of us into your way of thinking when we all know how lazy these Colored are."

A sharp intake of breath . . . then more gasps . . . and finally even some chuckles rang out.

"What did she say?"

"No way."

"Come on, that's too far."

Mrs. Johnston extended her finger to the door. "Suzie McFarland, you are dismissed from this meeting. And I will see you in my office."

Suzie stomped her foot, then stormed out of the room. Two other girls, who hung on Suzie's words like air and water, walked out with her.

"Now, as I was saying," Mrs. Johnston continued, "we are so grateful for Mary's above-and-beyond efforts and for the efforts of all who made this possible."

Mary determined not to let Suzie's sour attitude and disrespectful words ruin this moment for them. "We're getting a new reception hall!" She lifted her hands in the air and shouted the words.

Chatter came from all areas of the room.

"Will our rooms be refreshed also, or will it only be the reception hall?"

"Do we need to move the furnishings ourselves, or did we raise enough to pay for movers?"

"Can we start a petition to get a new cook?"

Mrs. Johnston raised a hand. "These are all great questions." She scowled at the girl in the back who'd asked about the cook. "Except for the insulting one about the delicious meals we receive here."

The girl lowered her head. "It was a harmless jest."

Mrs. Johnston tsk-tsked. "I do not have any further details at this moment. I only wanted to inform you that your efforts were effective."

As the group began to disperse, Mary whispered to Ida, "Did you see how Suzie stormed out of here?"

"She's spiteful and envious. I wonder if she even prays about her disposition during chapel." Ida's eyes rolled heavenward.

"That girl isn't jealous of me. She doesn't think I'm fit to carry her dirty shoes." Mary wasn't ignorant of the truth. Suzie was not superior to her in any way. However, Suzie believed the color of their skin was the only difference that mattered.

Janet walked over to them with a grin that lit up the room. "Mary Church, you are simply magnificent. You must join the Aeolian Literary Society."

Mary's mouth fell open. The literary societies were well respected among the students at Oberlin. She had wanted to join earlier this year but had shied away due to her studies.

Ida leaned forward and whispered in her ear, "Close your mouth."

The sheer shock of having the most popular girl at Oberlin ask her to join the most popular literary group on campus had left Mary speechless. Janet's father was richer than Mary's and everyone else's at Oberlin. She was White with red hair, smart as a whip, and always talked to Mary as if they were equals.

"What do you say?" Janet continued. "We could use someone with your gumption in the group."

Finding her voice, Mary asked, "What would I have to do?"

"As you know, we pick literary or cultural topics and

debate the Ladies Literary Society about once a month. We are far superior to that group, yet they have bested us the last two times."

Mary had attended those debates. She didn't know if she would say the Aeolian Literary Society was superior to the Ladies Literary Society in intellect. Both groups were well versed and exceptional. The one thing that kept her away from the Ladies Literary Society was that Suzie was a prominent member of that group.

Janet continued, "I believe you're the saving grace for our literary society. There's something special about you, Mary."

Flattered that Janet thought so well of her, Mary stuck out her hand, her friend took it, and they shook on it. "I'd be honored to join."

CHAPTER 9

December 1880

One week before Christmas, Anna's tears streamed down her cheeks like a relentless waterfall. The ache in her chest was as raw as it had been two years ago. When would it heal? When would the anguish unclench its grip? She sat alone with her sorrow, revisiting the sharp-edged memories of all the ways love had splintered her heart.

In the soft hush of winter's night, grief curled beside her like a shadow, and Anna could only whisper her love, praying the wind would carry it all the way to heaven.

She leaned her head against her pillow, eyes drooping, mind wandering back to the past when Christmas meant family and cookies and a baked ham . . . and sorrow and death.

"No, no, no! Stay with me, George." She cradled her husband's head in her lap. Heat from his body mingled with the chill of fear in hers. His chapped lips moved.

"D-don't try to speak." Tears flowed like a tide coming in,

washing out and then coming back to do more damage. Sorrow had wrapped itself around her like an old friend. "You're too weak, my darling. Rest, my love, and all will be well."

She doused him with water from the basin, hoping to cool his forehead. But the beads of sweat were ever present. Anna lifted her voice and began to sing:

"Oh George, don't get weary;
Oh George, don't get weary;
We're waiting for the Lord."

The original song title was "Oh Brother, Don't Get Weary," but Anna sang it with George's name, and she prayed it reached to the depths of his soul and revived him. But that was not to be the case.

Anna's eyes flew open. She sprang up in bed. Glanced around the room. She was not in Raleigh ministering to her dying husband. She was in Oberlin. She had started her new life. She'd left all her heartache and pain in the South. No sense dragging it here with her. Time to get out of bed and start the day.

She dressed in a long-sleeved white button-down cotton shirt and the long brown skirt her mother had made for her. She covered her shoulders with a thick wool shawl and put on the boots Mrs. Sarah had given her. Coming from warm North Carolina, Anna had taken no thought to the winter weather she would endure in Ohio.

But when the snow started falling last week, Mrs. Sarah had said, "*You can't go outside in those shoes you came here with." She handed her a pair of brown boots. "These are for Ohio weather."*

Grateful for the boots, Anna left the boardinghouse and slogged her way through two feet of snow. Being several blocks away from the school, her face was stiff and frozen by the time she arrived at her Greek studies class. Mary was seated in the back. Anna took the seat next to her and began taking notes voraciously as soon as the lecture started. Today they were studying Greek words with English roots:

- *Cosmos*: Meaning "order" or "world," as in a perfectly ordered universe.
- *Cynicism*: Derived from the Greek word for "dog" (*kynos*). Refers to a philosophy of skepticism and rejection of societal norms.
- *Anathema*: Meaning "something cursed or accursed."
- *Acrobat*: From *akri* ("tip or edge") and *vaino* ("to walk"), meaning "someone who walks on the edge."
- *Acropolis*: Literally "city on a hill" (*κορυφή*—"top," *πόλη*—"city").
- *Cemetery*: From the Greek *koimeterion* ("sleeping place").
- *Agios*: Meaning "saint."
- *Aidos*: A virtue representing respect, modesty, and humility.
- *Meraki*: Meaning "to put your soul into your work."

The professor finished the instruction, and Anna reviewed her notes before she put down her writing instrument.

As their classmates were filing out, Mary lingered behind, a paper parcel clutched in her gloved hands.

"What's this?" Anna eyed it warily.

"Oh, a few things I thought you might put to use." Mary pressed the parcel forward. "A couple of dresses and a sweater I no longer wear, but they're still quite fashionable."

Anna's stomach twisted. The words "no longer wear" landed like a slap. She eyed the parcel, the fine paper, the faint scent of rose water that always clung to Mary's things. For a heartbeat, Anna couldn't move. The bag sat between them like a secret everyone could see. "Oh." Her voice came out too thin. "You're giving me your clothes?"

Mary shrugged, the way people do when they're proud of being generous. "I figured . . . Well, they don't fit my style anymore."

Anna's fingers twitched toward the bag but stopped halfway. Why did this feel so awful? Mrs. Sarah giving her boots had warmed her to the core, boots that meant she could walk to school without her toes freezing, a simple kindness. But this . . . this wasn't kindness. This was Mary saying, "Here, you can have what I've finished with."

Anna's lips tightened. "I can't accept this." She quickly pushed the bag back.

Mary blinked, clearly confused. "It's of no consequence, Anna. Really."

But it was—the biggest consequence in the world. Taking that bag meant others would see what Anna was trying so hard to get away from. If she needed someone else's leftovers, she would be branded as a charity case. It meant she'd always be the girl standing a step behind Mary, never beside her.

"I said I can't," Anna whispered, the words trembling with a mix of pride and shame she couldn't untangle. She wanted to be helped, perhaps, but not pitied. Not made into someone's good deed. She folded her hands tightly before her, as if that might keep her pride from slipping through her fingers.

"Of course you can. You've worn the same blouse all week. You need something heavier in this weather or you'll catch your death from the cold."

Anna lowered her head. Heat rose to her face. She touched her cheek. Were people watching her? Did they know she had only one winter blouse? "I can't afford to pay you," Anna said quietly.

Mary dismissed that. "There's no cost. A gift from one friend helping another."

Anna peered into the bag and softly gasped. Nestled inside were two delicate blouses, crafted from fine cotton and trimmed with lace—fabrics far beyond anything she ever could have afforded on her own. Beneath them lay a soft wool dress in a muted gray and, folded with careful precision, a white silk gown that shimmered faintly in the light. Her fingers lingered on the gown.

Mary casually said, "They're last season," but Anna had never cared about the whims of fashion. What mattered was whether the garment fit and whether it was respectable.

At the bottom of the bag was a heavy jacket, lined and thick enough to block even the harshest winter wind. Warmth and grace bundled together in a gift she hadn't expected.

She swallowed past her pride and whispered, "Thank you."

Mary didn't seem to give it another thought as she changed the subject. "You seemed interested in the lesson. I could hardly keep up."

Anna nodded. "Greek studies have become a healing balm to me. I especially enjoy Greek poets. Have you read Sappho?"

Mary smiled. "I have. But I find that I'm more swayed by Hesiod and Homer."

"I did not study much of Hesiod in my hometown. Hopefully I'll be introduced to his work this semester."

Mary put a hand over her mouth and giggled.

"Did I say something amusing?" Anna's eyebrow jutted upward. She was having a hard time understanding this young girl. Maybe it was their age difference, or maybe it was their economic difference.

"Forgive me." Mary held up a hand. "I'm enjoying our conversation, but it does tickle me. Several of my friends informed me that I would have a hard time finding a husband if I took this class. They would surely believe there was no help in sight for me if they heard us talking."

A memory of George and her sitting on a blanket in front of the fireplace while she spoke Greek to him and he kissed her lips after each word caused Anna to bite her lower lip as the pain of losing her husband tore through her for the second time that day.

Mary's eyes grew wide. "Oh my goodness. My mother would take a switch to me for my rudeness. I shouldn't have said that considering your loss."

"I remembered something, that's all." Anna wiped her eyes and stiffened her shoulders. "My husband is in heaven voice and added, "The White men where I come from threaten Colored men within an inch of their lives if they go near that ballot box."

"Or they create ridiculous poll tests that only Colored men have to pass," Ida said.

"My father is working to make things better for our men. They will soon be able to vote without all this nonsense," Mary assured them.

Anna wasn't convinced. There were too many obstacles in the Colored man's way. How could things change for their good? And why was Mary always talking about what her father was doing? What about *her*? Did she feel obligated to do anything to help with the matter?

The ball was kicked over by Mary's feet. Mason ran to retrieve it. "Hello, Miss Mary." His eyes aglow, he picked up the ball.

Mary smiled. She nodded at him. Mason ran back onto the field and scored the winning goal. Mary jumped up, clapping loud. "Yay! Yay!" she shouted.

"I guess I was wrong," Ida said with a giggle. "You're not interested in that gentleman at all."

Mary shoved her friend as the crowd began to disperse. Anna lifted her chair and was about to take it back to Society Hall when Mary told her, "Leave it. The college will get someone to put them away for us."

Anna stared at Mary, took a deep breath, and exhaled her frustration. "I *am* that someone else." Anna's nostrils flared as she grabbed another chair.

Confusion danced in Mary's eyes. "What do you mean? The workers always put our chairs back."

voice and added, "The White men where I come from threaten Colored men within an inch of their lives if they go near that ballot box."

"Or they create ridiculous poll tests that only Colored men have to pass," Ida said.

"My father is working to make things better for our men. They will soon be able to vote without all this nonsense," Mary assured them.

Anna wasn't convinced. There were too many obstacles in the Colored man's way. How could things change for their good? And why was Mary always talking about what her father was doing? What about *her*? Did she feel obligated to do anything to help with the matter?

The ball was kicked over by Mary's feet. Mason ran to retrieve it. "Hello, Miss Mary." His eyes aglow, he picked up the ball.

Mary smiled. She nodded at him. Mason ran back onto the field and scored the winning goal. Mary jumped up, clapping loud. "Yay! Yay!" she shouted.

"I guess I was wrong," Ida said with a giggle. "You're not interested in that gentleman at all."

Mary shoved her friend as the crowd began to disperse. Anna lifted her chair and was about to take it back to Society Hall when Mary told her, "Leave it. The college will get someone to put them away for us."

Anna stared at Mary, took a deep breath, and exhaled her frustration. "I *am* that someone else." Anna's nostrils flared as she grabbed another chair.

Confusion danced in Mary's eyes. "What do you mean? The workers always put our chairs back."

Anna glared at Mary, then yanked another chair.

"What did I say that's so wrong?" Mary demanded to know.

Anna rolled her eyes heavenward. "You come from a world where being served is natural and easy. I would never burden someone else with doing what I could do for myself."

Ida pulled at Mary's sleeve. "Come on, we need to go study."

Mary pulled away from Ida and gave her attention back to Anna. "Are you angry with me because my family is wealthy, when all I've tried to do is befriend you?"

Anna's chest heaved with the anger that boiled within. "More like you've pitied me, giving me your clothes, as if I have nothing suitable for Oberlin society."

Mary got in Anna's face, her arms flailing. "I was only trying to help you as any friend would."

"Don't you yell at me, Mary Church."

"Don't be so dense."

Anna scoffed at that. "I'm not the dense one. You think your wealth is what separates you from me. But one day you'll come to see that our color forever joins us together"—Anna gestured at the White students leaving from the other side of the field—"and separates us from them."

"We don't have to stand here and listen to your insults. You're responsible for getting these chairs back into Society Hall, not us. There's no need for the outrage." Ida linked arms with Mary and pulled her away.

As Anna continued doing the job the college assigned her, lugging one chair after the other back into Society Hall, she thought back to Mary's expression as Ida pulled her away.

It was as if Mary hadn't recognized that some of her actions were offensive.

On her third trip back to Society Hall with chairs in her hands, Anna stopped for a moment and glanced around at the people milling about, having conversations with other students but ignoring the fact that she needed help. Did they not see her? Was her plight invisible to those of a higher status?

CHAPTER 10

February 1881

Mary stood barefoot and perched rather unsteadily atop a narrow table in the center of the gathering room while her seamstress frowned up at her. "Hold still."

Mary tugged nervously at the rose-colored polonaise gown that her mother had commissioned from a dressmaker in Poland and had shipped across the Atlantic with great fanfare. The gown, with its tightly fitted bodice and gracefully draped overskirt drawn up in three puffed swags at the back to reveal a finely embroidered petticoat beneath, was an elegant specimen of old-world taste. It was not, however, what Mary would've chosen for herself.

To her mind, the style leaned too heavily on tradition, lacking the freshness and simplicity she admired in newer American fashions. But her mother had declared it "the appropriate gown" for the distinguished affair Mary was to attend at her father's side—a reception for dignitaries and donors where appearances mattered nearly as much as one's words.

Around her, the gathering room hummed with activity. February's final days had brought with them a raw, persistent chill that crept through the brick walls and lingered in the corners of the room. Outside, a light snow dusted the earth, keeping most of the young ladies indoors. Several girls sat near the hearth, their hands extended in front of the flickering flames, while another circle of students, seated cross-legged on the floor around the low reading table, pored over textbooks in preparation for an upcoming examination.

The seamstress worked quickly, her mouth full of pins as she knelt and marked the hem, occasionally mumbling instructions or nodding approval at the drape of the fabric. Mary shifted her weight from one foot to the other, acutely aware of how conspicuous she must appear.

The door creaked open and Suzie entered, her eyes widening in astonishment as they landed on Mary in full display. "This room is for all of us. Why are you standing on the table, acting as if you're the belle of the ball?"

Mary ignored her, but Ida spoke up. "Mary's going to President Garfield's inauguration ball, so leave us alone."

Janet's mouth hung open as if she was awestruck. "You're going to the inauguration?"

"Hold still," the seamstress told Mary again while pinning another spot at the bottom of her dress.

Standing straight, Mary told Janet, "For some reason, my mother has decided not to accompany my father to this event, so he has requested that I attend."

"You don't seem happy about it. I would be over the moon. You get to meet our new president!" exclaimed Katherine, the leader of the Ladies Literary Society.

Mary nodded her agreement. "I'm excited about it. I'm concerned for my mother. Not sure why she would give up an opportunity like this."

"Maybe she's smarter than you. Garfield is the dumbest president this country has ever had." Suzie wrapped her arm above her stomach. "I wouldn't be caught dead there. They'll probably be serving watermelon."

"Watermelon is a summer fruit, so I doubt it will be on the menu," Katherine said.

Mary appreciated that Katherine would try to defuse Suzie's hateful comment, but those words stung nonetheless.

After emancipation, formerly enslaved Black people began to grow and sell watermelon, gaining economic independence. Some White Southerners resented that Black people were succeeding in this endeavor and sought to demean them by insinuating that watermelon was a symbol of Black laziness and simplemindedness.

They perpetuated these awful beliefs through caricatures featuring Black people eating watermelon in minstrels and newspaper articles. Mary never understood the desire to pull down people who were only trying to make an honest living, but when looking through the eyes of hate, evil men could turn good things bad faster than the devil was struck down from heaven. But Black people were more than the caricatures they'd been made out to be. That's why college was so important to Mary.

After they received their degrees, more Black women would come behind them. In Mary's mind's eye a sea of Black women would be holding up college degrees they'd rightfully earned. They would lift the banner of success and force this country to see who they were. And then they would sit down on a hot summer day and eat watermelon without fear of what others made of it.

That was the world Mary hoped for . . . and it was the world she would one day see.

March 4, 1881

"Freedom can never yield its fullness of blessings so long as the law or its administration places the smallest obstacle in the pathway of any virtuous citizen."

Even with her petticoat and white gloves, Mary felt a chill run up her spine at hearing newly elected President Garfield say those eloquent words.

Beneath the pale spring sky, the chill of March brushing against her cheeks, Mary Church clutched her father's gloved hand as they stood on the wide lawn of the National Mall, surrounded by a multitude of men and women, their faces lifted with hope. The wind carried with it the scent of damp earth and coal smoke, but Mary scarcely noticed. Her heart beat strong with pride, for she had borne witness to a moment that would echo through history.

President James A. Garfield, standing tall and resolute upon the inaugural platform, had spoken words that stirred the soul—words that affirmed the dignity and full personhood of the Colored race. Mary, not yet eighteen, let the weight and wonder of the moment settle deep into her spirit. A hundred other men might one day occupy the White House, but she would never forget where she was when Garfield promised a fairer deal for her people.

At her side her father stood silent, his eyes trained on the president with a mixture of scrutiny and restrained hope. He'd seen too much in his life to be easily swayed by political promises. President Hayes had tried to defend Southern Negroes, but that protection had been hollow at best.

Today, though, standing in the very heart of the nation, Mary allowed herself a flicker of belief that perhaps, with President Garfield in office, the tide might finally begin to turn.

"It's a spectacular building. I'm sure Garfield is thankful they finished construction in time for his inauguration gala." Mary's father waved an arm toward the Smithsonian National Museum.

When President Garfield concluded his speech, Mary lifted the hem of her gown and walked to the National Museum with her father. She should be thankful her mother had spent so extravagantly on her dress, but Louisa Church paid little attention to current fashion. Being forced to endure an inaugural ball in a beautiful rose-colored gown with a bodice that simply wasn't low enough and was last year's fashion was almost shameful.

"I don't know why Mama decided to stay home, but I'm enjoying myself."

Father patted her hand. "I wouldn't want anyone else on my arm tonight."

As their weary legs carried them closer to the National Museum, Mary's eyes filled with wonder. She didn't get to

Washington, D.C., often. This place, where the business of the country was handled, fascinated her.

As did this new National Museum, which had opened only recently so that President Garfield's inauguration gala could be held here. The exterior was constructed with geometric patterns of polychrome brick. A sculpture rested atop the main entrance. An iron truss roof covered the building.

The exterior was indeed impressive, but as Mary entered the museum, stepping onto the temporary wood floor that had been laid for the night's festivities, she let the hem of her dress drop to the floor as she twirled around, taking in the grandeur.

Thousands of gaslights flickered throughout the building, casting a golden glow that danced along the floors and echoed off the high arched ceilings. Every corridor was adorned with festive bunting, state flags fluttering gently from polished brass poles, seals gleaming like medallions of pride. In the heart of it all, the rotunda held its own glorious marvel: Two newly installed electric lights blazed steadily in front of the towering *Statue of America*.

The crisp white light cut through the haze of the gas lamps, casting a halo around the statue's face, lending her an almost divine brilliance. Mary stood transfixed, her heart stirring with joy. One day, perhaps, the soft hum of electric light would replace the sputter of lamps in Ladies Hall. But for now, America moved slowly, inching toward the promise of illumination . . . one bulb at a time.

"Isn't she a beauty?" her daddy asked while seemingly transfixed by the sculpted woman in front of them.

Mary's eyes drank in the sculpture of this glorious woman, holding an electric light in her lifted right hand, a sight that caused Mary to blink several times while taking it in.

"I was told about this piece. But it's more powerful than I expected," her father continued. "She stands for peace, justice, and liberty."

"And what is the meaning of the light she holds in her hand?" Mary wanted to know.

Before Father could respond, a tall man with salt-and-pepper strands of wool atop his head and dark, foreboding eyes answered. "The light, my dear one, is supposed to be an indication of American skill, progress, and civilization."

Mary pressed her clasped hands against her mouth. Her father had informed her that this magnificent man would be in attendance, but she could barely contain herself. She was standing next to Frederick Douglass, the man whose speech "What to the Slave Is the Fourth of July?" she had recited in class last year.

She curtsied before him as if standing in the presence of a king. He took her gloved hand and kissed it as she said, "I am a great admirer of yours."

"Are you now?" He appeared to be amused, as if silly girls said such things on each outing.

"Surely I am not as great an admirer as your lovely wife, Mrs. Anna Douglass, but I have studied your writings."

"You don't say." Mr. Douglass smiled at her.

"She means it," Father interjected. Then he nudged Mary forward. "Let Mr. Douglass hear a bit of his speech that you recited."

Mary didn't need further encouragement. She had reveled

in the words, feeling as if someone was finally championing the Negro cause for equality. She stood straight, forgetting about the tightening of her corset as she began, "'What, to the American slave, is your 4th of July? A day that reveals to him, more than all other days in the year, the gross injustice and cruelty to which he is the constant victim. To him, your celebration is a sham.'"

Frederick lifted his top hat and bowed to Mary. "I wrote that speech thirty years ago. I'm thankful that students are still studying it."

Mary grinned as if she had an audience with the president himself. "I've read everything you've written."

Mr. Douglass nodded his approval. "There is one thing you haven't read. Tell you what. I'll mail a copy of my newest essay to your father."

Mary put a hand to her heart, joy shining in her eyes. "Thank you so much for this kindness. I'll pore over every word. Will it include some of the progress Colored folks have made in the country?"

Mr. Douglass wagged a finger at her. "Remember, Mary, if there's no struggle, there is no progress."

His statement echoed in her ears until it seemed to embed itself in the crevices of her heart . . . *"If there's no struggle, there is no progress."* Was she built for such struggles? Or was she to remain a lady of leisure, only dipping her toes into the movement with high society parties, education, marriage to a suitable man, and children?

Her father leaned in slightly, lowering his voice. "It's time to go into the ballroom. We don't want to keep the president waiting."

"Yes, Father." As they walked away from the rotunda, Mary stared at the Statue of America once more. Did the progress the statue stood for include the Negro race as well? Her father's wealth granted her access to people and places others could only dream of. But what did that mean? Was she the progress other Negroes could point to and say, "If Mary can attend a college like Oberlin and sit in classes with White students like equals, then we can do great things too."

With the election of President Garfield, a man clearly in the Negro's corner, Mary prayed her people would be brought closer to equality. That would truly be progress.

CHAPTER 11

April 1881

Mary went to the dresser in search of her pearl necklace. The snow had melted with the rising sun and April showers, and she was ready to throw off her winter coat and enjoy the sun.

Ida sat up in her bed and scowled. "You can't be serious—why do you have your party dress on?"

Mary slipped on the necklace her father had given her for her sixteenth birthday. "The more important question is, where is your party dress?"

After getting out of bed, Ida sat down at her desk and lifted her history book. "I'm behind in my studies. I can't attend Mr. Danly's party. And you shouldn't either."

"There's going to be dancing. Of course I should attend." Mary lifted the hem of her dress and swayed from one side to the other.

"The Aeolian Literary Society selected you to present

our argument this week, and you know who you're arguing against, or did you forget?"

Apparently the moment Suzie discovered that Mary would be giving the argument for Aeolian, she asked to represent the opposing side. Mary rolled her eyes heavenward. "I'm not worried about Suzie. She can go stew in a sour sauce."

"I hope you won't be stewing after the debate," Ida warned.

Mary paid her no mind. She grabbed a sweater and headed to Mr. John Danly's home on Main Street.

Passing by College Park, Mary breathed in the oxygen provided by the beautiful oak trees surrounding the immaculately kept square. The weather had been so dreary when the leaves fell off the trees and the nights became a mix of cold and wet. But now that the sun was bold and bright again, and the leaves were once again swaying on the trees, the walk to Mr. Danly's was a pleasant one.

When she entered the Danlys' home, she was greeted by a Colored woman wearing a maid's uniform. It struck Mary as odd that a family of abolitionists, who even now were working to guarantee the vote for Colored men, had a Negro maid.

But then as she recalled that her own father employed several Negroes in their household, she admonished herself for minding matters that were not her own. A grand piano stood beside the hearth, its polished surface reflecting the fire's glow. A man sat at the keys, weaving melodies that shimmered through the room, while a violinist stood close by, her bow dancing in harmony with the rising notes.

"Did you come to the Danlys' to stand around so we can all appreciate your beauty, or would you like to dance?"

She'd been caught in a web as she listened to the poetic sound of each note. Blinking, Mary glanced up at Mason. Handsome. Smiling. Holding a hand out to her.

Mary studied the man before responding. His dress shoes appeared worn and the jacket he wore was a little too big across the shoulders. He was studying theology. From her experience at Oberlin, most of the theology men didn't concern themselves much with shopping for fine clothes. He would need a wife to handle such things for him. Mary extended a hand. "I'd love to."

Mary glided onto the dance floor. Her father had hired an instructor to teach her the waltz so she wouldn't be clumsy during social events. The music was soothing, capturing her mind and allowing her feet to move with Mason's as their bodies moved ever closer.

"You're a good dancer," Mason said.

"I've had great instructors." She twirled as he lifted their hands high and gave her space to move around him.

Mason smiled. "I finally got you to go out with me."

Laughing, Mary told him, "This is not a date. Mrs. Johnston would have my head if I was on a date without a chaperone."

"We're dancing, and there's music . . . so that's something. Right?"

She was in his arms, swaying to the music—it was something.

When the dance was over, Mason brought a cool drink of tea and a finger sandwich over to Mary. "See, I can take care of you, if you'd only allow it."

She smiled at him. Mason was the distraction she needed. "Thank you, kind sir."

Mr. Danly walked over to them, nodded in Mason's direction, then said to Mary, "Your father assured me that you would join us on our mission trip for voter rights, but I'm sure your studies are keeping you occupied."

Her studies were challenging, not to mention her activities with the Aeolian Literary Society. But in truth, she wasn't sure what she could do to aid in the fight for Colored men's right to vote when women still didn't have that right in this country.

Her father considered it a worthy cause, but Mary wasn't so sure it was *her* cause. "I've been occupied, Mr. Danly. I'm sorry if my father misled you concerning my activities. But I'm not sure which mission I will take part in yet."

Mr. Danly patted her hand. "Take all the time you need. Our mission is a worthy endeavor and we'd love to have you."

She nodded but didn't commit. Mr. Danly moved on to his other guests, and Mary allowed Mason to escort her to the dance floor again.

When the party was over, Mason walked her home. "I had a fine time with you this afternoon. I hope you'll allow me to see more of you."

"My studies keep me busy."

"Do you make time to eat or to take a walk?"

He was staring at her so intently that Mary couldn't continue to deny his request. "I'll have to ask Mrs. Johnston for a chaperone."

As they arrived at Ladies Hall, he kissed her on the cheek. "I shall call on you this Wednesday."

Mary touched her cheek, still warm where Mason's lips had grazed it moments before. A soft breeze tugged at the

CHAPTER 12

The days passed softly at Oberlin, like whispered prayers and hymns sung with joy. Anna moved from class to class, and in the evenings there was always another student waiting for her help, another lesson to explain, another small payment toward her room, her board, her fees.

Next semester's fees would be higher since Anna elected to take an extra language class. She would save up so she could pay for it. Anna appreciated the financial assistance she received. Without it she wouldn't be able to study at Oberlin. But she didn't like being considered a charity case.

Sitting at the kitchen table at Mr. and Mrs. Watson's house, Anna helped their son, Jerome, with primary school math. "I'll never get this!" He smacked his hand on his head.

"You're doing fine, Jerome. Arithmetic is a series of rules and operations. You'll get it."

Anna had not been fond of arithmetic when she was in primary school either. Much work had been put into the hem of her day dress, fluttering it against her ankles as she stood outside Ladies Hall. The redbrick building rose behind her, proud and proper, its white shutters gleaming in the late-afternoon light. Elms lined the gravel path like quiet sentinels, their branches rustling overhead in a gentle symphony of spring leaves.

She watched Mason's tall frame recede down the walkway, his stride easy, confident. Did she have a new beau? Her lips curved before she could stop them. One thing she couldn't deny—he was handsome, with eyes that sparkled when he laughed and a voice that could coax a smile from the gloomiest soul. And he listened . . . really listened. That, too, was rare.

But what did it mean? Could this thing between them blossom, or would it wilt under the weight of her father's expectations?

Mary glanced at the horizon, where the sun dipped low and golden behind the steeple at First Church. Hope, like the breeze, stirred softly inside her.

standardization of mathematical notations, and efforts to make mathematical concepts more accessible to a wider audience through improved textbooks and teaching practices had helped her master the skill.

Anna grew to understand and love the process of figuring out equations. She brought all of her hard-earned knowledge to her tutoring sessions.

"Would you like a piece of cornbread and the pinto beans I fixed for supper?" Mrs. Watson asked as she stood in front of the stove stirring the pot.

Anna's belly wasn't always filled with the two meals she received at the boardinghouse. So when she was offered an extra meal from time to time, she rarely said no. "I would be delighted to join you for supper." Those meals didn't make her feel like a charity case like Mary's last-season clothes did. This was more like people in the community watching out for each other. That was the way she had been raised. Her mother had always offered a bowl of soup or beans to someone in need.

Jerome finished his lesson, then Anna ate with the family. After that she walked back to the boardinghouse. She brought the broom from the back porch into the house and started sweeping. After sweeping she took the load of clothes Mrs. Sarah had put in a basket outside. Anna washed the garments and then hung them on the line to dry.

By the time she finally made it to her room, Anna's eyes drooped and exhaustion hung heavy on her frame. But she had a paper due in her history class the next day, and there was no way she was going to ask for more time for her assignment.

She took out her writing instrument and began her paper on the Roman Empire's influence on Europe.

One day she would travel to Rome and Greece and all the places she read about. Anna was not delusional about her circumstances. A former slave girl was not promised much in this world. But even so, if she worked hard enough and was smart enough, her dreams would have to come true.

She stayed up late into the night to make sure that her paper was perfect, writing until the oil in her lamp burned down. The next morning Anna got out of bed and performed her chores before getting dressed for class. She then yawned her way down Professor Street, feeling tired and wholly unprepared for all that was required of her at Oberlin.

She was about two feet away from Ladies Hall on her way to Society Hall when the door burst open and Mary, Ida, and several other girls ran out of the building, giggling and yapping.

"We're about to be late."

"We need to have a meeting about girls who linger too long in the bathroom."

None of those girls had extra chores in the morning or a job that kept them from working on their assignments until late into the night. They shouldn't be rushing to class as if their bathroom situation was keeping them from being timely.

Since she didn't run down the street with the other women, it took Anna a few extra minutes to get to class. Mary and Ida were seated in the front of the lecture room. Anna placed the paper she'd burned the midnight oil for on the professor's desk as he stood before the class giving his lecture.

Anna took one of the empty seats closer to the back of the room. Since getting into that argument with Mary and Ida, Anna kept her head down, staying out of the way of trouble or rich girls who dismissed hardworking people.

A White man was seated next to her. He stared at her as if he wanted to say something but then changed his mind and turned his attention back to the professor.

Katherine, the girl she studied with last week while avoiding Mary, was seated behind her. She leaned forward. "Another long night?"

Anna rubbed her eyes, then blinked to refocus. "Some nights are longer than others. But I finished my paper."

"I finished mine two days ago, but you have more responsibilities than I do."

The professor continued his lecture, and Anna tried her best to keep her eyes open and listen while she jotted down as many notes as she could about the Ottoman occupation in Greece during the eighteenth century.

Midway through the lecture a Colored man entered the room and sat in the only seat that was available, which was on the other side of the White man seated next to Anna. She continued taking notes until the White man stood and loudly declared, "Professor, I have an objection."

"What's your objection?"

He glanced in Anna's direction and then at the Colored man who moments ago entered the room. "I know this college is of the mind that Coloreds should be educated same as a White man. But I shouldn't have to sit next to 'em like this."

From where she sat, Anna heard Mary suck in her breath

as if shocked. Anna began gathering her papers and was about to lean against the wall or find a spot on the floor when the professor said, "Sit back down, sir. This is the way of things at Oberlin as you well knew before applying to this college."

Now Anna was shocked. Never had she seen a White man so forcefully stand up against another White man asserting his prejudice. After saying his piece, the professor simply went back to giving instructions as if he had done nothing remarkable.

Instead of Anna lowering her head and slinking away as she'd intended, the White man sat back down in his seat and took notes without saying another word.

When class was over, Anna stayed in her chair, waiting for the room to clear before leaving. She was thankful the professor had spoken up for her, but the incident had left a residue of shame. She didn't want to face Mary and Ida, who she doubted ever dealt with such belittling comments.

"Are you going to Ladies Hall for the debate?" Katherine asked.

Anna had forgotten about the debate. She wanted to go take a nap. But her literary professor had asked them to write a report on the debate between the literary societies. Anna sighed. "Let me review my notes and then I'll be right over."

Despite her better judgment, Anna went to Ladies Hall. The Aeolian Literary Society sat on the left side of the society room, while the Ladies Literary Society was on the right.

Since Anna was in neither, she sat in the back as close to the middle as possible, hoping she wasn't in anyone's seat or in the way of anyone who didn't want to sit next to her.

Suzie McFarland was the first to speak. She gave a speech titled "The Woman's Place in Modern Society." According to her speech, Suzie believed that women enjoyed being taken care of by their strong husbands. Suzie went on to say that most women only attended college to find husbands so they could have children and raise families. Therefore, in her opinion, universities were places for women to bide their time until potential husbands found them.

She hit all of her notes and seemed convinced of her argument. However, Mary's rebuttal was eloquent and forceful as she stated concrete reasons why women would do well to take their education seriously and concern themselves with accomplishing something meaningful outside of marriage and family.

As Mary spoke, Anna found herself agreeing with her rebuttal. It was heartening to realize that she and Mary were united in the cause for women's rights. They might be different in other areas, but in this common ground, she would give Mary her due. Anna stood and applauded as Mary finished.

Mary would win the debate, Anna was positive of that. But when the judges came back and scored the win for Suzie, the confusion on Mary's face caused Anna to feel compassion for the girl. At that moment it didn't matter to her how pompous Mary had been in the past. She had been denied her due, and Anna knew why—there could only be one reason.

As one of the only other Black women in the room,

Anna walked over to Mary. "If it's any consolation, I thought you won."

Mary pursed her lips together and shook her head.

Suzie glared at Anna. "Who are you to come in here and challenge the judges' decision?"

Anna stepped back, not wanting confrontation with these people. "You did well also, but Mary's rebuttal was . . . better." Anna lowered her head, then mumbled, "In my opinion."

"Who cares what you think?" Suzie swung around and spoke to one of the girls in her literary club. "They'll let anyone in here these days. No standards anymore."

Anna's face heated. What did she think she was doing, hobnobbing with these highbrow ladies?

Mary walked away from Suzie in a huff and picked up the papers she'd read her rebuttal from. "I need to get to my next class."

Anna's mouth hung slack. She'd thought Mary would tell Suzie that she had as much right to enter Ladies Hall for these debates as anyone else. But Mary walked out of the room without a backward glance.

Suzie clearly wasn't the only one who thought Anna had no business in a place that housed elite women; Mary must have found her unworthy also. Anna shouldn't have come . . . shouldn't have entered where she didn't belong. If only her teacher hadn't asked for a report.

Suzie turned back in Anna's direction and sneered. "Are you still here?"

Anna didn't respond. Her shoulders slumped as she walked out of the society room. Were all eyes watching each step she took as she walked down the hall, passing people who belonged in this most prestigious building? When she entered the common area, she ducked her head and rushed to the front door.

"Anna, how nice to see you," Mrs. Johnston said as she entered the room. "I hope you've been enjoying Oberlin."

Putting her hand on the doorknob, Anna gave Mrs. Johnston a weak smile. She wished she could confess that all was not right in her world. But would Mrs. Johnston care?

CHAPTER 13

"I can't believe it!"

"How did I lose to that evil ol' Suzie McFarland?" Mary stretched out across her bed the day after the debate and bemoaned to Ida the trials and tribulations of letting down her literary group.

"See what gallivanting around campus, attending those parties and allowing Mason to court you, caused?"

Mary shot up. "I'm supposed to meet Mason by the elm today. I almost forgot."

Ida's lips tightened as she stared at Mary as if to say, *You'll never learn.*

Mary planted her feet on the floor. "Mason and that party have nothing to do with it. The judges simply refused to vote for me. And my rebuttal was far superior to Suzie's speech. Her words kept women in bondage to their husbands' whims. I liberated them."

Holding *The Oberlin Review* while flipping the pages of the college newspaper, Ida chuckled. "My dear, you really should be more humble."

Mary folded her arms across her chest. "You were there. Do you disagree?"

"Of course I think your rebuttal was better than Suzie's speech." Ida lifted the newspaper, walked over to Mary, and sat next to her. "See here, even *The Oberlin Review* thinks you were clearly the winner."

Mary took the paper out of Ida's hands and read the piece that had been written about the literary debate. In the writer's opinion, Mary's argument was sound and delivered with force and precision. Clearly she'd won the debate. "See, my extracurricular activities had nothing to do with it."

Ida tsked as she walked back over to her side of the room, leaving Mary with the school newspaper. "You know what my father says: Colored folks have to be two times better than White folks in order to be seen on the same level. So you needed to work on that rebuttal until it was three times better than what Suzie could do if you wanted to win."

Mary's cheeks poked out in a pout. "That's not fair."

"When has anything been fair for us?"

Mary studied the article in *The Oberlin Review* once more. She had won that debate; others saw it. But those judges hadn't been willing to proclaim her the winner. Well, she wasn't going to let their blindness cause her to stumble. She was going to doubly prepare for the next debate. She would show them.

Later that day as she sat in the student hall with her journal in hand, writing a poem about the dangers of inequality, one of the White students in her English class ran over to her. "Mary, you've been nominated for class poet. If you win, you'll recite a poem during the Sophomore Exhibition."

The program for the Sophomore Exhibition was one of the major public events of the academic year, and she was being nominated to deliver the poem. The news was like a balm to her wounded heart. She leaped from her seat and hugged her classmate. Most of the students knew she loved both reading poetry and writing it. She longed to set the world ablaze with words. "Are you serious? Is this true?"

"As true as rain. I'm one of the students who nominated you."

Mary hugged the girl again. "Thank you."

"No need to thank me. You're sure to win."

A smile crept across Mary's face as her schoolmate walked away. She picked up her paper and other supplies and took them back to Ladies Hall to drop them in her room. Time had gotten away from her as she wrote her poem. She needed to meet Mason by the elm in College Park. And Ida was nowhere to be found. Her friend was supposed to come along and chaperone.

But Ida wasn't in their room and Mary couldn't wait on her to return. Like a flash, she rushed out and started running down the street until she reached her destination. She bent over, put her hands to her knees, and took a few deep breaths. She'd run too fast. Her mother would scold her for not being ladylike. But she hadn't wanted Mason to think she'd delayed on purpose.

"Are you okay? Should I get smelling salts?"

A couple more deep breaths and then Mary raised herself upright again. She surveyed Mason's dark complexion and compassionate brown eyes. Leaving Ladies Hall without a chaperone . . . not a good idea. But he was here and she was here.

"You needn't have rushed. I can assure you I would've waited." His eyes twinkled with amusement. Was he laughing at her?

She wrapped her arms around her chest. "Maybe I should rush back to Ladies Hall. I should have waited for my chaperone anyway."

Mason lifted a basket. "If you do that, I'll have to eat this fried chicken all by myself."

"You brought food?"

"And a blanket." He opened the basket, then spread the red-and-white blanket on the grass in front of the big elm tree. He then placed the basket on top of the blanket and held out a hand to Mary.

She glanced around at the people passing by. A faint frown crossed her face. "We can't sit out here in front of everyone."

"Why can't we? College Park is a public place for all Oberlin students." He touched her hand, pulled her closer.

Mary's foot stepped onto the blanket. Her professor from philosophy class passed by. She thought he'd admonish them to move along. When he did not, Mary's knees buckled. She allowed herself to be brought down. First her knees were on the blanket, then she adjusted her skirt and sat with her legs crossed at the ankle. "Okay, I'm down here. Let me taste a piece of this chicken."

Mason's smile lit up the sky. He opened the basket and took out a quarter leg and handed it to Mary. "I gave the lady at my boardinghouse a fourth of my earnings this week to fry these for us, so I hope you like it."

Mason's schedule with theology classes and study and church duties was rigorous. He wasn't able to work but a few hours a week, enough to pay his room and board and to have a little pocket money. Mary felt special realizing that he would spend what little money he had on her. She bit into the leg and found it to be juicy and seasoned to perfection. "Mmm. This is good."

"I'll let her know that you approve."

Wiping her fingers on the blanket, Mary leaned back on her forearm and let the warmth of the day settle on her like a dove perched on the branch of a tree. Students and faculty continued to pass by. A few of them glanced their way, but Mary wasn't paying them much attention. She only had eyes for Mason. He was not the man her father would approve of. He didn't come from a wealthy family, nor did he have lofty goals that would bring him wealth. But Mary was at home in his company.

"Tell me something." Mason placed his piece of chicken back in the basket and gave her his full attention.

"Why theology and not business or politics?"

"The simple answer is that I believe God has called me to His ministry. But you should also know that it's in my blood. My father and grandfather are both preachers."

"But this country is ripe for revolution."

"I don't disagree," Mason said.

The bass in his voice sent a trembling up Mary's spine. No man should be as handsome as Mason, and certainly not a man of the cloth. "What will you be able to do about it behind a pulpit?"

His head fell back as he let out a boisterous laugh.

"Don't laugh at me. It's a fair question."

As he recovered himself, Mason asked, "What do you think men of the cloth have been doing behind the pulpit since the end of slavery?"

"Preaching God's Word, of course."

"Yes, we are called to preach God's Word, but most Negro preachers also preach against oppression. This is how we do our part, by calling out the evil of inequality with the platform God gives us."

Mary was about to respond, but as she watched Mrs. Johnston approach, her words got caught in her throat.

"Well, Miss Mary, it seems you know better than I," Mrs. Johnston said with a stern face as she towered over Mason and Mary.

Mary's stomach dropped like a stone. Why . . . why . . . why did she think she'd get away with her disobedience? Mrs. Johnston surely would think she was without character. "I . . . I . . ."

"The rules, Mary. You do know the rules, correct?" Mrs. Johnston sighed. Her gaze slipped away as if she couldn't bear the sight in front of her.

Mary had never thought of herself as a disappointment, but clearly that was where they were now. "Have I offended you?"

"You have offended *yourself*. No courting without a chaperone, you know that." Mrs. Johnston clasped her hands together. "But thankfully, I was headed out for a grocery run that you will now be helping me with."

Two of the girls from Ladies Hall walked past them,

giggling and pointing at her. Another one of her professors strolled the other way, shaking his head. Heat rushed up Mary's neck. She stared at the ground as she stood and wiped off her dress.

Mrs. Johnston tapped her booted foot on Mason's blanket. "Come along."

The chicken and conversation with Mason had been lovely. But the shame of it all was too much for her. She turned away from him and began walking with Mrs. Johnston.

Mason picked his blanket and basket off the ground and ran over to her. "Let me walk you. I can help with the groceries."

"You've done enough to harm Miss Mary's reputation for the day." Mrs. Johnston shooed him away. "That will be all."

Mason stared at Mary, waiting for her to speak on the matter, but another group of girls from Ladies Hall glanced in their direction and laughed. Mary would not abide being a laughingstock for anyone, not even the handsome and charming Mr. Mason. "I'll see you around," she told him and continued walking with her chaperone.

CHAPTER 14

"Anna Cooper, what are you doing?"

Mrs. Sarah came into the kitchen while Anna was sweeping. "I'm finishing my chores."

"No, you aren't. If you keep working around the house, you're going to be late."

"I'll be fine."

Mrs. Sarah took the broom away from Anna. "You were late for class a few days ago. I'll not have you getting poor scores on account of housework."

Anna hated calling attention to herself by being late. Ever since that man made an issue of sitting next to her and another Negro student, she tried to get to class early enough to pick a seat in the corner of the room, away from those who might object to her presence.

"I have a little more time this morning." She reached out for the broom. "Let me finish sweeping. I promise I won't be late."

"I appreciate everything you do around the house. You

have more than earned your board and keep." Mrs. Sarah held on to the broom. "Go . . . be early to class today."

"You're too kind to me." Anna hugged Mrs. Sarah. "I'll stop cleaning if you'll answer a question for me."

"What do you need to know, dear?"

Anna glanced around the room, then leaned closer to Mrs. Sarah. "Where did you hide the runaway slaves?"

A big, boisterous laugh roared through the room as Mr. Wilson entered the kitchen. "I suppose you think we have a hidden door we slid open and stuffed our guests in."

"Don't laugh, Mr. Wilson. It's an honest question. I've only lived in a place where the enslaved ran away from, never in a town that they ran to. How did you hide them?"

Wilson Bruce Evans sat at the kitchen table. Mrs. Sarah put a cup of coffee in front of him. "Eggs?" she asked him.

"Thank you, my dear." Mrs. Sarah went to the stove.

Anna stood next to the table. She held her breath as she stared down at Mr. Wilson's bushy white beard and head full of white hair. This man possessed wisdom she knew nothing of. She had wanted to ask this question the day she arrived, but that seemed too forward.

He glanced up at her. "You're right; slavery was no laughing matter. I would've done anything to remove someone from that scourge of senseless suffering."

Mrs. Sarah turned toward them while scrambling the eggs. "We weren't the only ones who helped. The Bardwells and John Scott, to name others in this town who opened their doors to runaways. And I doubt any of them had hidden doors either."

Mr. Wilson said, "We figured out the best way to hide

a person was to do it in plain sight. So the runaway slaves lived in our home, like you do. Or they stayed in the area out back that I use for my woodwork. They walked the streets of Oberlin, like you do every day. They were here temporarily, until we could get them to the next site that would take them to Canada."

Mrs. Sarah put the eggs and buttered bread in front of her husband, then shooed Anna away. "You've got your answer; now go get ready for school."

"Yes, ma'am." Anna took the stairs two at a time. The blouse she brought from Raleigh was dirty. She hadn't had time to wash it last night. She opened her dresser, hesitated a moment, then pulled out the white blouse Mary had given her. It had buttons down the front with lace on each side of the buttons.

Anna had never worn a blouse with extra frills. After fastening the last button, Anna let her hand run down the side of it. The smoothness of the silk caused an easy grin to spread across her face.

But even with the richness of the silk cloth pressing against her back as she walked to the college, Anna wondered if she had made a grave mistake. The grass was green in Oberlin, and the homes were modest. Nothing flashy like those plantation homes back in Raleigh. The people were mostly pious and humble, but Anna was like a bird stuck in a cage.

Should she have stayed in Raleigh and attended Shaw University with people who looked like her? People who weren't offended by her presence?

Each day she witnessed things on campus that struck her

as outside of what the founders had intended. She'd thought the White students would welcome her with open arms. Had thought that getting out of the South would soothe her soul. But Northerners hated them the same as the Southerners.

It was as if the people of Oberlin were in tune with Colored folks receiving their freedom, but not with higher education or equality of the races. Anna's heart hurt. The North was no better than the South in the way Whites thought of Black people.

Glancing up at the sky, Anna was surprised at how big and bright the sun was so early in the morning. She was used to heat invading her walks in the South. She thought it would be a bit cooler here since it wasn't yet summer but the second week of May.

As she came upon the Soldiers Monument, she stood there for a moment and soaked in the shade that shadowed the monument. Anna began reading the names that had been inscribed on it.

Ever since Mary had told her about this structure, Anna had tried to wrap her mind around why ninety-six men from these parts, fifty-six of them being Oberlin students, had given their lives for the cause of freedom if they didn't want the Negro man and woman to be all the way free.

Or did the idea of freedom fall out of favor once these fine, upstanding White folks understood that the Negro aspired to the same lofty goals as they did? The semester was almost over and Anna was contemplating her path and dreaming about going home. Sighing, she tried to muster the courage to get through the day.

"This monument is special. I stand here at least once a

week and remind myself of all that was lost for the cause of freedom."

Anna had been deep in thought and hadn't noticed anyone approaching. Katherine Smalls, the newly elected president of the Ladies Literary Society, came up behind her.

Anna stepped to the side and allowed the girl to move closer. Katherine thrust a finger at a name inscribed on the monument. "Henry McNair was my uncle. My mom still grieves for him."

Anna understood the sorrow weighing on Katherine's mother, a deep, unyielding ache that clutched the heart and refused to let go. "I'm sorry for your loss."

Katherine's eyes dimmed a bit, but she gave Anna a small, distant smile while memories danced in her eyes. "It was a long time ago. I was only four years old when it happened, so I didn't know him well. But I'm proud of what he did."

Many lives were lost during the War Between the States. Black lives and White lives. Anna was sure that the Black men thought they were fighting for a better life for their families. Some things became better, but most had stayed the same.

"You don't feel at home here at Oberlin, do you?"

How could one feel at home when people kept letting her know that she didn't belong? But Anna couldn't bear the gaze of pity on her mother's face if she came home a failure. She couldn't be found lacking at Oberlin or anywhere else. "I've been gathering my bearings. I'll be fine."

"Well, the Ladies Literary Society is in need of another member. Maybe you should join us."

Join them? A lot of ladies in that group were not friendly

to Coloreds. Why would Katherine suggest such a thing? "I don't know."

"What worries you? You're brilliant. We could use a person like you."

"What about the people who don't think I should even be on this campus?"

Katherine scrunched her face so hard, lines appeared on her forehead. "Who thinks that?"

Katherine had been nice and polite to Anna. But she doubted the girl was as naive as she appeared at this moment. "Suzie, for one. She doesn't want people like me around."

Rolling her eyes heavenward, Katherine said, "Sue is not the leader of our group. I take over that responsibility next year. And I would be honored to have you join."

She was barely getting her assignments done with all of her chores and tutoring. "I'm not sure if I can fit one more thing into my schedule."

They started walking up Professor Street, headed to French Hall. Katherine said, "We only have two more weeks before our summer break. Why don't you come to our last debate as my guest and then think about joining us at the beginning of the fall semester?"

What had Mr. Wilson said? Something about staying safe by hiding in plain sight. Had she run away from her home in the South to hide in Oberlin? "I'm signing up for extra classes during fall semester, but I'll think about it."

"Make sure you do. Being a part of the Ladies Literary Society might be the thing you need to fit in here."

When they arrived at French Hall, Anna told Katherine,

"I don't mean to be rude, but I don't understand why you care if I fit in or not."

A beat of silence followed, then Katherine offered a faint encouraging smile. "I told you about my uncle. But what I didn't say is that I overheard a conversation between him and my mother before he left for the war. She wanted to know why he had to fight . . . why this was so important to him. I'll never forget what he said."

As Anna stared at Katherine, waiting for her to finish her statement, it seemed as if the girl traveled back in time and was drifting on a memory before she said, "'None of us are free until all of us are free.'"

Anna needed to challenge Katherine's thinking on freedom. "But you do understand that being free without equality is its own kind of bondage."

Katherine nodded. "So the fight isn't over."

No, the fight wasn't over. Katherine was doing her part by befriending her, and Anna appreciated the olive branch that was being extended. But friendship alone wasn't enough to change the world . . . or the whispers that followed her down these storied halls.

Anna had a part to play as well. She wasn't sure yet what that would be, only that doing nothing wasn't an option anymore. Her pulse quickened with something that felt like courage—or maybe defiance. *Then we fight on*, she thought, and smiled. The two walked into literature class shoulder to shoulder.

CHAPTER 15

Mary could hardly sleep the night before the election results. Becoming the poet for the Sophomore Exhibition meant everything to her. She'd already written to her father to tell him of her nomination. She couldn't wait to tell him of her win.

Her father didn't want her getting ideas about employment after college. But if she could show her father that she excelled in the things that mattered to her, maybe she'd be able to convince him that work, even for a woman of means, was a worthy endeavor.

"Hey, sleepyhead, it's time to get up." Ida nudged her.

Mary rolled over and rubbed her eyes. "Morning came too fast."

"You should've gone to sleep like I told you last night."

After getting out of bed, Mary stretched and yawned. "My nerves got the best of me."

"What are you so nervous about?" Ida rolled her eyes. "You're the only poet in our class. Of course you're going to win."

Mary gathered her bathroom necessities from the top of her dresser, then pulled a white dress out of the drawer. "Thanks for your vote of confidence."

"You'd better hurry. A line was forming in front of the bathroom when I came out. Reverend Brand is about to announce the poets for the exhibitions, and then you'll see how many others voted for you as well."

The exhibitions were always held at First Church, so Reverend Brand did the honors of announcing the winners. Mary headed for the shared bathroom, but as a thought dropped into her spirit, she swung back to Ida with her day dress pressed against her chest. "What if they don't pick me?" A rare moment of self-doubt seeped in and strangled Mary's hope.

"Who else would they pick? You get excellent marks on the poems you turn in for Literature, so stop worrying." Ida shooed her out of the room.

"You're right." Mary's heart lifted until she stepped into the hall and came face-to-face with seven women standing in line for the bathroom. Not today. "Ladies, I need to cut the line. Will one of you please help? I have extra cookies I can share."

The third girl to the door told her, "I have Professor Martin, and he won't let me take my exam if I'm late, so I can't get out of line."

But the sixth and seventh girls said, "We'll take those cookies. You can get in front of us."

Mary moved up in line as the bathroom door opened and the first person waiting ran in. She was now fifth and prayed she wouldn't miss the announcement. Two of the girls in line only needed to use the toilet, so they came out quickly. After fifteen minutes of standing in line, Mary finally got her turn.

She went into the bathroom and refreshed herself, then pulled her day dress over her head. Soon she and Ida were walking to First Church, where several other students had already gathered. Janet rushed over to her and whispered, "You're sure to win. I know of at least three others in our literary group who voted for you."

"Thank you. It'd be my honor to serve as class poet."

"You deserve it." Janet took her seat at the front of the room, then eyed Mary with a conspiratorial grin.

Mary wasn't sure if she should sit up front so she could quickly make her way to the pulpit area when Reverend Brand announced that she would be the class poet, or if she should sit in the back of the sanctuary so she didn't seem so presumptuous.

Ida tilted her head toward two seats in the middle of the room, and the decision was made for her. "Your father will be so proud," Ida whispered as they took their seats.

"I hope so. He needs to see me as more than his daughter." Mary was growing . . . exploring . . . figuring out who she was. More and more, the liberation of women was becoming top priority. Men had far too many rights that weren't enjoyed by women. She needed to figure out the best way to express her thoughts to her father.

Reverend Brand entered the sanctuary with the ballots in his hand. Mrs. Johnston and the principal of the Men's Department followed him to the pulpit.

"I won't hold you long," Reverend Brand said. "We're always happy to host the Sophomore, Junior, and Senior

Exhibitions." He lifted the envelopes with Mrs. Johnston standing on his left and the principal of the Men's Department on his right. "And now we'll see who our poets will be."

He allowed Mrs. Johnston to open the first envelope. "Well, this is a surprise." Mrs. Johnston's eyes scanned the room.

Ida poked Mary's side. Mary's heart rate sped up. She sucked in air, put her hands on the edge of the pew, and began to lift herself.

Mrs. Johnston gestured to the back of the room. "Mr. Peter Hanover, can you please come stand beside me? You've been voted sophomore class poet."

The room shifted. Mary's legs wobbled as she fell back into her seat. Her mouth parted, but no sound came. She blinked once, twice, as if the words hadn't yet landed. She wasn't the class poet? Had she heard correctly?

A hush fell over the room, and several eyes drifted in Mary's direction. Her chin lifted even as her heart sank. How could Peter have bested her? She was in two classes with him, and he hadn't so much as written two lines of verse in their philosophy or literature classes.

Ida nudged her. "I can't believe this," she muttered.

Don't cry . . . don't cry, Mary admonished herself even as hot tears formed in her eyes. She quickly wiped the disobedient tears away, then squeezed Ida's hand. "What happened? Why did this happen?"

Tears leaked from Ida's eyes too, as if Mary's pain was her pain. "I don't know. I thought you had enough votes."

The president of the Men's Department called off the name of the junior class poet, and then Reverend Brand announced the senior. Everything was a blur as Mary glanced around the room, noting smirks from a few of the students. Why were they so cruel? What had she done to them? What was her sin that they would vote for a person with no poetry experience to be the class poet rather than her?

Mrs. Johnston's lips pinched as she and Mary locked eyes. The students began to stand, getting ready to leave the sanctuary. Mrs. Johnston's eyes flashed as if she suddenly remembered another detail, then she lifted her hand. "Wait, don't leave yet."

The students reclaimed their seats.

Mrs. Johnston said, "We will need decorators for the exhibitions. I'm asking that Mary Church and Susan McFarland work together to make this the most festive exhibition Oberlin has ever seen."

The students clapped, then stood and began filing out of First Church. Katherine and Janet ran over to Mary. Janet hugged her. "I'm so sorry. We thought you would surely win."

The hurt of it all stung like nothing else Mary had experienced. If Peter had been her equal or even if his poetry bested anything she could do, then she would understand this slight from her peers. But he wasn't and everything about the selection seemed wrong. As a Colored woman she doubted many in her class would believe she was superior, so she said, "I'm sure Peter will do a fine job."

"He doesn't even like poetry. They nominated him to spite you," Katherine said.

"And he won." Wetness filled the corners of her eyes. Mary needed to remove herself before the tears rolled down her face. Ida grabbed her arm and moved her forward.

Mary stepped outside and drew in a shaky breath of the

crisp afternoon air, hoping it would steady the storm inside her. *Why? . . . why? . . . why?* pulsed in her chest like a heartbeat. She wanted to scream to the heavens, to anyone who might listen. Poetry had always been her refuge, her joy, her rebellion. To stand before a crowd and give voice to one of her verses would have meant everything. But her chance had been stolen, snatched away by those who saw her not as gifted but as less than.

Her throat tightened as hot tears welled in her eyes. She turned her face to the wind, ashamed of the way rejection burned so deeply, as if it had peeled back her skin and exposed the raw and aching parts. She wanted to run, to disappear into a shadowy corner where no one could see her shame. How could they not see her worth? Hadn't she been born to rise? Wasn't she destined to walk among presidents, ambassadors, and great men like Frederick Douglass?

The lie of that promise echoed louder than any truth. If she belonged in such rarefied company, then why was she not even permitted to deliver a simple poem in front of the White students at Oberlin? Her spirit crumbled beneath the weight of that question and the cruel silence that followed.

But this was not her truth. She would not let them steal victory from her. Today's tears did not change who she was. If she had to work harder, fight harder, it didn't matter. One day her peers would know the truth. They would know she was their equal in every way.

CHAPTER 16

They called it buck breaking where Anna came from. Before emancipation, when a slave got too big for his britches, the slave owner would publicly flog and humiliate him in inhumane ways that only the devil himself could have devised. Slaveholders would force other slaves to witness their vile acts as if they were proud of the degenerates they had become.

The White students who voted against Mary thought she needed to be brought down a peg or two. Needed to show her that despite her wealth she was not, and never would be, one of them.

Anna didn't know why it was so important to Mary to be accepted by those idiots. Didn't understand why Mary thought attending First Church and putting herself in proximity to whiteness would prove anything to people who didn't want her there.

Things weren't perfect at Second Church. They didn't have the funding that First Church had. The walls were in need of painting. Oil lamps were used to provide light inside the small church, and the cookstove heated the building during the cold winter months.

In the heat they were currently experiencing, Anna and many other parishioners used their hands or pieces of paper to fan themselves. But even as sweat dripped from her forehead, Anna didn't want to be anywhere else on campus.

She'd come to the weeknight service, needing to be among like-minded people—people who knew the burden of being wrapped in skin that was deemed unworthy, people who kept striving against all odds. Those were her kind of people. It was easy being with them. Easy to clap her hands and sing along with the choir.

"Wade in the water,
Wade in the water, children,
Wade in the water.
God's gonna trouble the water."

Had God troubled the waters when He allowed her to apply to Oberlin College? Was this good trouble or the worst trouble she'd ever gotten herself into? Why did the people up north seem no different than the ones who enslaved her and her mother down south?

When the choir took their seats, Pastor stood behind his wooden pulpit. His eyes were ablaze with the fire of a man who'd seen evil and was about to stomp on its head. Gripping the pulpit on each side, he leaned forward and sang, "Not much longer, I say, not much longer."

The congregation shouted back, "God's coming to see about His people."

"Not much longer, I say, not much longer," Reverend Nunon repeated.

And then the congregation shouted again, "God's coming to see about His people."

Goose bumps went up Anna's arms. This was the third time this chant had been done since she'd been attending Second Church. It was normally followed by a message that set the tone for the rest of the week. Anna needed to be inspired. She needed something to encourage her to keep moving forward. She shifted in her seat and prepared for the message that was about to be delivered.

Restless, Mary left her dorm and set out for a stroll around the campus when she ran into a second-year student in Oberlin's Business Department. He was tall and fair skinned with a cleft chin.

"Hey, Miss Mary, what you up to on this lovely evening?" Timothy Jones tilted his hat as she walked by.

"Out for a stroll." She didn't know him well. They didn't have any classes together. The only place she ran into him on a regular basis was at chapel on Tuesday and Thursday mornings.

"I'm strolling over to church. We have service tonight. Do you mind if I walk with you?"

First Church didn't have service tonight. She hadn't seen him in attendance at her church anyway, so Mary presumed he was referring to Second Church. He gave her a lopsided grin, and she smiled back. "I guess I can walk that way."

Mary hadn't been in Mason's company since her thorough embarrassment from that crazy picnic idea. She had stuck to her studies. Right now, gentlemanly company might be what she needed.

As they were approaching Second Church, music and then chanting seemed to encircle them. It sounded like a war cry being sent up to God.

"I don't recall seeing you at the gentlemen's tea. Were you there when we hosted you all at Ladies Hall?"

He shook his head. "Family emergency."

Mary's brow furrowed as her voice dipped. "I hope everything's okay."

"All is well."

She liked the sound of his voice. It was a deep baritone that sounded warm and smooth. Mary could listen to him talk for hours.

They were a few feet away from Second Church. The music thumped so loudly the ground shook. "What's going on in there?"

He faced her. "God's coming to see about His people."

His comment was so random that she stopped walking and stared at him. As she listened, those same words came from inside the church. He grabbed her hand. "Come with me."

Mary pulled back. "I attend First Church. Not sure about this."

"You can still attend your regular service on Sunday. Join me for this weeknight service."

Mary had never attended services here. She hadn't seen the need for a Colored church when there was still so much work to be done to unify the races. But today an overwhelming desire to be around like-minded people swept over her, and she allowed him to pull her forward.

The moment Mary walked inside the church, she took note of the disrepair. Paint chipping off the walls, open cracks between the wide boards on the floor, and worn fabric on the chairs. Mary watched her step, fearing she might fall through the floor and twist an ankle.

He squeezed her hand. "Let's sit over here." He indicated two seats in the back of the small building.

Sitting down, Mary caught sight of Anna at the front. The girl seemed to be soaking in every word as Reverend Nunon read from the Bible.

When the pastor finished reading, he faced the congregation. "Brothers and sisters, I have a dilemma before me. I want to preach a hopeful message. I want to believe the words we chant and the prayers we send up to heaven.

"While much has changed, so much has stayed the same. Even in this town where men like Wilson Bruce Evans and so many others went to prison for the right of one man to live free.

"Here in Oberlin, we are proud that our actions ignited a war that eventually freed enslaved people. But our work is not done. As long as Colored folk still bow their head to a White man . . . our work is not done. As long as convict leasing laws still exist in the South . . . our work is not done. As long as we're still seen as the lesser race . . . our work is not done."

Reverend Nunon sighed before adding, "So I ask you, my brothers and sisters, what are you willing to do to ensure that Colored people are seen as equals in this country we all live in?"

His message chilled Mary. She'd read about the shameful practice of convict leasing in the South where they arrested Colored men for the crime of sitting around, minding their own business. Judges were in on this scam that brought money to the state and free labor to former plantation owners, coal mines, and anywhere White folks needed labor they didn't want to do themselves.

In Mary's estimation the answer to this shameful practice would be getting more Black men *and* women the right to vote. Reverend Nunon's message left her wondering what she could do to effect change. But she was a girl without any rights in this country. What could she do that would make a difference?

CHAPTER 17

Mrs. Johnston stood at the bottom of the stairs and yelled, "Mail's here!"

Mary's ears perked up. She hadn't received any correspondence from her family in over a month. The school year would end within ten days, but she still hadn't received her train tickets to Memphis. After putting on her shoes, she and several other ladies caused a stampede as they rushed down the stairs.

Hands outstretched, they eagerly asked, "Anything for me?"

Mrs. Johnston passed out the mail, and to Mary's delight a package had arrived from her father. Mary thanked Mrs. Johnston, then ran back up the stairs to her room. Ever since she was eight years old, Mary was only permitted to be with her family in Memphis during the summer months or when they came to visit her.

Mary was thankful for the yearly visit from her mother and father during Christmas or springtime. They would stop in to see her at her boardinghouse before vacationing in whatever part of the world they fancied. There were times when she and her brother were allowed to vacation with them. It was always a joy to be with her family, but she most enjoyed the summer months. It was the only time she felt at home.

When she opened the package and pulled out the train tickets, she twirled around the room with delight. "I'm going home."

Hugging the tickets to her chest, Mary pictured the frilly white drapes in her bedroom. Her warm blanket that had ruffles of lace on the top and her fluffy rug that warmed her feet as she got out of bed. There were no extra frills in her room at Ladies Hall. At Oberlin College, excess was sinful. But she would soon be back in Memphis, even if only for the summer. Lying on her soft mattress would feel like heaven.

Mary placed the train tickets on her desk and then pulled the letter out of the package. It was written by her father:

My dearest Mollie,

I pray that all is well with you and that you are rising to every occasion at Oberlin. You have always been a stellar student and I'm sure your professors enjoy having you in their classrooms.

Unfortunately, I must tell you that when you come home this summer, we will not be at the house you were born in. The city of Memphis hosted a demonstration of fire equipment on our street a few weeks ago. During this demonstration, they burned down our home. It was a clear act of revenge on our mayor's part. My activism as it relates to Black voter rights has sparked his hatred. Nonetheless, we shall march on.

I will be at the train depot to pick you up when you arrive and will escort you to our temporary home. I am sorry that you have to come home under these circumstances. But I will not give up my quest, and I hope you can understand my zeal.

Your loving father,
Robert Church

Her family lived in a wealthy mixed-race neighborhood. It was a peaceful place where nothing exciting ever happened. How could the mayor hate her father so much that he'd burn down their home and run the risk of burning down the homes of others in the neighborhood?

She didn't understand that kind of hatred. Why didn't her father consider the harm his actions were causing the family? They had lost their home due to her father's efforts. But then she remembered Reverend Nunon's words. *"As long as we're still seen as the lesser race . . . our work is not done."*

While thinking on the things that troubled her, Mary lifted her notes from her desk and went to the society room. She had been asked to give the argument at their literary meeting today. Honestly, Mary didn't know why her fellow literary society members still trusted her to compete against the other society. Her plan was to run for office next year and leave the debates to those more eloquent than her.

Actually, the debater didn't have to be eloquent. But she did have to get enough votes from the Ladies Literary Society to win a debate. Most of Mary's votes came from the literary society she belonged to; she received few votes from the other side. She figured Suzie's being a member of the other literary group might have something to do with that.

"Are you ready?" Ida asked when she entered the room.

"I hope so." Mary gave her friend a tight smile. She took her place behind the podium on the right. As she glanced to her left, she saw Suzie standing behind the other podium, smirking at her.

Mary took a deep breath and laid out her first argument: "The enemy of progress is the ballot box that has been denied to women of all races. Susan B. Anthony and Lucy Stone knew this. That is the reason they traveled to the American Anti-Slavery Society meeting and suggested that they combine forces to bring equality to all citizens. If the AASS had merged with them, women would probably already have the vote and our Colored men would not still be fighting to register."

Mary continued on with her sound argument. She watched as heads nodded in agreement. Ida clapped as Mary concluded her argument. Surely Suzie would not be able to refute an argument that was built on facts and research.

Suzie's rebuttal was not built on facts. She informed the group that White women should not concern themselves with the problems of Coloreds and proceeded to rant about the inequality of the races. Her rebuttal made no sense. Surely the judges would see that. But once again, the Ladies Literary Society took the win and Mary was undone.

Humiliation colored her face. Her peers scored a rebuttal for the inequality of the races higher than her argument for equality through joining forces. At that moment she was eleven years old all over again, standing before the class, reading about slavery and realizing that she herself was the descendant of those former slaves. How could she ever compete when her skin color was ever-present?

"Wipe that expression off your face, Mary Church. You did your best and that's all that matters." Ida squeezed Mary's hand.

Mary sighed deeply. "I let my team down . . . again." And this time she had canceled a date with the gentleman she went to Second Church with, locked herself in her room, and studied all weekend long.

"You didn't let anyone down. You're harder on yourself than you need to be," Ida said.

Mary's eyes watered. She wiped them, then left the society room with what little dignity she had left, but Suzie picked that moment to walk over to her with a triumphant glee. "Why, oh why does your literary society keep pitting you against your betters?"

"Leave me alone, Suzie." Mary tried to walk away from the hateful girl, but Suzie wouldn't step aside.

"You're not intelligent enough to beat me in a game of wits. None of your kind could ever better a White person."

Mary scoffed at that. "I earn higher marks than you in literature and language. You needed a tutor to earn decent marks. I don't see how you could ever think you're more intelligent than I am."

Suzie stepped back as if struck. As she recovered herself, she narrowed her hate-filled gaze on Mary. "You know why you didn't win class poet?" Suzie put her mouth close to

Mary's ear. "We voted for Peter so Oberlin wouldn't have the stain of a nothing Colored girl representing us."

A tidal wave of emotions boiled inside her. Mary's chest heaved. She spewed out words a proper young lady would never utter. As classmates stared, Mary added, "I will not stain Ladies Hall further with my presence. I will not live with you hateful people anymore."

Mary stretched out her arm and moved Suzie out of her way so forcefully that the girl stumbled and fell into a chair. "How dare you! I will not stand for being touched by the likes of you."

The hairs on the back of Mary's neck stood. She opened her mouth to respond, but she was at a loss for words in the face of such hate directed at her. She had been taught to expect doors to open for her based on her status. But these girls only cared about the color of her skin. Mary closed the door behind her as she walked out of Ladies Hall. She didn't know where she was going or where she wanted to be.

Why had she listened to her father and moved into Ladies Hall to live among girls who were offended by her presence? Ladies Hall was not for her. She wasn't making lasting friendships that could be useful later in life. If they weren't attending the same school, none of those girls would give her the time of day. But then she thought of Katherine and Janet and the other girls who'd always treated her with kindness. No, she wouldn't lay this hatred at all of their feet.

Stopping at the edge of the path, she allowed her gaze to trace the familiar windows. How many nights had she stared out of them, believing this place would shape her . . . make her stronger? She had given so much—her time, her hope, her faith—believing that fairness could be built brick by brick. For a while it seemed to be working.

But the whispers had never stopped. The stares, the laughter, the small cruelties. You-don't-belong had crept into so many corners, she could no longer tell where the Ladies Hall ended and the pain began. Even now, she could still hear their laughter echoing off the walls.

Mary had planned to stay here four years. She'd thought the work, the kindness, the patience would matter. But Ladies Hall had taken more from her than it ever gave back.

Her chest ached as she lowered her head. It wasn't simply a place she was leaving; it was the version of herself who'd believed she could belong here.

As she entered College Park, Mary took note of the chairs that had been left on the lawn. Most likely they were left after the soccer game ended last night. The door to Society Hall opened and Anna stepped out. Mary watched her take hold of two chairs and carry them to the building. She opened the door, then pushed it with her back as she held on to the chairs.

Anna moved slower as she reappeared. She massaged the back of her neck and then attempted to lug two more chairs into the building. But this time she stumbled and fell against the door before opening it again.

A big stick was on the ground. Mary picked it up and walked over to Society Hall. She opened the door wide and stuck the stick under the door so it would stay open. She went back to the lawn, carried two chairs into the building, and left them in the room the students normally took them out of.

Anna's eyes widened when she saw Mary with the chairs. "What are you doing?"

"Helping" was all Mary said, then she went back outside and grabbed two more chairs.

Anna and Mary continued working in unison to move the chairs back into the building, neither saying anything to the other. When all the chairs were back where they belonged, the two women sat down to catch their breath.

Mary put a hand to her heart, breathing hard, and used her free hand to wipe the sweat from her forehead. "That was a lot of work."

"More work than you've probably done in a lifetime," Anna said and then giggled.

Mary shoved Anna. "Not funny."

"But seriously, I know you have better things to do than physical labor. Why'd you help me?"

"You shouldn't have to do all of that work on your own."

"I get paid to do it," Anna told her.

"Okay, well then, I guess it was my way of apologizing to you for being so insensitive all those months ago."

"You're not the only one who owes an apology. I never should've yelled at you the way I did. I was angry that you and Ida didn't understand. I would've expected that from the White students, but not you."

Mary nodded. "Can I tell you something?"

Anna wiped sweat from her face. "Of course."

Putting a hand to her chest and gulping back her pride,

Mary said, "I've always believed that my high-society social status carried more weight than the color of my skin, but this has been a trying year."

"Is this the first time you've been treated poorly by White students?"

"It is. It seems as though many of the newer students, who've never lived in the area before, aren't invested in Oberlin's values. It's gotten so bad that I'm planning to move out of my dorm for next semester."

"After all the work you did to bring attention to the repairs needed at Ladies Hall? You should be the last one to leave."

"I can't stay there anymore." It brought Mary joy to know her efforts to secure better living quarters would benefit the others who lived there. Well, all but Suzie. But Mary would not stay. "I always thought that people should be judged by their character and their work ethic, but to some people we will only be recognized by the color of our skin."

"They probably think that for a Colored girl, you've been given more than your share of good and to give you any more would be unfair to their race."

Mary's cheeks puffed with hot anger at the thought of charity being bestowed on her. Her chin lifted with the air of who she was. "No one has given me anything. I work hard for my grades. I contribute to each committee or group I've been a part of."

Anna stared at her for a moment, then her eyes clouded over. "I'm sorry that this world is so cruel that even a rich girl like you can see and feel the injustices that plague our race."

Mary leaned back and eyed Anna. "I don't know how to take that. Do you have sympathy for me now, or is that another insult?"

Anna shook her head. "I don't want to insult you. I'd actually like to be friends if it's not too late."

Anna was a hard worker, and she was smart and ambitious. She was the exact kind of person Mary wanted to befriend. Mary stuck her hand out. "It would be an honor."

Part 2

A SUMMER OF CHANGE

[The colored man] has ceased to be the slave of society. He may not now be bought and sold like a beast in the market, but he is the trammeled victim of prejudice, well calculated to repress his manly ambition, paralyze his energies, and make him a dejected and spiritless man.

—FREDERICK DOUGLASS, "THE COLOR LINE," 1881

CHAPTER 18

Back in Memphis for less than a day, and Mary's mother had suggested a dress fitting. "Seriously, Mother? We're living in temporary housing and we're hosting a party?"

That didn't seem like the most prudent thing to do with their summer. The home they were staying in was, of course, in her father's portfolio of real estate. But it was half the size of the house the fire department "accidentally" burned down.

"Our summer party is the talk of the town. There's no way your father would cancel it."

Mary stood on the platform stage in the dress shop, the full-length beveled glass mirror before her as she admired the lime-green gown the dressmaker helped her into. "As long as Father understands that I'm not interested in adding any of his protégés to my dance card."

When she didn't receive a response, Mary glanced over her shoulder to see her mother staring at nothing in particular, her fingers absently tracing the rim of her teacup. "Mother?"

Her mother jumped, as if startled. Recovering herself, she

asked Mary, "What do you think of the handkerchief dress, dear?"

Mary studied herself in the mirror again. The tunic of her dress fell in points over a narrow pleated skirt. Running her hand along the front of the dress, she nodded her approval. "This is fine for morning wear, but I thought you brought me here to pick out my gown for our midsummer ball. I cannot wear this, Mother. I simply cannot."

Admiringly, her mother said, "The dress is perfect on you, but this will not be your ball gown."

Mary exhaled her relief. "I'm not trying to catch the eye of a suitor, but I must be presentable. We can't raise funds while the daughter of Robert Church looks as though she can't afford a proper gown."

Each year, her father used his midsummer party to raise money for the cause of the Colored vote. While funds were being raised, all the eligible women in the city danced the night away, hoping that a courtship from one of the handsome young men would be forthcoming.

Mary had been introduced to society two years ago. Her father had planned to find her husband that summer, and then four years of college wouldn't have been necessary. Those were his plans, but Mary had other ideas. And if her father had another suitor in mind, Mary was going to disappoint him again. School first. Marriage would come much later.

"We know your studies are your first priority." Mother smiled at Mary. "And if I'm being honest, I'm proud of the decisions you've made for yourself."

Mary's head tilted slightly at the way her mother said "yourself." As if Louisa Church hadn't been able to make many of her own decisions. But that couldn't be true. Mary was about to ask her mother if something was on her mind, but the dressmaker came back into the room carrying a champagne-colored gown.

It had a fitted bodice and an overskirt that was draped and swagged at the back. It was the style that was all the rage this season. Her mother stood, took the dress, and handed it to Mary. "You didn't think I'd make the same mistake twice when it came to your attire, did you?"

Mary leaned forward and kissed her mother's cheek. "I should've known you'd find the perfect dress."

After Mary tried the dress on and had it fitted to her form, Mary's mother patted the seat next to her. "Come sit with me."

"Of course, Mother." Mary handed the dress back to the seamstress, donned her day dress again, and sat on the padded bench.

Mother lifted her hand and touched Mary's face. For a moment the two sat there, saying nothing. Being mother and daughter was enough. "Are you enjoying school?"

"I enjoy learning and discovering new disciplines. Can't say I enjoy all of the people I attend school with."

Her mother waved that off. "You'll forget about those hateful girls once you graduate. The important thing is what your graduation will do for other Black girls in this country."

Mary clapped with delight. "The fact that it's not only me but two other Black girls graduating with a four-year degree—this has never been done before from a mixed-race school. Anna, Ida, and I, well, we're making history." The thought inspired Mary. In a way Anna's unexpected enrollment had been a godsend. One day history books would speak of their accomplishments. "I won't let anyone stop me from completing what I started."

Her mother nodded. "I know you won't. Now tell me: What do you want to do after graduation?"

The question surprised her. Louisa had been there when her father strongly suggested that she not obtain employment after graduation. "Well," she began slowly, "Father thinks I would be taking a job from others who need the income, so I'm not sure if I should apply for anything."

Her mother leaned closer to Mary. "But what does your heart want?"

Her heart certainly didn't want marriage, at least not now. Her heart didn't want to become a socialite who threw parties for the glory of others either. "Truthfully, Mother, I want to write."

"Then do it, Mollie. Don't let me or your father talk you out of what's best for you. Trust me, you can't live someone else's dreams without being crushed in the process."

Would her mother agree with her dreams if she knew that Mary also wanted to teach? She wanted it as badly as she wanted to breathe. She had suppressed her dreams in order to be the daughter her father expected, shaped by the dictates of society.

It was a given that Anna would become a teacher. Ida was even thinking about teaching. Mary had kept quiet about her desire to inform young minds and mold them so they could go out into this world and become all they were meant to be. Mary believed she could inspire the next generation of women . . . if given a chance.

They left the dress shop after purchasing three dresses.

Their coachman, Mr. Barnes, was waiting for them. He tipped his top hat. "Ladies, has shopping gotten the better of you?"

"Yes, Barnes, please take us home." Mother climbed into the covered buggy.

Mary and her mother normally went for tea after a day of shopping. But when they got in their buggy, her mother put a hand to her head. "I'm not feeling well today. Do you mind if we go back to the house?"

"Of course, Mother. I'll make tea when we arrive home." It was strange, calling the house they were staying in home. But that wasn't the only strange thing about the temporary space her family shared.

There were three bedrooms in this house. Mary's clothes and toiletries had been placed in the bedroom at the top of the stairs before she arrived in Memphis. Her brother, Thomas, took the middle bedroom, and her mother had the bigger bedroom at the end of the hall. But only her mother occupied that bedroom. Her father slept in his office.

Mary knew this for a fact due to her father's long-standing late-night snack routine. Tess, their maid, would place cheese, crackers, and whatever fruit they had available that day on a plate and take it to their parents' bedroom at around nine every night.

The first night she was home, Mary found herself in the kitchen at night. Tess made the snack and then took it to her father's study. The next night the same thing occurred. Mary knocked on her father's door. When he opened it, she asked, "Would you enjoy company this evening?"

He widened the opening and allowed her to step in. "Can't sleep?"

His mahogany desk was in the middle of the spacious room. A gray filing cabinet stood against the wall on the right side and an Elizabethan sofa was on the left. A pillow was on the armrest of the sofa and a blanket stretched across it.

"I was in the kitchen." She spotted the tray on the desk. "Have I been gone so long that you've changed the way you receive your nightly snack?"

"No. No. Of course not."

Mary placed a hand on his desk. "Tess always used to bring your snack to your bedroom. But for the past two nights, she's brought it in here."

He put a hand to his mouth and coughed. "I've got a bit of a cold. Don't want to get your mother ill."

"How thoughtful of you." Mary clasped her hands together as she pondered this. Her parents had always shared the same bedroom, and now her father was sleeping in the study and claiming to have a cold. "Well, I'll take my leave."

"Wait. Before you go . . ." Father walked over to his desk and shuffled a few papers until he held a manila envelope. "I almost forgot that this came for you."

Mary took the envelope. It was from none other than Frederick Douglass. Her eyebrows rose.

"At the inauguration ball he said he would send you his latest article."

Nodding, Mary smiled. "I forgot about that. Thanks for giving this to me." She left the room, fully intending to engross herself in Mr. Douglass's newest article, but the day had been exhausting. And her parents' odd behavior was weighing heavy on her mind. She placed the essay on her nightstand and endured a fitful sleep.

The next day while Mary was still thinking on the changes in her family since arriving in Memphis, her parents sat her and Thomas down in the dining room. Her father said, "We know that you two are concerned about the burning of our home, so we wanted to take a moment to talk with you."

Mother chimed in, saying, "We don't want you to be afraid."

Mary actually thought they were going to explain the new sleeping arrangements. But she did wonder why someone would set their beautiful house on fire. "What I don't understand is why the fire department was allowed to do this demonstration with their fire equipment so close to our home."

"I'm not going to lie to you. The mayor wants me to stop fulfilling my mission. I refused his request and now the house is gone," her father said matter-of-factly.

Mary greatly admired her father, but this was too dangerous. "You've used your influence and connections for the greater good. But maybe you've done enough. Maybe it's time for others to step up."

"I'll never stop trying to advance our people. If I wasn't a wealthy man, I would be in the same predicament they find themselves in."

"We understand that, Father," Thomas said. "But your safety is of utmost importance. At least hire armed men to guard you while you're out surveying your properties."

Father nodded as if in agreement with his son.

But Mary didn't see how that solved anything. "What about Mother? How will she ever be safe if hateful men are burning down our home? Don't you fear they'll try again?"

"Calm down, Mollie." Mother stood. Walked over to Mary and pulled her close. "Your father and I already have all of this planned out."

Glancing back at her father, Mary watched his shoulders draw inward as though he was trying to become smaller. "What plan?" Mary eyed her mother. "Why does it seem as if the two of you are keeping secrets?"

"Well, I . . . I . . ." Her mother stepped away and stammered over her words.

Father filled his smoking pipe with tobacco and lit it. "No one's keeping secrets. We wanted to wait until you were settled for the summer before giving you our news."

Mary glanced over at Thomas. "Do you know what's going on?"

His lips tightened.

Mother clasped her hands together. "Well . . ." she started off, "you needn't worry about me getting tangled in your father's *affairs*." When she said the word *affairs*, there was an added lilt to her voice. "I'll be moving to New York in the coming weeks, so these hateful people in Memphis won't concern me." Her mother finished the statement as if she had announced that she was moving her hair shop two streets over.

Thomas jumped out of his seat. "I'm not moving to New York!"

"Of course you're not," her father answered. "You're going back to college."

"I don't understand." Mary looked to him. "Are you moving to New York or staying in Memphis?"

"My business dealings are here," he said as if that answered her question.

Mary glanced from her mother to her father and then back again. "Who will we spend our summers with?"

The doorbell rang and her father jumped out of his seat as if he'd received a welcome reprieve. His assistant, Mr. Mackey, came into the house. "Sir, a telegraph came for you. I thought it prudent to bring it posthaste."

"Thank you, my good man."

Mary rose from her chair, her skirts rustling softly against the polished wood floor as she moved toward the foyer. The scent of pipe tobacco mingled with the faint trace of lavender oil from the parlor. Mr. Mackey stood stiffly near the coat stand, his flat cap clutched tightly in his hands, eyes fixed on the floorboards as though he couldn't bear to meet anyone's gaze.

He cleared his throat, voice low and strained. "The news isn't good, sir. Not good at all."

Her father took the folded telegram with a tentative hand. Mary caught the tremble of his fingers, a rare and unsettling sight. As he read, the color seemed to drain from his face. The crinkling of the paper was the only sound in the room as a silence thickened around them.

When he glanced up, his usual steady eyes were wide, clouded with disbelief. "This can't be," he murmured. "I was to meet with him next month . . . We were to discuss the plight of our people."

His voice cracked on the last word, and a chill settled in Mary's chest.

"It's madness," Mr. Mackey said.

"He's only been in office four months. I can't believe this . . . He's been shot?"

"Shot!" Mary stepped farther into the room. "Father, who's been shot?"

Concern was etched across his face as he blurted out, "President Garfield."

Mary's hand went to her heart. How could this be? President Garfield was good and noble and a friend to the Negro. Why would anyone shoot him? Worse yet, what did this mean for all the programs President Garfield was putting in place to help Colored folks with education and Southern White resistance to their progress?

The room shifted under Mary's feet. She put a hand on the wall to steady herself. The winds of injustice were surely blowing their way. Would this shooting bring Blacks and Whites together to fulfill Garfield's mission, or would it tear them further apart?

CHAPTER 19

President Garfield's attempted assassination had shaken the nation, but to Anna, it paled in comparison to the heartbreak that awaited her in Raleigh. As the train hissed to a stop and she stepped onto the familiar platform, the stifling Southern heat wrapped around her like a damp wool blanket. But it wasn't the weather that stole her breath; it was the sight of her mother.

The once-sturdy woman who had scrubbed floors and mended garments with tireless hands was now ghostly thin, her skin drawn tight over hollow cheeks. A gray pallor clung to her face like ash. Her eyes, once sharp, had dulled to a weary glaze. Still, she managed a faint smile and waved as though nothing were amiss.

Anna rushed forward, embracing her mother gently, as though the woman might crumble in her arms.

Despite her visible decline, her mother waved away any mention of rest or medical attention. "Ain't got time to be sittin' down." She brushed aside Anna's concern with a trembling hand. "Work don't stop 'cause I'm feelin' poorly."

Anna had longed for a bit of peace in coming home, a brief reprieve from the rigors of school. She'd scrimped and saved enough to afford the train fare, a small triumph that filled her with pride. The rhythmic clatter of the wheels, the distant scent of coal and iron, had stirred dreams within her. Today, it was a ride to Raleigh. But one day—yes, one day—it would be a grand voyage across the ocean to Rome or Greece, where statues whispered stories and marble streets echoed with history.

But all her fantasizing about her somedays was put on hold the moment she arrived home. There was no comfort or reprieve from weariness for Colored women in America.

This was especially true for her mother. At forty, her mother had no one to care for her but instead had to care for others even while ill and obviously in need of rest.

"It's nothing—stayed out in the rain too long picking those vegetables for Mrs. Saddie," Mama said.

Saddie Haywood, George Haywood's wife, was demanding and unrelenting. Even all these years after slavery ended, her mother was still working in the home of the man who had enslaved her. "Why didn't you send Rufus to the train station? You should be in bed."

Mama slid a bony arm around Anna. "Hush your fuss. Let's go home so I can get you a good Southern meal."

"I've had plenty of good meals at Oberlin," Anna said, not wanting her mother to busy herself in the kitchen when she needed to lie down.

"Stop it. Those Northerners don't know nothin' about seasonings and you know it."

They got in the wagon. As Anna sat down she asked, "Whose wagon is this?"

"Mrs. Haywood allowed me to use it to pick up groceries and supplies for their manor."

"Mighty generous of her," Anna mumbled.

Her mother flicked the reins and the horse trotted down the road. "Don't be like that. The Haywoods aren't all bad. They—"

"Why do you always take up for those horrid people?" Anger burned through Anna's veins. "Why do you even stay in this town?"

"Where am I supposed to go? I don't know anyplace else but right here. You and your brother have your fancy dreams . . . and that's fine. I'm happy for you. But the only dreams I have left are for y'all."

Her mother's words sounded so final, like she was figuring on that upper room in the sky. Anna didn't like that at all. She needed her mother to be with her when she finally accomplished her dreams.

"What's your schedule for the rest of the week?" Anna asked.

"Usual. Picking up groceries today, then cleaning the Haywoods' downstair spaces tomorrow, then cooking the next day and cleaning upstairs the following."

"Sounds like an awful lot to do for a person who should be lying down rather than running errands." Exhaustion had rested on her dearly departed husband right before he took ill. She feared the same was now her mother's fate.

"I'll be fine. I've got my daughter home with me, so I'm happy." Mama smiled at Anna. "We'll let the good Lord handle the rest."

The Lord was not going to come down here on earth and handle all the chores that her mother was required to do whether she was sick or well. Anna would have to do that. "Pull the wagon over, Mama. Let me guide us home. Then I'll fix dinner and I'll go to work for you at the Haywoods' as long as you promise to rest."

"You'd do that for your mama?" Her mother's face scrunched as if she were about to shed real tears. Hannah Haywood had rarely experienced kindness from others but still somehow always managed to give it.

"Of course I would," Anna said.

Mama pulled the wagon to the side of the road. She scooted over to the passenger seat. Anna held the reins, and the horse made its way to the house. Her mother leaned her head on Anna and fell asleep.

The very next day, Anna donned her mother's housekeeper uniform and went to work. It was like a bruise to her soul to walk through the back door of Haywood manor. If she had to return to the place where she had worked with her mother as a little girl, scrubbing floors and washing dishes, why did it have to be like this?

She didn't want to live in this town again, but Anna had imagined that one day she would visit Raleigh in honor, having everyone fawn over all that she had accomplished.

"Well, well, look at you. That maid uniform suits you well."

Anna's back arched as the tingling sensation of disdain seeped up her spine and lodged in the crevices of her heart. George Haywood's daughter was standing in front of her with a belly full of baby and eyes full of contempt.

Elizabeth was either her half sister or cousin. They used to play together in the yard in front of this very house when Anna had finished her chores. But as they grew older Elizabeth began to hate her and despise the fact that Anna had been allowed to pursue her education while Elizabeth had been told to marry and have babies.

Leaning back on her heels, Anna put the towel she'd been scrubbing the floors with in the bucket of sudsy water. "How are you doing today, Mrs. Elizabeth?"

Raising one eyebrow slightly higher than the other, Elizabeth put a hand to her belly. "I've been fine. This is my second baby. But you wouldn't know anything about family life since you were such a failure at producing a child before your husband died."

"No, I wouldn't" was all Anna said as she wrung the rag out and began scrubbing another section of the floor.

Elizabeth harrumphed, then walked away. Her hateful words trailed back to Anna. "Lot of money wasted on college to become another Negro scrubbing floors."

Fury surged through Anna, making her hands tremble as she scrubbed and scrubbed. Her mind swirled with words she longed to hurl. Cutting, cruel words sharp enough to knock Elizabeth down a peg. *Fight back . . . fight back.*

Those words echoed in her head. But there were no fair fights for Coloreds in the South. From what she could see from her time at Oberlin, there weren't many fair fights up north either. Mary fought against that hateful Suzie, but in the end she'd decided to move out of Ladies Hall as the torment became too heavy a cross to bear.

Mary could fight against the evils of prejudice if she chose to do so. She had a rich father who took care of her and could easily spend his money at another college if Mary decided to leave. Anna didn't have anyone in her corner. Best to keep her mouth shut. Scrub these floors and survive another day in this White man's America.

The front door opened. George Haywood himself walked in. He stepped into the foyer that she had scrubbed, took off his top hat, and placed it on the table. His lusty eyes glanced her way, then went wide with surprise.

Without offering her the smallest greeting, he lifted his gaze as Elizabeth came back into the room and ran into his open arms.

"Papa, you've been gone way too long. I feared I wouldn't see you before my time draws near."

"You needn't have feared. My first priority was coming back home so I would be in residence when my grandchild comes into this world."

The two walked off arm in arm, their footsteps light with ease and laughter trailing them like acrid perfume. Anna remained on her knees, scrubbing the floor until her fingers ached and the scent of soap made her stomach churn. In the distance down the corridor, they burst into laughter. It was bright, unburdened, full of the kind of joy that had always been out of her reach. They would never know how deeply their small, thoughtless gestures—an entwined arm, a shared smile—so completely destroyed her.

They would never see how, with each echo of their happiness, they scraped away at the tender parts inside her, wreaking havoc down deep in her soul. It wasn't envy alone; it was grief for a kind of belonging, a kind of lightness, she had never been allowed to possess.

Work . . . Keep working.

"It was awful. I hate being at that house," Anna complained to Rufus that evening.

"I hate this whole town. All I want is to play my music. I don't want to serve people who wouldn't lift a finger to help me."

Anna shook her head. "You don't have to stay here if this is not where you want to be. Go and pursue your dreams."

"Easy for you to say, Miss Oberlin scholar." He playfully poked an elbow into her side.

"It's not easy for me. And it won't be easy for you." She took her brother's hand in hers and looked him square in the eyes. "But the life we live here is harder than anything the rest of the world will throw at us. Things are hard at Oberlin. But I feel human . . . like I could actually become somebody and do things that matter on this earth."

"I'm happy for you, Sis."

"Don't be happy for me. Your music is beautiful and passionate. Don't let it die inside you. Get away from this godforsaken town where the people only see us as servants."

After encouraging Rufus to spread his wings, Anna went to her mother's room and sat with her. The rest didn't appear to be doing her any good. Her eyes were hollow, cheeks flushed. And as she lifted a hand to place it on Anna's arm, it shook as if the movement was more than her body could handle.

"Thank you for taking my place today. I'll try to get over there myself in the morning." The words her mother spoke were but a whisper. As if her strength and vitality were being sucked away.

"It was like old times, being at the Haywoods' today. Think I'll finish out the week for you."

Her mama patted Anna's arm. "You're a blessing to me." Then she closed her eyes and drifted off to sleep.

Anna would never tell her mother the truth. She'd never tell her that she hated seeing George Haywood with his legitimate daughter. Hated feeling invisible when she was in the presence of a man who should love her. But her mother was not well enough to do the kind of work the Haywoods required of her. So Anna would suffer in silence.

CHAPTER 20

A heaviness hung over Mary's house after her family learned of the attempted assassination of President Garfield, but once they discovered that the gunshot did not kill him, their minds settled on the midsummer ball, which was always the talk of the town.

Last year Sojourner Truth and Harriet Tubman attended the affair. They both spoke on women's suffrage and the duty to get Colored men registered to vote. The ball had raised five thousand dollars, and all the money went to organizations that would provide the poll tax Black men were required to pay in order to vote.

White men had invented all sorts of tricks to stop Colored men from gaining the right to vote. The literacy and civics exams given to Black men were nonsensical and meant to deprive them of their rights.

However, Black men began compiling lists of the questions on those so-called civics tests and passed the information around. This enabled organizations to provide a cheat sheet of sorts to the men before they went off to the polls.

Tonight's party would no doubt be a blessing to the men

in this struggle for equal rights. Mary was proud of the small part her family played in making life better for those who couldn't do it for themselves. But her mind was on other matters as Tess helped her into her evening gown.

"Will Mr. Douglass be at the party this evening?" Tess asked.

Mary slid an arm into her gown. Tess walked around to the side and helped pull Mary's other arm through. "I'm not sure. Father mentioned that Mrs. Anna Douglass has been feeling poorly of late. He might not be traveling this summer."

"I'm always so impressed with the highfalutin folk that attend your father's events." Tess giggled. "I work on my off nights, helping to serve at the events so I can see all of them too-fine-by-half Colored folks strut into the room."

While Tess buttoned the back of her dress, Mary said, "I don't think Daddy's guests consider themselves 'highfalutin.'"

Tess chuckled. "You know what I mean . . . important folks."

Mary had not discussed the guest list with her father. She had been too busy plotting with her brother on ways to get their parents to sit together for a meal or to accompany them to the drawing room as she or Thomas played the piano. But tonight would be different. They wouldn't want polite society knowing of their rift. Mary had it all planned out in her head. She was going to get them to dance together. They would gaze into each other's eyes as they used to and realize that they still had love.

Thomas left for the event hall with Father. The men felt the women would need more time to prepare themselves, so their coachman, Barnes, stayed behind to ensure their safe arrival. Which was perfectly fine with Mary. Barnes fancied himself a music maestro and often played his violin during social events. He would help with her plan.

"You're quite lovely tonight, Mother. The lavender in the gown suits you," Mary said as they sat in the covered buggy on their way to the midsummer extravaganza.

Her mother glanced down at her gown and gave a half smile. A second later, the light in her eyes dimmed a bit. "This may be the last event such as this, so I wanted to ensure that I leave a favorable impression with your father's friends."

"They're not only Father's friends. You have many connections in this city as well," Mary reminded her.

"Be that as it may, they won't be friends much longer." Mother shifted her gaze to the window. "That's the way these matters go."

Mary wished her mother wasn't so set on giving up. Why wouldn't she fight for her marriage? When they arrived at the event hall, Barnes helped them down from the buggy. Mother went ahead of her. Mary whispered to Barnes, "Are we all set?"

He nodded. "Anything for you, princess."

Wearing the champagne-colored gown with its frilly lace and long petticoat, Mary was a princess on her way to the ball to save what was left of the Church kingdom.

Immediately when she entered the event hall, she recognized her mother's handiwork. An arch in the entryway was covered in purple irises, her mother's favorite flower. She also loved the design of archways, always had. The same kinds of flowers in the arch were also in vases on every table, sitting atop the silver tablecloths.

Even with an impending divorce, Mama had made sure

her husband's midsummer extravaganza was decorated to perfection. That had to mean something. A smile crept across Mary's face. This might not be as heavy a lift as she'd previously thought.

"Mary Church, you are certainly a sight to behold," Charles Landon said as he approached her.

Charles's father was in real estate, as her father was. "Thank you, Charles. It's so good to see you."

He admired Mary's dress. "I swear you get prettier and prettier every summer."

"And you are quite dashing yourself." Charles was one of the handsomest boys in Memphis with his mustache, chocolate skin, and hazel eyes.

"If I'm so dashing, why won't you allow me to court you?"

Mary playfully shoved him away. "Go on with yourself. You have too much of a wandering eye for my liking."

He touched his chest. "You wound me. I've only had eyes for you since we were eight years old and you ran off to Ohio on me."

Mary laughed at his antics. "You know very well that I didn't run anywhere."

Even though she'd left for Ohio at a young age, she and Charles still became friends as their families spent time together during the summers when she was home. Her father had even been her chaperone on a few outings with Charles two summers ago. But her old friend flirted brazenly with his eyes. She'd decided then and there that they would always be friends and nothing more.

"Save me a dance tonight?" he asked.

"Of course," she told him. When Charles stepped away and

then stopped in front of another young lady, Mary grinned, then walked around the room, greeting the attendees. She glanced in the direction of the band. Barnes was talking with the other musicians. He winked at her.

Delighted, Mary clapped upon discovering that they had two special guests tonight: Susie King Taylor and Robert Smalls. Both were heroes for their bravery during slavery and Reconstruction. And their fearlessness in the face of the Jim Crow South.

Mrs. Susie King Taylor had escaped slavery by way of the Union army. She had been a nurse and a teacher during the War Between the States. Her dedication was the reason many Black children were educated in the South.

Mr. Robert Smalls gained fame during the war as well. Hating being enslaved, Smalls commandeered a Confederate transport ship in Charleston Harbor and sailed it from the Confederate-controlled waters of the harbor to the U.S. blockade that surrounded it. He had tricked the captain into allowing his family and the other crew members' families to stay on board so they could all escape together.

At the helm of the ship, mimicking his captain's commands, he guided the ship to the Union-controlled enclave in Beaufort–Port Royal in the Hilton Head area, where it became a Union warship. In the process he freed himself, his crew, and their families. Mr. Robert Smalls was currently running for the United States House of Representatives from the state of South Carolina. If they could get enough Colored men registered, he'd have a great chance of winning.

The music started and Mary danced with the son of a grocery store owner. She was careful to listen for the start of the song she'd asked Barnes to play. It was her mother's favorite and would surely bring fond memories of yesterday to her parents.

But when the first song ended, Mrs. Taylor spoke to the crowd in attendance. She stood a little over five feet tall, but her words carried the weight of a giant. Her speech flowed with a bold elegance that filled the room.

She trailed a finger down her face as she said, "My dark skin tells most Americans that I'm not worthy of the same treatment that is afforded to White Americans, and yet I was taught to read and write before slavery ended. During the Civil War and for some time after, I taught my 'children of freedom' in schools that I opened."

Where the beginning of Mrs. Taylor's speech was uplifting, her next words served as marching orders. "But I didn't come here to talk about education. We have other problems that plague the Negro race. The constant lynching of Blacks and these Southern laws that have been drawn up against us must come to an end. How do we accomplish this? By showcasing excellence in all of our dealings. Other races will open their eyes one day and see our humanity. Excellence is the way to equality."

Mary was mesmerized by the forceful manner in which Mrs. Taylor spoke of the way Colored folks needed to conduct themselves. For a moment she'd forgotten her schemes and stood there daydreaming about all the ways in which she displayed excellence at her school. But was that enough?

Thomas came over to nudge her. "The song, Sis. Are you ready?"

Mary's mother loved the instrumental version of "Oh, Dem Golden Slippers" by James Bland. Mary had asked Barnes to make sure it was played early in the night, before her mother or father could feign tiredness. "You go get Mother. She will accept your offer to dance, I'm sure of it."

"Got it." Her brother nodded.

"I'll dance with Daddy and then we'll meet in the middle of the floor and switch off."

Thomas nodded, then went off in search of their mother. Mary didn't have to search for her father; he was standing next to Mrs. Susan King Taylor, speaking to her as if he were a great admirer.

Mary extended a hand to Mrs. Taylor. "Thank you for speaking at our event tonight. Your words were illuminating. I have often said that as more Colored folks showcase excellence, the dominant group will have no choice but to see us for who we are." Mary would have loved to speak with this woman further, but she had one mission in mind for tonight. She extended her hand to her father. "Might I have this dance, Father?"

"But of course." He excused himself from Mrs. Taylor as he took his daughter's hand. The joy in his eyes showed the pride of a father escorting his daughter to the dance floor. "I would've thought you'd prefer one of the younger gentlemen in attendance tonight."

"The night is young, Father. I can dance with anyone I choose later, but for now I can think of nowhere else I'd rather be than right here with you."

He laughed, clearly amused by her. Father twirled Mary around and then two-stepped with her on the dance floor.

Thomas and Mother were all smiles as they moved ever closer to Mary and Father. He twirled Mary once more, and she made sure to step backward. Her father followed her. They locked hands once more. Mary said, "You must be the best dancer in town."

Father nodded at Thomas. "I think your brother has me beat by a mile."

Mary two-stepped toward Thomas. She watched her brother's form as he made his way closer to her. She told her father, "You might be right. Think I'll dance with the other Mr. Church."

Mary swung around in Thomas's direction. Thomas swung Mother into Father's arms, and then Mary and Thomas danced together, heading for the other side of the floor. Thomas gleefully said, "It's working. They're dancing and laughing together."

"They may be laughing at our antics, but at least they're together."

Charles approached them, grabbed Mary's arm, and whisked her back onto the dance floor. "You are too smooth for your own good, sir."

"Too smooth for you, maybe. But most of the young ladies like what they see," he boasted.

As they two-stepped around the dance floor, Mary watched her parents. The song was ending, and they broke apart. "I saw the young lady you were speaking to earlier. You might want to be careful with her. Several gentlemen were after her last season."

He twirled Mary around, then brought her back to him. "I'm always careful."

Charles was charming. He was handsome. But he wasn't

careful. "You'd better hope that a suitor for one of these girls doesn't fatten your lip."

When the music stopped, Charles brought another dance partner to the floor and Mary did likewise. She watched as her parents walked off the floor. Mary's hopes for reconciliation waned once the two parted and then stood on opposite sides of the room for the rest of the night.

CHAPTER 21

Standing at the grave site of her dearly departed husband didn't seem so all-consuming as it had before Anna left for Oberlin. She still missed George terribly. He was on her mind often. But she was making new friends and believing for better days.

Bending down, she placed the flowers she brought with her from her mother's garden on the grass where his headstone should've been. Instead of dwelling on her impoverished situation, she started talking to her husband as if he were sitting on the grass listening to her.

"I wish you could've seen Oberlin and met Mr. Evans. He's a cabinet builder . . . Well, now he builds coffins. But before slavery ended, he and several other men from the town saved a runaway slave from the slave catchers. I'd never met anyone who helped with the Underground Railroad, but he and his wife did.

"Their home is so beautiful. One day I'm going to have a home where people in need are welcomed. It's going to be a nice place. Clean and well kept." Her eyes misted over at the experiences she would have that George would never see. "Still miss you, though."

After leaving the burial site, Anna donned her apron and went to the Haywoods'. The upstairs bedrooms needed to be cleaned today. Anna hummed the hymns from church or recited Greek poetry as she worked—anything and everything to keep her mind off her daily tasks and the withering away of her mother.

"Stop that incessant humming," Elizabeth said as she entered her bedroom. She flopped down on her bed and raised a hand to her forehead. "I can't rest with all the noise you're making. It's time for my daily nap."

Wiping down the drapes, Anna said, "I apologize, Mrs. Elizabeth. I was singing a few songs while I work."

"No one wants to hear your Negro spirituals." She shooed Anna away without glancing at her. "Finish up in here and go clean the nursery."

"Yessum, ma'am." Anna hated the sound of her voice as she reverted back to that old slave-speak with head bowed low, trying not to be seen as she picked up her bucket and headed to the nursery to freshen it up.

By the time she wrung out the rag and began wiping down the walls, the song in her heart had left her alone. All she had now was a throbbing pain on the right side of her head.

She swept the floors and mopped. Did everything that was required of her without ever having a kind word spoken while she worked. Rather they jutted a finger at her and said, "You missed a spot" or "Hey, get that" after they dropped this or that. They told her what to do with as few words as possible, and then the residents of Haywood manor would walk away as if she wasn't a person with feelings or dreams of a better life.

By the time Anna was able to leave, she wanted nothing more than a quiet night. She boiled water when she got home and made two cups of tea, one for her and the other for her mother. But when she stepped into her mother's room, Mama was sprawled on the floor, twisted awkwardly beside the bed.

The world narrowed to a single, terrible heartbeat. For a moment Anna couldn't move. Couldn't breathe.

The cup slipped from her hand and shattered, but she didn't hear it.

"Mama!" She ran to the bed. Lifted her mother's frail body, feeling the weight of bones.

Her mother moaned, "I couldn't get up. I tried."

The bed was soiled. Mama was wrapped in a blanket of urine and excrement. "I'll get you cleaned up. I'm sorry I was gone so long." Anna unraveled the blanket from around her mother, then brought washcloths and the water basin to the room.

If God would let her mother heal and regain her strength, Anna would give up everything—the Haywoods' approval, her own pride, even being seen at all. She'd stay invisible forever, if only her mother could live.

Divorce was an evil that only the devil could have come up with. Mary's heart ached at the demise of her parents' union. But there was no saving it. Her mother moved to New York shortly after the ball. Thomas went with her to help their mother get settled. Mary stayed at home, which wasn't much of a home without their mother.

This morning as she woke to the wetness of her pillow

once again, Mary wiped her eyes, then sat up in bed and wrapped her arms around herself. Nothing was going the way she had imagined it.

Her father wasn't a perfect man. But Mary believed her parents loved and respected each other. They were supposed to be happily building their separate empires. She never imagined that something like this would happen. And if her mother and father couldn't manage to stay together when they had all the resources in the world, how then could anyone else find lasting love?

"Get out of that bed, Mollie. This is no time to sleep and slumber. We have a luncheon to attend," her daddy called out to her.

Mary put the pillow over her head and inwardly groaned. She didn't want to get out of bed today. Her mother should be the one attending these business lunches with her father, but he'd allowed her to slip away. Now Mary was expected to be his hostess.

If she knew one thing about Robert Church, it was that he wouldn't let up. He'd come back to her door if she didn't get out of bed. Mary threw the covers back and got up. "Give me a moment."

She put on the day dress her mother had purchased for her when she first arrived home, then left the house with her father.

She attempted to climb into the buggy. A man on a horse was trotting toward them. Her father nervously glanced down the road and then yelled at her, "Go back in the house!"

She glanced around. "What's wrong?"

"Do as I say, Mollie. Don't dally."

She rushed back inside and peeked out of the front window. Her father reached for the gun on his holster as the White man on horseback eyed her father, then passed by.

When the man was farther down the road, Mary opened the door and ran back over to the buggy. "Who was that, Daddy? Was it the Klan? Thomas told me they've been threatening you."

Her father straightened his jacket. Then leaned forward and gave Mary a helping hand into the buggy. "Might have been an innocent passerby. But I wanted to make sure you wouldn't be in danger."

As they headed down the road, Mary took note of the worry lines on his forehead. His head swiveled this way and that, like he was trying to find trouble. "Do you think this business with voting is worth everything it's costing you?"

Daddy's eyes were set on her. "I know what it is to be powerless, Mollie."

Her parents had never talked to her about the years they spent in slavery when she was younger. She wished they had.

"I'm able to speak with presidents and other government officials. My voice helps to change unjust laws that have been enacted to harm Black folks. But for most Black men, the only power they will ever have in this country will be their vote. So I fight for them."

His words held conviction . . . passion. He might not be able to hold on to a wife, but her father had found something in this world that mattered to him. "You're like a real and true freedom fighter, huh?"

He smiled at that. "I'd never thought of it that way, but yes, seems like I'm fighting for our freedom all over again."

"What would you rather be, a freedom fighter or a man of means?"

A rumble of laughter escaped as he held on to the reins, his head tilted backward. "Terrible things to choose from, Daughter."

"Why's it so terrible? Pick one."

"If I wasn't who I am, no one would listen to a word I had to say, so I can't choose one over the other."

Shame crept up her spine as she sat next to this man who was willing to endure hardship for a cause bigger than himself, when she was already tired of fighting against the discrimination at Oberlin.

"Father, can I talk to you?"

He gave a small nod of understanding. "I know you want your mother to come back, but she's set on living in New York and building her business there."

"That's not what I want to talk about." She hesitated a moment. "I'm thinking about moving out of Ladies Hall. Would you be okay with that?"

His brow lifted. "You like it there, don't you? What about this group that you've joined . . . that literary club?"

"I don't have to live in Ladies Hall to be a part of the Aeolian Literary Society."

"But what about the connections you're making on campus? Sometimes that's more important than a stuffy old degree."

After a long-suffering sigh, Mary told him, "I'm sure your accountant told you that I've already requested to move. This is not a negotiation, Daddy."

He sucked air through his teeth, then gave Mary a look that would have silenced her in the past. She wasn't one to be disagreeable with her father. She normally did as she was told, believing that he had her best interests at heart. But neither he nor her mother cared how their divorce was breaking her heart, so she wasn't going to be led astray by either of them anymore.

"I don't understand the fuss, Mollie. You're letting go of an opportunity to build relationships with women who may marry important men who could further our cause. You're making a mistake."

"I'm tired of always being talked down to for being a Colored woman. And men aren't the only important people. One day this country will respect women and understand our importance. I promise you that."

The horse came to a stop. They pulled in front of the dining establishment. He faced her. "Do you know why I sent you to a school with mostly White students?"

Mary shook her head. There were several prestigious universities in the South for people of color where Mary would've fit in and not stood out. Fisk University was in her home state of Tennessee. Southern University opened last year in Louisiana. And this year, Tuskegee opened its doors with none other than Booker T. Washington as its president. With so many opportunities for higher learning in the South, why her father chose to send her to the Midwest boggled the mind.

"I sent you to Oberlin to learn how to fight." He got out of the buggy, walked around to her side, and helped her down. As she stood next to her father, staring up at this giant of a man, he added, "I won't live forever. One day you will continue my legacy of fighting for those who can't fight for themselves. My dear Mollie, one day you will change this world."

He said those words with such power and force that they embedded deep in Mary's soul. The privilege that she had from being born into a wealthy family was not for her alone. It was so she could shake a nation and open its eyes to the plight of Colored folk.

They had lunch with one of her father's business associates and his wife. Mary had expected to see Mr. and Mrs. Landon, and when she asked about their absence, her father and Dr. Hinge exchanged sorrowful glances. Her mind was still stuck at the spot where she stood by the buggy as her father told her she would change the world, so she almost missed the exchange.

"Is something wrong with Mr. or Mrs. Landon?"

When no one answered, she tried again, glancing at each person. "Will someone tell me what happened?"

Her father's business associate cleared his throat. Then exhaled. "We had another lynching last night."

Mary's hand went to her mouth. "Goodness gracious, why does this keep happening?" Now she understood why her father was acting so strange when they left the house and almost shot that White man who'd been passing by.

Her father wiped the sweat that had gathered at the top of his head. He reached for Mary's hand. "The thing is . . . this lynching has hit home."

"Home?" Mary's brows furrowed. Why was her father holding her hand and looking like he was about to shed tears? Mary went still, preparing her heart for what was to come.

"It was Charles Landon, Mollie."

"Charles!" A few heads turned in the restaurant. She stood, wrapping her arms around her stomach. "But Charles was at our summer party. He can't be dead. We haven't had our outing for the summer yet."

What was she saying? What did their normal summer outing have to do with whether or not Charles had been lynched? She wasn't making sense . . . This whole matter didn't make sense.

Her father stood and pulled her into his arms. "A few White boys were angry about the building he purchased. They didn't like the way he spoke to them, so they cut his tongue out and then hung him in the tree outside of his new building."

"Nooo!" The word tore out of her throat before she knew she'd spoken. For a moment the world blurred. The light, the tables, the faces—the whole world was wrong without Charles in it.

Her hand clutched her chest as if she could hold her heart still. "*I'm always careful*," he'd told her. "Not Charles. Not my Charles . . . He was so full of life." The tears came hot and blinding, and she let them.

"I'm sorry, Mollie. I know you and Charles were great friends."

She couldn't stop crying. Didn't want to stop crying. Charles had such a quick wit. They cut out his tongue. "I want t-to go home . . . T-take me home."

She ran out of the restaurant and waited for her father to help her into the buggy, and all the while her heart was breaking and hardening at the same time. How could she change the world when she was beginning to hate so much of what she saw? Could hate change anything in a good way? She broached this question once they were back in the buggy and headed home.

"You can't fight this kind of evil with hate. You fight it with your intellect . . . You fight it by being better than what they say you are."

"Charles was better, and they killed him for it."

"Trust me, Mollie. What I'm telling you seems off-kilter, but I know what I'm talking about. My life has testified to this."

All those debates in which Mary had been judged the loser smarted. She didn't know what to believe anymore. "Even when I best them, they say I don't . . . They see my skin color and find me lacking."

"Those are the words that fall from foolish mouths." He pointed at his chest. "Deep inside, they know that their argument against us is full of holes."

Her eyes were still moist, but the tears were no longer flowing uncontrollably. Even so, a deep kind of sorrow clawed at her. "I hear what you're saying, Father, but it doesn't seem that way. They're convinced that we're inferior."

He conceded, "You won't reach everyone. Your job is to find reasonable-minded people. Very rarely will you convince a person who hates you that you're not their enemy. But for those who have been told that they *should* hate you, with no real validity to the argument—those are the people whose hearts and minds you'll win over by being who you naturally are."

"What about those who continue to hate us without cause?" A tear fell again as she thought of the hate those men who'd lynched Charles must have been possessed with.

"Let them."

Mary's eyebrows scrunched. "Let them?"

He nodded. "I'm a businessman. Do you think I would continue exerting energy and spending money on a cause I didn't believe in?"

As Mary stared into her father's eyes, she heard the melody of his heart. Robert Church did not exert energy on things he no longer believed in, and that was the reason her mother now lived in New York.

This realization shifted Mary's heart to her mother. No woman should have to give up everything for a man who could so easily decide where his energy and effort were most useful and then not pick the one who'd been by his side through it all.

Mary didn't have much experience with men. She briefly courted Mason and later took a walk to church with a fellow student. She'd imagined finding love with a man she could build a life with. But after her parents' divorce, she wasn't in a rush for love or marriage.

After Charles's death, she wasn't even interested in making friends with anyone who could be snatched away by those who could snuff out lives as if they meant nothing to anyone. Lynching was an evil that had to be eradicated. One thing was for sure: Charles's death was not in vain. It had woken her up to the fact that she needed to do more to help her people escape the evil of hatred.

When it was time to go back to school, Mary packed her bags and headed to the train station, not with love on her mind but this fight for equality that surely must be won.

That was where she would choose to exert her energy.

CHAPTER 22

The doctor had hung a bag of asafoetida around Mama's neck to ward off respiratory issues. The stuff smelled like death, which was the reason it was referred to as the devil's dung.

Anna had started giving her mother okra soup in the morning before going to work. When she arrived home in the evening, she would sit in her mother's room once more and tell her about her time at Oberlin and feed her okra soup and whatever herbs she could find to put in her cup of tea.

Mama had gotten thinner, but the soup and the devil's dung seemed to be working miracles, as each day her mother gained a little more strength. Tired of dealing with the Haywoods, Anna stayed home and fed the soup to her mother every few hours until she finally refused.

"I'm glad you got away from here. No matter what happens, I want you to go back to that college," Mama said softly.

Anna had to lean closer to hear her mother. Her words were strained and shallow. But what bothered Anna most was hearing the words, "*No matter what happens.*" She said,

"You're getting better, Mama. You need to concentrate on regaining your strength."

Later that evening, the oil lamp flickered low, casting golden shadows across the bedroom walls, their edges soft and trembling. Even with the heat of the summer, her mother had complained of a chill that went all the way through to her bones.

Anna had thrown wood chunks into the woodburning stove that morning. The fire had long since dwindled to glowing embers, its warmth barely stretching from the living room into this small bedroom. "Do you want me to add more logs to the stove?"

"No, I'm warm."

Outside, the wind rustled the branches of the oak tree, whispering through the cracks in the windowpanes. Anna sat quietly, her skirt tucked under her legs, hands folded around her mother's frail fingers. The ticking of the clock on the mantel marked the passing moments with an aching precision.

"Mama," Anna said, voice barely above a breath, "you've lost so much weight. I need you to eat."

Her mother, once a woman of strength and fire, now lay small and sunken into the feather bed. Her hair, a mix of black and gray once tightly pinned or braided, now spilled like coarse threads across the pillowcase. "Stop worrying. I'm getting better. I can feel it."

"Then eat." Anna lifted the bowl of okra soup. The doctor said it would help her heal, but Anna wanted to fix a meat and potatoes meal so her mother could put back on the weight she'd lost.

Her mother took the bowl and slowly scooped the soup into her mouth. "I taught you about seasoning. Don't go forgetting my lessons. Being up north is no excuse."

Anna smiled. If her mother was getting on her cooking skills, she must be turning the corner on this illness. "I'll add more seasoning tomorrow. Finish your soup, and then I'll let you get more rest."

"I wouldn't have been able to get an ounce of rest if you hadn't come home."

"George worked himself to death for a worthy cause." George pushed himself beyond exhaustion, even knowing he wasn't feeling well. He so believed in the church and the work they did at St. Augustine's. "What you were doing was not a worthy cause to die for."

"I'm thankful you came home and made me rest." Her mother handed the empty bowl back to Anna. "You're a good daughter."

"And you're a good mother. I need you to take care of yourself when I go back to school. I'm going to send word to the Haywoods that you need another month to heal. I don't want you going back to that awful place before you're ready." Anna's face tightened when she mentioned the name that rarely crossed her lips, and she immediately regretted it.

A tear slipped down her mother's cheek, trailing into the deep lines that time had carved. "Don't fret over the Haywoods no more," she murmured.

"I don't care about them, Mama," Anna choked out, her voice breaking as she kissed her mother's hand. "You've been mother and father to me. Thank you."

Her mother's lips curled into the faintest smile. "You're better than ten thousand Haywoods. Get them off your mind." She squeezed Anna's hand. "Go do what makes you happy."

Anna waited for her to continue, but her mother's chapped lips closed as she rested her head against the pillow. Anna lingered by her mother's bedside. She didn't have much time left to spend with her mother. Anna's train for Oberlin pulled out next week.

Watching her mother sleep, Anna decided that she'd spent the last day of her summer vacation at the Haywoods'. Let them find someone else to push around. She was spending the rest of her time with her mother.

As she finally got out of the chair and walked out of the room, her mother lifted a hand. "You need me?" Anna asked.

"Make me some cornbread tomorrow; no more of this okra soup."

Joy like sunshine breaking through fog filled Anna's heart. "Yes, ma'am. I'll get right on that."

Her mother always tied a gray piece of cloth around her head before getting to work in the kitchen or the yard where she grew collard greens and tomatoes. It used to embarrass Anna that her mother's favorite accessory was a shredded old rag, but today she smiled as she tied it around her head.

Anna spent the morning tidying up and cooking her mother's famous meatloaf, greens, and cornbread. Her mother felt good enough to eat cornbread, and she was going to get a whole meal.

After putting the cornbread in the oven, Anna started sweeping the kitchen floor. There was a knock on the door and she went to answer it, her eyes widening when she glanced out the window. George Haywood was standing on her porch. After leaning the broom against the wall, she opened the door.

"Mr. Haywood." Anna's jaw tightened. The name soured in her mouth. She snatched off the rag she'd tied around her head. "I didn't expect to see you today."

"That is evident, but I'm not sure why." He put a hand on the door and widened the entry as he stepped inside the house. He glanced around, then followed Anna into the living room. "I was glad to hear that your mother is on the mend."

She indicated the high-back chair. "You're welcome to take a seat, Mr. Haywood."

"I have no time to sit. I'm on my way out of town, but my home is in disrepair and you haven't come to clean in two days."

Was she hearing him correctly? "I sent word through your staff that I need to take care of my mother. Why didn't you hire another maid?"

He gave an exasperated sigh. "My wife is ill and in Elizabeth's current state, she simply can't be expected to manage my household while I'm traveling. She has requested that you continue on with Hannah's duties."

"And what of my schooling? How can I be expected to take over my mother's duties when I'll be back at Oberlin next week?"

Setting his steely eyes on her, he ran his tongue over his front teeth. "We've always been good to you and your family. I would expect you to help us during our time of need."

Anger boiled inside Anna. "You need a maid, so I have to give up my dreams?"

He stood there not saying a word as he waited on Anna to see things his way.

"My mother is ill. She almost died." Anna's voice rose with each word. What was she saying? This man didn't care about anything that concerned her or her family.

"We're all sorry for Hannah's illness. She's the best servant we've ever had."

"That's all she was to you—a servant?" Anna lifted her hands, then brought them down as if she was striking a blow against the cruelty her mother had endured. "Do you lay down with all of your servants?"

He stepped back as if struck. "How dare you!"

"Either you or your brother is my father, yet you've never said one kind word to me. Barely even glance my way. Then you have the audacity to come here and tell me about your delicate little daughter. How dare *you*!"

Had those words come out of her mouth? *Fight back . . . fight back.* The words rang in her head, and this time she didn't fear them.

"Things such as this are not spoken of. This is not the way we live in the South. Oberlin may have been the worst choice of schools for you."

"I thank God for Oberlin. It got me away from this town and people like you. Who only think of people like me as servants to be used and misused."

George Haywood harrumphed, stiffened his neck, and then walked to the door.

Anna followed behind him. But this time she would not

be silent. "I'm going back to Oberlin, and I will make something of myself. You and your precious children will only be a footnote in history, but this world will know that I was here. I can promise you that."

He scoffed. "I'll have you know that the Haywood family will be remembered for all we've contributed to the great state of North Carolina before a slave girl ever will."

"Your whiteness and your manhood are the only reasons you believe that. But you, Mr. Haywood, have done nothing to contribute to the good of this state or the nation."

Standing on the porch, he stomped a foot in anger. "You will not speak to me in this manner."

"But for the inability of White men in this country to see the humanness of people of color, you, sir, would be hanging from a tree for the crimes you have committed against my family." With that she slammed the door, confident she would never lay eyes on the man again. And that suited her fine.

Part 3

BACK AT OBERLIN: TIME TO FIGHT

This same spirit, which promptly assumes everything against us, just as readily denies or explains away everything in our favor. We are not, as a race, even permitted to appropriate the virtues and achievements of our individual representatives. Manliness, capacity, learning, laudable ambition, heroic service, by any of our number, are easily placed to the credit of the superior race.

—Frederick Douglass, "The Color Line," 1881

CHAPTER 23

Never in her wildest imagination would Mary have conceived that coming back to Oberlin would be less stressful than being in Memphis with the ones she loved. But things had gotten too complicated at home, leaving her feeling as if she had to choose between her father and her mother. How could she decide who to spend summers with when she loved them both?

On the train ride back to Oberlin, Mary told herself that she would never put her future children through anything like this. Divorce was too harsh. Although Mary had enjoyed her flirtations with some of the college boys at Oberlin, after her summer break, one thing was for certain: Marriage was not for her . . . at least not yet. Her focus would be on graduating and then deciding what she wanted to do with her life. Marriage and children would have to wait.

As she was going through one of her bags, her hand skimmed across the envelope that Mr. Douglass had mailed to her. With everything that had happened this summer, she never made time to read it. And therefore, she hadn't written to thank him for this kindness. Mary was appalled at her thoughtlessness.

She took the envelope out of her luggage and sat back down to read the essay. It was called "The Color Line" and was published in *The North American Review* in the month of June. Turning to the first page of the article, she began reading.

> *Few evils are less accessible to the force of reason, or more tenacious of life and power, than a long-standing prejudice . . . It is a moral disorder, which creates the conditions necessary to its own existence, and fortifies itself by refusing all contradiction . . . As those who believe in the visibility of ghosts can easily see them, so it is always easy to see repulsive qualities in those we despise and hate . . . The great Daniel Webster once told the people of Massachusetts . . . that they "had conquered the sea, and had conquered the land," but that "it remained for them to conquer their prejudices."*

Fascinated by the text, Mary read the entire article in one sitting, all the while wondering how Black folks would ever dispel the dominant group of the prejudices that caused them to see what they expected of Colored folks rather than the reality that stood before them.

If those White men who came against Charles had only seen him as a man who took pride in ownership rather than as someone to hate—a Colored man who'd gotten above himself—then Charles would still be alive, thriving and flirting.

Those men didn't have the right to take the life of a human being simply for the crime of excelling while being Black. Something had to be done; Mary was convinced of that. Her prayer was that President Garfield recovered soon and could carry on with the plans he was putting in place.

After spending hours engrossed in Frederick Douglass's words and wondering if the color line would always be in their way, Mary got out of her seat and reached for her luggage in order to put the envelope back in her suitcase.

"I can help you with that," a gentleman said as he approached her.

Mary turned toward him. His eyes, dark and intriguing, seemed to pierce through her with a glance. Her hands shook as he tipped his hat to her.

He took Mary's bag and placed it back in the slot she had removed it from. "Thank you, kind sir."

"My name is Robert Terrell. I didn't mean to startle you."

She rubbed her hands together, making sure they weren't moistened from sweat, then held one out to him. "You didn't startle me. My name is Mary Church."

"Well, Miss Church, I'm on my way back to college. Are you traveling to see family?"

His mustache intrigued her. How old was this young gentleman? "I'm on my way back to college as well. I attend Oberlin in Ohio."

"You don't say." A small, appreciative smile tugged at Robert's lips. "I'm in my second year at Harvard University."

An eyebrow jutted upward before Mary could tell herself to remain unmoved. But Harvard? It was the oldest institution of learning in the country. Very few men of color were admitted. If this man standing before her was a Harvard man, then she counted him a man of substance. "It's nice to meet you. I'm in my second year also."

"Sounds like we have a few things in common."

"Only our grade level and the fact that we both attend college." She wasn't going to let him know that she was impressed. He would have to earn that with a little more conversation.

Mary had the most delightful conversation with Robert that by the time the train pulled into Ohio, she inwardly groaned at the thought of leaving her travel companion. She'd told him about Frederick Douglass's "Color Line" essay . . . about her troubles at Oberlin . . . and even about her friend's untimely death at the hands of wicked men.

"Perhaps you might be able to bring about a measure of change with your newfound knowledge."

Mary wasn't sure if there was anything she could do to change the hearts and minds of the people who saw only color when they looked at her, and not her intellect. But she could protect her peace. Which was the reason she did not return to Ladies Hall when she stepped off the train. True to her word, she had moved out.

Her father had paid a company to transport her items from Ladies Hall to Mr. and Mrs. Vaughans', the couple she had boarded with while in primary school. Mary enjoyed living with them in Yellow Springs, and now that they were in Oberlin, she was thrilled to join them. It was a heap better than being in Ladies Hall and being treated poorly.

Walking toward Oberlin College, Mary crossed over onto East Vine Street. As she reached the home of Mr. and Mrs. Evans, Mary waved at Anna as the young woman swept the front porch steps. "Good morning. You going to class this morning?"

"Finishing up." Anna laid the broom against the wall in front of the house. "I have another hour before my class begins."

"So do I," Mary told her. "Thought I'd check on you before going to school, since I now live the next street over."

"You stuck to that, I see."

Mary nodded. "Even the distance of summer break couldn't dissuade my resolve to get away from those nasty girls I shared living space with."

Anna sat on one of the porch chairs and invited Mary to do the same. "I hope your summer was better than mine." Anna's face took on sorrow. "My mom almost died while I was at home."

"Oh, Anna, I'm so sorry to hear that." Mary leaned forward and hugged her friend.

Anna wiped her eyes. "She's doing better, but she might have died if she didn't get the proper rest."

"I'm sure you're thankful that you were home during her time of need."

Anna nodded. "Anyway, how was your time at home? Filled with galas and suitors, no doubt."

Mary wished her life was filled with only frills and no pitfalls as Anna seemed to believe. But sorrow didn't care which door it knocked on. "My parents got divorced. And a close family friend was lynched, so I didn't enjoy my summer break in the least."

Anna's eyes widened. "I'm sorry about that. And here I

was thinking you were in Memphis having the time of your life while I was being treated like a servant rather than a scholar."

The two sat in silence for a long moment, then Mary shrugged. "Sounds like we both had an awful summer."

"I'd prefer to have a new summer break where I could pick the experience."

Mary nodded in agreement.

Anna sighed deeply. "After my mother took ill, the man who used to own her . . . the man who is most likely my father . . ." She said the words as if they were nothing more than statements of fact. "He came to the house and demanded that I give up college and take over my mother's cleaning duties at his manor."

Mary harrumphed as her nostrils flared. "How could he expect that of you?"

Anna shrugged. "I slammed the door in his face. It felt so good. But my mother chided me for being disrespectful." Her lips twisted. "George Haywood deserves all the disrespect I could give him." Hate blazed in Anna's eyes.

"Was he one of those sadistic slave owners? Did he harm your mother?"

"I don't like talking about the Haywoods, but the truth is, they caused me and my mother great harm. My mother was too ashamed to ever talk about it." Anna glanced back at Mary as her lips tightened around the shame that lingered.

They sat beside each other in solidarity, then Mary said, "Yours isn't the only family to deal with a slave master taking advantage of a slave girl. My father and my mother are mulatto. Both of their fathers were White . . . so you see, we aren't so different after all."

Anna smirked. "We're very different, Miss Mary Church."

"No, we're not." Mary shook her head.

"Okay then, tell me, how many parties did you attend and how many gown fittings did you have in Memphis?"

"Our summer season does involve dances and fundraisers. And my mother did take me for a fitting before she left for New York," Mary admitted.

"I spent my summer scrubbing floors for the people my mother worked for, so we're not the same." Anna grinned. "But it's okay. I'm glad to have such a high society lady as a friend. It gives me hope."

"Are you being serious, or is this more sarcasm?" Mary never knew which way the conversation would end with Anna. She didn't want to offend her, but sometimes offense came in the least little thing she said.

Anna stood and took the broom back in her hands. "I'm serious. I'll admit, I was jealous of all you have when we first met. But you've proven to me that you're not some shallow rich girl. And I like being around you and Ida."

"Speaking of Ida." Mary stood too. "I'm supposed to meet her at chapel."

Opening the front door, Anna told her, "I'll meet you at school. Let me freshen up."

Mary stepped down from the porch, but before leaving she told Anna, "We won't be at Oberlin forever. Let's make the most of these years."

Anna agreed and then headed inside.

As Mary walked to the college, the years she'd spent in this town rolled through her mind. She'd lived in Oberlin since turning twelve and entering Oberlin Union School. It was a peaceful place with welcoming people. All of her teachers had been decent except for the one who took a board to her knuckles.

An older couple sat on their porch sipping their morning tea. They lived outside the walls of Oberlin College. Mary raised a hand. "Good morning. Fair weather we're having today."

"The way we like it," the man of the house said.

Then his wife asked, "Returning from summer break, Miss Mary?"

"I am."

"Well." The woman waved her toward the porch. "Come have tea with us."

"I have chapel, but I'll arrive earlier tomorrow so we can have tea together." Mary waved goodbye as she entered the college.

They were a lovely family she'd met when she first arrived in Oberlin. They'd always been so welcoming and encouraging to her. She'd see more of them now that she would be walking to her classes every morning.

As she made her way to the chapel building for morning prayer, Mason exited his dorm across the street and began walking in her direction. Her mind had not changed on Mason since he caused her to look so foolish.

She cut a path through the yard and walked behind one of the other dorms before making her way to chapel. Avoiding Mason was silly. She would have to speak with him eventually, but not now. She wasn't ready to deal with all that.

Reverend Brand clasped his hands together and peered out at the group of about a hundred students. "Thank you all for attending the first prayer time at Oberlin as we begin the fall semester. Today, we're not praying for the college or our city. Please join hands as we pray for the president of the United States of America. Mr. Garfield needs healing and we will endeavor to lift our voices unto God at least once a week until he makes a full recovery from that evil attempted assassination."

Garfield was supposed to be on the mend, but they'd been informed that he was still bedridden. Mary joined hands and prayed like everyone else. But deep inside she was praying extra hard. President Garfield had proven himself a friend to the Negro when he appointed Frederick Douglass as the recorder of deeds in Washington; Robert Elliott, special agent to the Treasury; John M. Langston, Haitian minister; and Blanche K. Bruce, who was now registrar to the Treasury. Progress was being made, but if Garfield didn't fully recover from his injuries, what would become of their progress? "Help us, Lord."

CHAPTER 24

The first day back on campus, Anna walked past Council Hall, a men's dorm, as Katherine Smalls, president of the Ladies Literary Society, stepped out of the building.

"And what are you about today, young lady? Did you have official business in Council Hall?"

Katherine put her hand over her face as she giggled. "You caught me. I took Roy Davis a slice of cake."

Anna bit down on her bottom lip, then stared at Katherine. "Isn't that the boy you were sweet on last year?"

Katherine leaned against Anna's arm and whispered, "We're courting now. He might be the one."

"And you think sneaking into his dorm with cake baked by hands other than yours is going to reel him in?"

"Oh, Anna, don't be so pessimistic. A few more cakes and cookies and I'm sure to win his heart."

The two women walked down the street together. Anna said, "The food trick. It's worked for many women." She wagged a finger at Katherine. "Make sure you're being genuine.

If this fellow wants a cook and that's not what you aspire to be, don't start off pretending."

Katherine stopped walking in the middle of the road and gave Anna a hug. "Thank you for that wise counsel. I should've come to you with my plan in the first place."

Anna was shaken. Not due to the fact that Katherine hugged her, but that she was willing to take advice from her. She hadn't seen the girl since they'd left campus for summer break, but she proved to be the same warm and kind person Anna had come to know. "Katherine Smalls, you are a caution."

"And you sparkle like a sunshiny day. Your summer break must've been good for you." Katherine continued down the street.

Anna smiled at Katherine. "I wouldn't say that, but I'm happy to be back on campus. How was your summer?"

"Delightful, as always." Katherine giggled. "Unless you count all the fussing my grandparents did during our Sunday meals. I swear, the older those two get, the less they seem to agree on anything."

Never in her life had Anna sat at a dinner table with grandparents. Katherine's declaration made Anna yearn for a world with grannies and papas no matter how ornery they were. But alas, her mother's parents had been sold off before Anna was born. She didn't know, to this day, if they were dead or alive. "Still must have been nice to be around your grandparents."

"It was," Katherine admitted.

Once they were outside of the college grounds, Anna asked, "Are you headed into town?"

"I'm actually on my way to your house. I need to speak with Mr. Wilson Evans about a paper on the abolitionists who lived in town during slavery."

"And what made you want to write a paper on such a thing?" Last year, several of the Black students had written papers about abolitionists, but most of the White students had focused on other aspects of American history. She was curious why Katherine was going in this direction.

Katherine shrugged. "I don't know . . . guess I've always admired what was done in this town during those terrible days."

The fact that Katherine could openly admit that slavery was a terrible thing brought joy to Anna's heart. Made her want to let Katherine in on a few other things she'd discovered about the town. Anna swept a hand in the direction of a house on East College Street. "From what I've been told, Mr. Burrell's home was used by the Underground Railroad."

"Mr. Burrell never verified if that was true or not, but his brother over in Yellow Springs participated in the Underground Railroad for sure," Katherine said.

Anna nodded her approval. "I see you've done your homework."

Katherine's eyes crossed as if she was caught between a thought, then she said, "Why on earth would anyone attend Oberlin unless they had a fascination with this whole idea of freedom for us all?"

"I've asked myself that very question a time or two since coming to Oberlin," Anna told her as the two continued on.

When they arrived at the house, Mr. Wilson was seated on the porch, rocking back and forth, as if enjoying the last few days of summer. Anna waved at him. "Mr. Wilson, how are you doing today?"

"I'm right fine for a Monday," he told her and kept rocking.

Anna gestured to Katherine. "A friend of mine from Oberlin would like to talk to you about some things. Can you spare a moment for her?"

He glanced in her direction. "I s'pose I can spare a moment." He lifted a hand. "But I'm going right back to rocking when we're done."

Stretching out her hand to him, Anna's friend said, "I'm Katherine Smalls. We met during open house a year ago, but I doubt you remember me."

Mr. Wilson ran his hand through a piece of his white beard. "I've lost a bit of my eyesight, but the mind is still good." He snapped his fingers. "You're the niece of that fellow who went off to war to help us fight against them Confederates."

"If you remembered that about me, I'd say your mind is pretty sharp." Katherine sat on the porch step. "This will be very helpful. I need some information about the years before the war."

He stopped rocking. "This is going to take a while. Sarah was finishing supper when I came out here. I reckon you should join us." He stood and opened the door, then waved Anna and Katherine into the house.

Katherine jumped up and rubbed her hands together. "Thank you for saving me from Cook's meatloaf. It's usually dry."

Anna watched the young woman to see if there was any hesitation about sitting down to dinner with Colored folks. Katherine surprised her yet again. Could there be such a thing as a White person without preconceived prejudices against other races?

"I smelled the cabbage cooking from the porch. You're in for a treat," Anna told Katherine. "Mrs. Sarah's food is always good."

"I'm glad you approve," Mrs. Sarah said to Anna. "I cooked a big pot of stew also. Way more than we could eat this week."

Anna enjoyed most all of Mrs. Sarah's meals, especially her macaroni and cheese and fried chicken. The way Mrs. Sarah's pots were filled with goodness and love, it was a travesty that she'd lost four of her seven children to illness early on. Anna wished all of Mrs. Sarah's children could sit around her dinner table and enjoy all she had to offer. But life had been unkind to them.

After their bellies were full, Mr. Wilson sat back on the porch with Anna and Katherine. He was patient and answered every question Katherine threw at him. With glee he told her about the men in this town who'd been on the right side of the slavery issue. "It wasn't only Black men, you know. Plenty of White men were abolitionists."

Anna wasn't sure how to feel about all the things that went on in this town during slavery. Oberlin was different these days. When Anna could hold it in no more, she said, "I don't get it."

Lines creased Mr. Evans's forehead. "What troubles your mind?"

Anna rubbed her temple with her index finger. "If the White people in this town hated slavery so much, why are some of them so against advancement for Colored people?"

"My generation fought the evil of slavery." Mr. Wilson stood, stretched his legs, and rubbed his knees. He eyed Anna and Katherine as he added, "This mountain of equality is a worthy cause that your generation must climb."

After speaking his piece, Mr. Wilson went back inside the house, leaving Anna and Katherine staring at each other with concern. "And how does he suggest we climb this mountain?" Katherine asked.

"I think he was directing that comment to me."

"On this, you're wrong." Katherine put her arm around Anna's shoulders. "For a movement to be successful, it'll take all willing hands, and I promise you, my friend, I'm willing."

Anna gazed at this White woman whose arm rested on her as if they were friends. But could they ever truly be friends? "So you're telling me that you would take up a fight that's not yours?"

She nodded. "If it's a worthy cause, I'd do it in a heartbeat."

In Katherine's eyes she saw the unmistakable presence of an ally. When Anna ran into Katherine that day that she stood in front of the Soldiers Monument questioning their actions, she had no way of knowing she'd gained a friend.

As they sat on the porch at the home of an abolitionist, with a framed photograph on his mantel that spoke of allyship, for the first time since arriving at Oberlin, Anna felt peace sweep over her. She'd finally found her people. For the cause of equality was not the cause of a race or a sect, a party or a class. It was the cause of humankind, the very birthright of humanity. And they would climb this mountain together.

CHAPTER 25

September 16, 1881

"You did it, Mary! You did it." Ida's eyes glistened with joy. She put a hand to her heart. "I can't believe this." They stood behind a table in the society room at Ladies Hall, confused and befuddled by what had transpired.

Anna hugged Mary and admitted, "I'm a little shocked myself. But this is the absolute best day!"

Mary couldn't control the grin that spread across her face. For the past few weeks she had run a campaign to become the recording secretary of the Aeolian Literary Society, and after the votes had been counted, it was announced that she had won. She actually won.

Placing her hands on her cheeks, Mary plunked down in her chair. She opened her mouth, then closed it. Then opened it again. "I—I hoped I'd win. But after all the other disappointments, I didn't know if it would happen."

Glancing around the room at the faces of smiles and happiness brought Mary joy. Even though there were others who clearly didn't like the fact that she was now the first Colored woman to be voted recording secretary of the Aeolian Literary Society. It showed in their crossed arms and downward-twisted lips. The hostility wasn't coming from her society, who'd unanimously voted her in, but from the Ladies Literary Society.

Mary chose not to focus on the people who weren't for her. Today, she was a winner and those who despised her could do nothing about it. She got out of her seat and made her way around the room, smiling at and hugging those who saw her value. "Thank you all so very much for your kindness. I'll do my very best in this new role."

Janet nodded her agreement. "You'll do a fine job. You might even take my role next year."

Mary shook her head. "I wouldn't dare run against you. I'll wait until you graduate. Next year I'll set my sights on the vice president role." The two got along so well that there was no need to compete with each other.

Knowing that Janet had that much confidence in her made Mary want to work ten times harder for the literary group. "For now, if you let me know what you require, I'll make sure it gets done posthaste."

"And that's the reason you won the election. People know they can count on you," Janet told her.

Mary, Ida, and Anna gathered their belongings, preparing to leave Ladies Hall. They walked into the gathering room, and Mary waved at the girls she used to share this space with. They were seated on the floor with books open or on the sofa holding conversations.

A few girls ran down the stairs and joined the group in

the gathering room. Mary found herself gazing longingly at those steps. Days gone by flashed through her mind, but she kept on walking.

Ida told them, "Mrs. Jones is cooking a big meal tonight. She said I could invite friends if I wanted to."

As Mary had moved out of Ladies Hall, so, too, had Ida. She was now living with the Joneses', two streets over from where Mary resided. "She makes the best homemade rolls. I'd love to come."

"Count me in as well," Anna said.

They'd reached the door and Ida had placed a hand on the doorknob when they heard, "How nice it is to see you young ladies."

They turned to see Mrs. Johnston standing in the middle of the gathering room. "Hello, Mrs. Johnston," Ida and Anna said simultaneously.

Mary said, "It's good to see you too. I meant to stop by last week, but my schedule was overwhelming."

"If you have a moment, I'd like to speak with you in my office." Mrs. Johnston stared pointedly at Mary so there was no mistaking who she was extending the offer to.

"Of course." Mary followed her to the small office she'd been called to on numerous occasions.

Mrs. Johnston nodded to the seat in front of her desk. "Please."

Mary sat down. Folded her hands in her lap.

"I hope you're enjoying the hospitality of the family you're boarding with."

Mary nodded. "They've always been good to me. I'm thankful for them."

"I wanted you to know that your absence is felt at Ladies Hall. We wish you well, but we miss you."

The smirk that appeared on Mary's face was pronounced. "I'm not sure how many of the residents miss me."

"Maybe not all," Mrs. Johnston agreed. "But you have many friends here; I hope you know that."

After today's vote, Mary couldn't deny the truth of that statement. "I know. Thank you for saying so."

"If you ever decide to return to Ladies Hall, know that the door is wide open for you."

"I appreciate your kind gesture."

"That isn't the only reason I wanted to speak with you." Mrs. Johnston picked up a piece of paper from her desk. "*The Oberlin Review* is in need of an editor for the Lifestyle section of their paper. I suggested you for the position."

"Me? Why?" Mary leaned forward. Tapped her index finger to her jaw as she waited for a response.

"Don't think I haven't noticed your love for writing. And I spoke with your literature professor." She handed the paper to Mary. "The job is yours if you want it."

Glancing down at the advertisement, a frown creased the corners of Mary's lips. The Lifestyle section was frill and society. "I don't know, Mrs. Johnston. Are you sure I'm the right person for this position?"

"Of course you are. As principal of the Ladies' Department, I've personally read several of your papers and poems. Your writing is exquisite."

Her peers would think her shallow. It would be different if she were given editorial license over the Communication or Commentary section. She'd be able to call out issues she'd witnessed on campus. "Thank you for noticing the work I put into my papers. But I don't know if the Lifestyle section is for me."

Mrs. Johnston straightened in her seat. "The Lifestyle pages may not be your heart's desire, but it's a start . . . something to build on for the day you write your own stories and have them published."

Writing her own stories was something Mary had only dreamed about. Could she be a voice for her people? The only thing that held her back was her father's image of her as a socialite who threw parties and raised funds.

But after the divorce, Mary wasn't so sure that Robert Church's advice was as sound as she once believed. Her mother told her not to let anyone stand in the way of her dreams. That included her father. He would have to accept who she was becoming. "Okay, Mrs. Johnston, I'll do it."

She left Ladies Hall feeling good about her decision. And now that she was recording secretary, she'd make sure to include her literary club in articles for *The Oberlin Review*. There were many things about life at Oberlin she could add to her column. The sports outings, the teas and parties hosted on campus, and so much more. Ideas were flowing. This would be good.

Mary held on to her exuberance all weekend long. Not only had she won the election to become the recording secretary of her literary group, but she was now editor of the Lifestyle section. Her peers were showing respect and that was all she'd ever wanted.

On Sunday she went to church, still floating on a cloud. After praise and worship Reverend Brand gripped the pulpit with both hands and asked everyone to rise. Once they were standing, he said, "Church, we need continued fervent prayer for President Garfield. I've received reports that he's had a setback due to an infection."

Not the news she wanted to hear . . . not good at all. She'd prayed and prayed for President Garfield. He had survived the shooting, and he simply had to survive this terrible infection. Her people were depending on him.

She was so lost in thought as she made her way out of First Church that she bumped into someone. "I'm sorry, please forgive me," she said without looking up.

"How can I forgive you when you've been ignoring me since I shared my fried chicken with you?"

Her head jerked up. "Mason, how are you doing?"

"Poorly." He poked his bottom lip out and pouted. "Will that cause you to take pity on me?"

Her lips twisted as a few parishioners passed by. "You aren't doing poorly and you certainly don't need pity."

He took hold of her arm and moved her over by the window close to the door. "Tell me what I did that was so wrong. Why do you avoid me like this?"

Mason was a gentleman. She had enjoyed being in his company, but some things should never be done. "That picnic idea of yours caused me great humiliation. As the minority race, we need to be doing things with excellence. We can't allow ourselves to be laughed at by the dominant group."

Lines creased Mason's forehead. "What dominant group?"

Mary waved a hand at the parishioners as they walked by. "When I say dominant group, I'm speaking of the White race."

"No race, no matter the color, will dominate me," he said with a lilt of pride.

"I'm not saying they're better than us. It's merely that there are more White people than Colored people in this country. And I don't believe we should make fools of ourselves in front of them."

"That's the difference between you and me. I don't live and breathe based on what others think of me."

Mary's hands went to her hips. "Neither do I, but there is still decorum that we as the Colored race must adhere to if we want to be acknowledged as equals."

He stepped away from her, folding his arms. "And you think such a thing will happen in our lifetime?"

"My father says that if we comport ourselves in the right manner, others will soon come to see that we're good citizens of this country and will respect us."

Mason's lips twisted. "You care too much about what your father thinks."

"That's not true. I have my own mind and my own way of thinking. However, on this matter, my father is correct."

Mason blew out hot air. "Correct or not, I'm not changing who I am to impress people who don't care anything about me in the first place."

"I figured as much. This is the reason you and I should go no further."

He walked away from her without uttering another word.

Mary stepped out of the church, the cool air pressing against her face. The gravel crunched unevenly beneath her shoes. Mason's voice echoed somewhere behind her, a sharp edge she couldn't shake. She drew her shawl tighter, as if that might hold her together.

She'd worked so hard to build a good name—for herself,

for her family. For her people. That was the point, wasn't it? To make them proud, to show what they could be? Her thoughts tangled, each one slipping away before it finished forming. What was so wrong with that? With her father's words? She slowed, but her pulse didn't.

That night she went to sleep with the betterment of the Colored race on her mind. By morning when she went to chapel and discovered that President Garfield had died, even after all the prayers they'd sent up on his behalf, it was as if her world had crashed in on her.

President Garfield . . . gone. She blinked hard, but the tears came anyway. On the street outside, church bells tolled, slow and heavy, each note landing like a stone in her chest.

Around her, students stood silent, hats pressed to hearts, eyes fixed on nothing in particular. "He believed in us," a young Colored man whispered. She swallowed against the ache rising in her throat. Who would speak for them now? Who would fight for the educational reforms for Blacks that he'd promised?

Her accomplishments, which had made her so proud on Friday, seemed insignificant and hollow on Monday. What difference did it make to her people that she had won a recording secretary position or editor of the Lifestyle section of *The Oberlin Review*? Could either of those things help with the advancement of her race, or was she engaging in frivolousness that would serve no one but herself?

CHAPTER 26

After the storm of tears had passed, after her body had shaken itself empty of grief for a good man who had wanted only to do good for her people, Mary sat in her room, feeling hollow and ashamed.

How easy it had been to wait. To hope. To let others fight while she stayed safe on the fence, telling herself that the tide of justice would turn without her hand upon it.

Her father was a fighter. Mary had always admired the work he'd done for people who couldn't help themselves. His voice rose in her mind, clear as if he were standing beside her. *"I sent you to Oberlin to learn how to fight."*

She'd believed in President Garfield, believed that his plans for the education of Colored people might open a door wide enough for all of them to walk through. But now he was gone, and with him, that fragile dream.

Her father . . . President Garfield. Mary had put her hopes in two men, never asking herself what she could or would do to lift a people.

It would take all willing hands. Every woman, every

man, standing, pushing, bleeding if need be, until equality was more than a word whispered in prayer. More than hope for someday. Until Colored folks were judged by who they were inside and their work ethic rather than the color of their skin or the lies about their character . . . the work would not be done.

And Mary, at last, would no longer wait on others to do what only she could do—no more. Her part was what she would do, then leave the rest for other willing hands.

The next morning she dug deep, discovering what mattered to her. Lynching. That mattered. Colored folks being seen as humans worthy of respect. That mattered. Women being seen as more than wives, mothers, and cooks. That mattered. All of the things that mattered to her boiled down to equality. White men wouldn't lynch Black men if they feared being brought to justice for their crimes. The problem facing Colored folks and women in this country also could be solved if the dominant group saw them all as equals.

She was only one person. She couldn't tackle all things at once. *Pick a problem and work on it.* Later that day she designed flyers that were anti-lynching pleas.

Most of the lynching was done in the South, but Northerners had turned a blind eye to it, believing the lie that the Colored men being lynched had raped White women. However, out of the hundreds of Colored men and women who were beaten, burned, mutilated, and hung on trees, only a handful of them had been accused of rape.

More White men had raped poor defenseless slave girls in the South than any Colored man ever thought about doing to a White woman, and yet not one White man hung from a tree for this crime. It was the greatest hypocrisy ever perpetrated on American citizens.

Mary was tired . . . past tired of the silent complicity that had aided in Charles's death and the deaths of other Colored men who'd done nothing but exist in the dominant group's world. At the top of the flyer she wrote, LYNCHING IS WRONG. And at the bottom she added, DO SOMETHING OR BE JUDGED FOR YOUR SILENCE.

She cut a picture of a man hanging from a tree out of a newspaper and pasted it in the middle of the flyer. The reporter had received the photograph from a White man who'd brought his wife and children to the site of the lynching so they could see what happened to Coloreds in America. They brought a picnic basket and made a day of it. Even in death, the Colored man had to provide entertainment for degenerates who had no hearts.

She had a hundred copies of the flyer printed at the newspaper she worked for. With the flyers in hand, Mary stood directly in front of Tappan Hall where most students walked during the day.

"Excuse me, can I hand you this flyer?" Mary said again and again as students and faculty passed by. "Lynching is wrong. We must fight against this evil!" she shouted.

Ida and Anna were about to pass by. Ida approached her first. "What are you doing?"

Mary handed her the flyer. "I'm trying to get people to understand that lynching is a scourge that needs to be eradicated."

"Give me a few extra. I'll help pass them out," Ida told her.

Anna stuck her hand out as well. "I can help too. You should've told us. We would've been here with you."

"Well, you're here now and that's what counts." Mary

handed Anna and Ida a few of the flyers. Then Katherine and Janet joined them as well.

When Mary came up with the idea of passing out flyers about lynching, she never imagined others would help. Most people knew that lynching was wrong, but the few who had spoken out against it had suffered consequences such as losing political appointments, jobs, and even their lives.

"You're doing this all wrong," Mason said as he walked over to her.

The hair stood up on the back of Mary's neck. If he was going to criticize her again, she was going to let him have it. "If you have a better way, I'd love to hear it."

"Of course I have a better way." He was wearing overalls today. He put his thumbs around the straps and leaned back on the heels of his feet. "But I wouldn't want to cause you utter mortification."

A hand went to her hip as she huffed. "If you're going to be a pest, why don't you move along?" Mary handed a flyer to another passerby. She repeated her catchphrase: "Lynching is wrong. We must find a way to fight this evil."

When she swung back around to shoo Mason away, he was already gone. Good. Who was he to tell her she was doing anything wrong?

She and her group continued passing out the flyers until there were no more. Then they huddled on Tappan Walkway, trying to decide their next steps.

"This was good, but I feel like we need to do more. This is such an important issue," Janet said.

Ida nodded her agreement. "I'm sick to death of hearing about our people being strung up for the smallest of infractions."

Mary nodded too. "More has to be done. I'm thinking about a few other things, but I need to figure out what's most effective." But as she watched more people pass by, she wished she had printed more of those flyers.

Anna was about to speak when a booming voice shouted, "Lynching is wrong. Help us fight this evil!"

The sound rang out over by Council Hall. Mason was standing in front of the building, holding up a large paper sign with the words *Lynching Is Wrong* written on it.

He walked toward her, still shouting about the evils of lynching while holding on to several other white poster boards. He handed one to each of them. Mary's board said, THE WORLD IS WATCHING—SPEAK UP NOW.

Anna's said, EVIL MEN DO EVIL DEEDS.

COLORED FOLKS JUST WANT TO LIVE were the words on the sign Janet was given.

Ida picked the one that said, NO HUMAN SHOULD HANG FROM A TREE.

YOUR SILENCE SPEAKS VOLUMES were the words on the final board. Katherine took that one. Then the group held up the signs and marched around the area in front of Tappan Hall, shouting, "Stop the violence! No man, woman, or child should be lynched!"

As they marched around this small section of Oberlin, shouting and holding up their signs, a changing tide washed over them. When Mary was passing out the flyers, people took them and went on their way, but as they held up these posters and shouted, the people didn't walk away. They stopped, stared, shouted with them. The crowd grew . . . and a movement grew.

The following week Mary added sticks to their posters so they could raise them high in the air. And a funny thing happened: More students showed up in front of Tappan Hall and asked to join them.

Mason held up his sign and protested with them again.

Mary walked over to him to eat crow. "Okay, I fully admit that you were right." It hurt Mary's heart to capitulate to Mason. But his idea had sparked more than Mary had ever dreamed of on the Oberlin campus.

"The flyers are definitely needed also. Now that we're getting crowds to pay attention to this issue, we could pass out the flyers with a call to action on them."

Mary smiled. "I'm beginning to like the way your mind works."

His eyes were aglow as he stared at her. "And I like the way you've let loose recently. Not sure what's happened, but you've been different lately."

She was not as stiff as Mason imagined her to be. But life had a way of pausing what was and bringing one into reality—her parents' divorce, Charles's lynching simply for being a Colored man of excellence. Women being able to do little about their circumstances since they didn't have a voice in the voting booth. Those were the things that wouldn't let Mary go. Those were the things that had scarred and changed her forever.

She couldn't tell him about all the ways her heart had been broken by this country while they stood in the open air with crowds of people milling about. So she simply said, "I guess I'm growing."

"Have you grown enough to have dinner with me again?" His eyes sparked with hope.

Mary exhaled and held out her hand. "Not dinner, Mason. But I'd like to call you a friend."

He took the offered hand. "Then friend it is." They shook on it, and then he walked away.

Mary sighed deeply and watched him leave. In that sliver of a moment, she wished she believed in happily ever after. Forever was a long time, and if her parents couldn't make it, then she wasn't going to take a chance on young love. Mary was more determined than ever to live life on her own terms. She wanted to fight for the good of her people. She was learning how powerful her voice and the voices of others could be when they united. Love would come one day. Right now, she had other things on her mind.

"We did it." Ida's voice held surprise and pride at the same time. "The people responded to our protest today."

"I had a few people ask when and where the next protest would be," Anna said.

Mary exhaled. Tired and hungry yet still energized. "I like the sound of that. Let's grab lunch and discuss our next protest."

The three women walked away from Tappan Hall arm in arm, headed to Ladies Hall. They couldn't have known they were about to walk right into their next fight.

CHAPTER 27

Anna rarely ate lunch in the Ladies Hall dining room, preferring to go home and enjoy Mrs. Sarah's company when she had time between classes. Mary stopped at the bathroom while Anna and Ida entered the dining hall.

The smell of baked chicken with gravy wafted in the air. Anna put a hand to her stomach as it growled. "Smells delicious in here."

"We'll see. I prefer the food at my boardinghouse," Ida told her.

Janet and Katherine were seated at a table near the front of the room. Anna and Ida grabbed their plates, then sat down with their friends. "Whew!" Anna sighed. "I'm so tired, I might sleep the entire weekend."

Katherine rubbed the back of her neck. "Picketing is hard work. But so rewarding."

Anna cut into her chicken and took a bite. Many of the students complained about the cook's food, but it was actually good, though not make-you-moan-while-eating good. But she wasn't spitting it out either.

Ida said, "I have a gown fitting this weekend for a party my parents are throwing next month, so no rest for me."

Two White girls walked over to their table, plates in hand, fire in their eyes. "What are you doing? Your table is back there." One of the girls waved a hand at a table in the back of the room where three Black girls were seated.

"Excuse me?" Ida glared at the girls.

Katherine said, "They're with us, so leave them alone."

Eyes shifted from the table in the back to the girls demanding that they move. Then they turned to Katherine.

"What are they talking about? Why do they want us to move?" Anna asked.

Janet huffed. "Since Mary and Ida moved out, several of the girls decided that Black students needed to eat together at a table in the back so no one else had to sit with them."

Ida stood and snatched her plate off the table. "So the work Mary and I did to get funding so Ladies Hall could be remodeled doesn't matter? My appearance at a table you didn't pay for bothers you." Ida shot each one of the girls a disparaging glance. "Thank you for letting me know." Then she went and sat with the girls whose coloring was more like hers.

Anna stood, chest heaving. "Why are you girls always fighting against us when we're not your true enemy? We should be fighting together to ensure women have the full rights we deserve in this country. But you'd rather feel superior to a Colored woman."

Anna picked up her plate, but Katherine grabbed her arm. "Don't leave. Those girls don't run anything in this dining hall."

"The only seat I will ever fight for is a seat at tables where men sit and smugly deny women access." Anna sighed, her shoulders rolling forward as she smirked at the girls waiting on her to move. "One day you will realize that I'm not your enemy. Until that time"—Anna stepped away from the table—"have a seat and keep fighting the wrong battle."

The dining hall smelled of baked chicken and gravy. A haze of steam hung above the serving counter, and the steady clatter of utensils rang out like a regiment of tin soldiers. Sunlight fell through the tall windows in bright rectangular patches, gilding the white linen and catching on the silverware.

"Why are y'all sitting back here?" Mary's voice carried a note of disbelief as she paused beside the last table in the room. "We normally sit at the second table." She indicated the front where several White students—Janet, Katherine, and the others from the literary society—were already gathered, chatting and laughing as if nothing in the world had shifted.

Ida shrugged, though her eyes flicked nervously toward the front. "We were told that Colored folks now sit at this table."

"That doesn't make sense." Mary glanced again at their usual table, at the familiar chairs that now seemed strangely foreign. Her stomach tightened. "They're separating us by race?"

Anna gave a dry, humorless laugh. "Apparently our color offends them so terribly that they can't bear to eat their baked chicken alongside us."

"I for one don't care." Ida waved a dismissive hand, though the tremor in her fingers betrayed her.

Mary's foot tapped against the floor, quick and sharp. Heat climbed into her cheeks. "Well, I care. I didn't come to Oberlin to sit in the shadows. This isn't Memphis. This is supposed to be different."

The next morning Mary gathered the Colored girls who boarded at Ladies Hall, pulling them aside in the narrow hallway that smelled faintly of coal smoke and starch.

"Why are you letting them push you to the corner?" she demanded.

One girl shifted her books in her arms. "I'm only here until the end of term. Then I'll have my certificate. No sense stirring up trouble now."

Another murmured, "They're so hateful, Mary. Best to stay out of the way."

Mary leaned closer, her voice low but fierce. "If we keep out of the way, they'll keep moving the line until there's nowhere left for us to stand. I have an idea, but it'll take courage."

By noon her plan was set. The smell of roast beef and green beans drifted through the corridor as she entered the dining room half an hour before the bell. Her palms were damp, but her steps were sure. She accepted her plate from the cook. Mary then carried her plate straight to the second table from the front.

The room was cavernous in its silence. She could almost hear her heart thudding against her ribs.

Moments later, the three Colored girls she'd spoken with that morning came in. They exchanged wary glances before approaching. "Are you sure about this?" one whispered.

Mary smiled faintly and gestured to the empty seats. "Please. Join me."

The scrape of their chairs on the floor sounded louder than thunder.

When Katherine, Janet, and several White girls from the literary group entered, they glanced over at Mary, grinned like conspirators, then took their plates and sat at the back table, the one newly designated for Colored students.

"What's going on?" a girl exclaimed.

"We're eating," Mary replied evenly, though her pulse raced.

"You know what I mean, Mary Church. Why are you sitting up here while White girls sit in the back?"

The way she said her name—*Mary Church*—cut like a sneer. As though she were something scandalous, a disturbance in their genteel order.

Mary forced her tone to remain calm, though anger simmered beneath her ribs. How dare they. How dare they! What made them so clean, so holy, that her presence contaminated their meal?

Anna and Ida walked over to the table, trays in hand. They sat beside her. Voices murmured and hissed across the room, like wind stirring dry leaves. Someone muttered the word "shameful." Another said "uppity."

Mary kept her eyes on her plate. "Keep eating," she told her friends softly. "Ignore them."

Suzie marched over, fists clenched. "You've got a lot of nerve, Mary. I know you put them up to this."

Mary set her fork down, slow and deliberate. "They're eating their lunch. I believe that's what one does in a dining hall."

"Then eat back there!" Suzie's voice rose, brittle with fury. "You don't even live here anymore. You have no right to come stirring up disorder."

Ida smirked, unable to help herself. "Looks like the table in the back is full."

A ripple of laughter, soft, nervous, ran along their table.

Suzie's face flushed crimson. "You put Katherine and Janet up to this foolishness."

Mary didn't glance up. She speared a green bean, swallowed slowly, and went on talking with her tablemates about their upcoming recitations as if Suzie and her indignation were no more than a passing draft.

When the meal ended, Mary did not rise. Instead, she opened her book, the pages quivering faintly in her hands, and began to read. One by one, the others did the same. Across the room, Janet and Katherine copied their example.

By the time supper rolled around, Mary's back ached, but she refused to yield.

When the White girls entered again, their voices rang sharp with disbelief. "Why are you still here?" one demanded.

This is my table too, her mind shouted. But she said nothing aloud. Her silence was armor now.

Suzie stormed out and returned moments later with Mrs. Johnston and President Fairchild. Her index finger stabbed toward Mary like an accusation. "President Fairchild, I'm sure you didn't realize what's been happening."

Mary rose to her feet. "Good evening, President Fairchild. Mrs. Johnston."

"How are you young ladies today?" the president asked mildly.

"We were enjoying our meal"—Mary gestured at the cluster of scowling faces—"until these girls insisted we move to the back."

President Fairchild glanced at Suzie. "Did you bring me here to ask these ladies to move when there are empty seats aplenty for your group?"

Suzie stammered, "Th-the Colored girls sit in the back. Mary's being difficult—"

Mary stepped forward, her voice clear as glass. "Were you aware, sir, that Colored students are no longer permitted to sit where they please in Ladies Hall?"

His brows drew together. He pivoted sharply to Mrs. Johnston. "What's the meaning of this?"

Mrs. Johnston's hand flew to her chest. "I certainly never approved any such arrangement!"

Mary could feel the room's air shift. Shrinking, uncertain girls stood by their tables now. She pressed on. "I only wondered, sir, whether Oberlin's ideals have changed. Shall I write my father to tell him that Negroes are no longer treated as equals here?"

The president's voice boomed, "Certainly not." He stepped forward, commanding the space with ease. "Ladies, Oberlin opened its doors in 1835 with the belief that Black and White students should learn, dine, and live together. That ideal remains unchanged."

The silence that followed was heavy and absolute. One by one, the White girls unclenched their arms and took their seats elsewhere. Suzie's mouth opened as if to protest, but Mrs. Johnston lifted a hand. "Enough. Let us remember why Oberlin stands."

Mary sank back into her chair, the tremor of relief mingling with pride and exhaustion. The taste of victory was bitter and sweet all at once. She had won the battle, but the war within her heart, the one that measured hope against anger, had only just begun.

CHAPTER 28

Enough was enough, simple as that.

Something had to be done about the way this new group of students conducted themselves. Mary sat at her desk with paper and her inkwell. Exhaling her frustrations, she regurgitated them on paper.

> Is there a color line at Oberlin? Have the students and faculty lost sight of the principles this college was built on?
>
> We think that the faculty, as a whole, maintain the same principles upon which the institution was founded fifty years ago. It is, to a great extent, a different class of students and a different class of people that have made the color line more distinct. But whatever its cause, if it continues as the old professors pass away and new ones take their places, who can tell to what it may lead?
>
> The assertion that it is the wealthier class of students who are more prejudiced to color seems to us false. Wealth is generally supposed to bring with it refinement.

It is certainly not the refined man or woman who slights a person on account of race or color. Even in the South during slavery, it was a noticeable fact that the wealthier class were far more humane than so-called poor Whites. A few years ago, before the election of speakers for the Oratorical Contest, some of the students made an agreement not to vote for a man simply because he was a Negro. Then the wealthy and more refined students were those who vigorously opposed such an unfair scheme and exposed the plot.

Twenty years ago a respectable Negro student could find board at any private boarding home in town. Can he now? This is the fault of the students and citizens. But the Ladies Hall belongs to the institution. It should be governed by the principles of the institution. It should be known that those who are in authority there will maintain those principles at any hazard.

It is true that the faculty cannot change each student's heart, but can they demand that this principle of the institution be carried out in the Ladies Hall at least? This principle that requires that men of all nations, regardless of color, shall receive an education on an equal footing here? What other race would be requested to eat at the same table on account of their nationality?

We doubt that under such circumstances Irish and German students would ask to sit together as that disgusting article in the News section claimed. However that may be, there is some difference in being granted a privilege to do something and in being compelled to do it, at least for so slight a cause as having dark skin.

We expect to endure some slights here, to meet some

prejudice, but when it comes to a separate table at the Ladies Hall dining room in liberal Christian Oberlin, it is more than we ever conceived of. And we are thankful to say that through the decision of our president, there is no longer any cause for complaint at the Hall. Although nearly all colleges are now open to Colored students, there are supposed to be some advantages to studying at Oberlin. We hope that these advantages will increase as only the students can increase them, and that the day will soon dawn when it will require not so much "forbearance" as "brotherly love" and "charity" to tolerate the Negroes' presence.

The inkwell was dry by the time Mary finished her article. She stared at the last period, a small black mark that seemed to carry the weight of her whole heart. Her fingers trembled as she set the pen down. No rewrites or second-guessing. The words had spilled out on the page . . . words that needed to be said.

Swallowing her fury, she pushed back her chair and stood, her knees stiff from hours of sitting. The air in her bedroom was heavy with the scent of ink and resolve. After grabbing the pages, she left her boardinghouse and made her way to the office of *The Oberlin Review.*

She had worked twice as hard, stayed twice as quiet. But silence was a kind of surrender and she was done surrendering. She slapped the pages down on the desk of the editor in chief. "Can you please add this to our next printing?"

"You've already turned in your column for this week. Do you want to replace it?"

She picked up the papers. "This isn't for my Lifestyle column. I have something to say to our community, and this is the best way I know to get the message out."

He bent his head toward the paper, reading. Then he eyed her. "Are you sure about this?"

"I've never been surer about anything." Covering social or weekend activities provided needed information that would help the students live a well-rounded life on campus. This article was an open rebuke, designed to change how comfortable students were with their actions while living on campus.

"I'll put it in the Communication section with your byline."

Byline? Everyone would know she wrote the article? Would they take it seriously, coming from the Lifestyle editor? "Why don't we do this one anonymously?" In Mary's estimation, if her peers read the article without having someone to single out as an agitator, maybe they would sit with the message rather than crucify the messenger.

Heads bent downward with *The Oberlin Review* opened wide. The students were supposed to be preparing themselves for philosophy class, but their minds were far from it. White students were whispering, and Black students had wide, appreciative eyes glued to the paper.

"Have you seen this?" Anna asked Mary. "What am I saying? You write for the paper. Of course you've seen it."

Mary glanced over Anna's shoulder at the page she was referring to. "I read it and I agree with it."

Anna's eyes were wide with amusement. "Who wrote it?"

Mary shrugged. "It's anonymous. I guess the writer doesn't want credit for the article."

One of the White students who held the paper said loud enough for everyone in class to hear, "I shouldn't be forced to sit with Colored students if that's not what I want to do."

Another one said, "If Oberlin is dead set on having these Coloreds, they should create space for them away from us."

Mary huffed. "Why should we be taught separate from other students? We have as much right to be in these classes as anyone else."

"Your father's wealth doesn't make you equal to us," another White student with the fire of hatred in his eyes said as he popped out of his seat.

"My father has nothing to do with it. I'm not merely equal to you all; I'm better."

Laughter thundered around the room.

But Mary would not be shunned into silence. "Laugh if it makes you feel better, but my marks prove it." Bragging was in bad form, but the men in her philosophy class would never make her feel less-than, not when she knew the truth.

"Doesn't matter if you cheat and score higher than us on a few tests," one of the White men said. "You're still Colored."

With a heaving chest, Anna said, "Why do you men always accuse us of cheating when we score higher than you? Try studying rather than living in the land of mediocrity."

A Black male student stood and directed his question to the White man holding the newspaper. "Why did you all register at Oberlin if you don't appreciate its moral stance of equal education for all? Did you come here to cause trouble?"

"Did I say you could talk to me?" one of the White men snarled.

The other said, "Why don't y'all register at one of those Colored schools? Weren't they built for people like you?" He flung *The Oberlin Review* in the air. "Instead of writing drivel no one cares about."

Shouts tangled in the air as students pressed against each other, faces tight, voices sharp. A few fists rose, punctuating the noise. Mary bit down on her lip, her pulse thrumming in her ears. She'd hoped the article might open conversation; now it seemed more like a spark setting the campus ablaze.

The professor walked over to his desk and slammed a book against it. The loud thud exploded throughout the room like a clap of thunder. "Hello," he said while waving to everyone. "It's time for class. Please take your seats."

Anna leaned closer to Mary as the two sat down. "I'm guessing this is why the writer wanted to remain anonymous."

The melee in her classroom shook Mary. If people were that riled over seeing the truth, maybe they needed more of it. Maybe the anger would turn into conviction and change would come to Oberlin.

The first article she wrote on the subject did nothing but add to the hatred and entitlement on campus. The following month, Mary wrote another article about the color line. In this article she spoke of the time President Fairchild and Mrs. Johnston had to remind the girls in Ladies Hall about the principles of the school. She remained anonymous.

Since President Garfield's death, Mary had picketed, staged a sit-in, and written articles for the betterment of her people. She'd do it all again, a thousand times over, if any of her efforts would take blinders off eyes that didn't want to see clearly.

"Mary, can I speak with you a moment?" Mrs. Johnston asked as she was nearing the door to exit the Ladies Hall.

"I'm on my way to philosophy class, but I have a few minutes to spare." She followed Mrs. Johnston to her office. She hadn't been in this room since the day Mrs. Johnston told her about the Lifestyle editorial position with *The Oberlin Review.* She sat in front of the desk, folded her hands in her lap, and waited.

Mrs. Johnston cleared her throat. She shuffled a few books and papers around on her desk. She picked up *The Oberlin Review* and set it in front of Mary. "I've certainly been enjoying your Lifestyle column. I knew you were the right person for that job."

"Thank you. I'm enjoying my work." Mary kept her voice even, though her stomach gave a nervous twist. Had the principal called her to the office for more than her Lifestyle column? Had she guessed that Mary was the author of the Color Line articles? Was she angry about those articles? Was this the moment she'd be banned from the Ladies Hall?

Mary forced a polite smile, but her mind raced. She wasn't sorry. Not for a single word. Everything she'd written was true—uncomfortable, maybe, but true all the same.

Mrs. Johnston clasped her hands together. She leaned forward. "And are you enjoying your time at Oberlin?"

"I'm learning a great deal."

"But are you happy here?"

Mrs. Johnston's voice was so full of care that Mary could not ignore the woman's plea for the truth. "I used to be happy at Oberlin, during my preparatory years. I was happy at Ladies Hall in the beginning, but—" Mary turned away, eyes watering, thoughts spiraling.

Mrs. Johnston handed her a tissue. "You know what, Mary?"

Wiping the tears, Mary glanced over at her.

"I don't think I should've asked if you're happy. I tend to believe that some people were born to make a difference."

Mary stood. "I'm going to be late for my class." She headed for the door.

Before she reached it, Mrs. Johnston said, "You are."

Mary stopped. "I'm sorry, what did you say?"

Mrs. Johnston stood. "I said you are making a difference. And I'm proud to serve as your principal."

Those words were all the encouragement Mary needed to take her next step toward showcasing her excellence in any room, no matter who tried to convince her she wasn't worthy. Oh, she was worthy all right.

Mary began her campaign to become vice president of her literary group. VOTE FOR ME—I'M THE ONE YOU CAN COUNT ON were the words Mary put on the flyers she passed out to her peers.

Janet told her, "You've got my vote."

Others assured her that they would vote for her as well. She'd lost so many votes at Oberlin that Mary couldn't believe this would work out until the votes were tallied. Becoming the first Black vice president of one of Oberlin's prestigious literary groups would be a great accomplishment. But would her detractors deny her this?

The election was held the week before the end of Mary's sophomore year. She sat in the society room with friends surrounding her. Mrs. Johnston held two envelopes in her hand. She opened the first and announced the winners of the different positions for the Ladies Literary Society.

Eyes on the other envelope, Mary ran her hand through her hair. She crossed her legs, uncrossed them, and still kept staring at that envelope.

"Now for the offices that will be held next year for the Aeolian Literary Society." Mrs. Johnston's voice carried through the room as she opened the envelope.

Mary clapped along as names were called—new recording secretary, treasurer, historian. She smiled until her cheeks hurt. She was proud of them, truly. But a small part of her, the aching, breath-holding part . . . waited.

"And the new vice president is . . ." Mrs. Johnston paused long enough for Mary's heartbeat to climb into her throat. "Mary Church!"

For a moment she couldn't move. Couldn't breathe.

Then Ida grabbed her hand and squealed, "Oh my goodness, you did it again! You actually won another election!"

Mary heard her, but the words floated somewhere far away. Vice president. The title rolled through her mind like a hymn. She rose slowly, then suddenly couldn't help herself. She jumped from her seat, her voice rising bright and sure.

"I'm vice president!" she cried. "Me . . . Mary Church!"

Laughter and applause filled the room, but Mary's heart was too full to take in either. Her mind traveled back to every time she'd been told Colored girls didn't belong where decisions were made. Every smirk that said someone must've taken pity on her.

No pity had carried her here. No man's favor, no White woman's indulgence. She'd fought for every inch.

She'd spoken when they'd tried to hush her. Debated when they plotted against her. Written speeches until her fingers cramped, taken minutes, planned events, served as recording secretary and historian, and now, she'd earned her place.

Her chin lifted, pride threading through her like steel.

Vice president.

As it should be.

Part 4

THE COST OF PROGRESS

Can this prejudice against color, as it is called, be accounted for by circumstances outside and independent of race or color? If it can be thus explained, an incubus may be removed from the breasts of both the white and the black people of this country, as well as from that large intermediate population which has sprung up between these alleged irreconcilable extremes.

—Frederick Douglass, "The Color Line," 1881

CHAPTER 29

June 1883

"Gather 'round, ladies. It's the time you've all been waiting for." Mrs. Johnston placed a manila folder on each of the six tables in the front of the assembly room. She held one of the folders.

At the beginning of their junior year, Mrs. Johnston informed them that they would receive extra credit for graduation if they participated in a mission trip the summer before their senior year. Mission trips were for feeding the hungry, spreading the gospel, or even helping with voter registration. When they were informed a few months ago that four students would be going to Europe this year, Anna almost needed smelling salts to recover herself.

Anticipation grew in her so mightily, she thought she might burst wide open with the possibilities she'd been dreaming about ever since she'd signed up for the European mission trip. In her wildest dreams Anna never imagined she would be this close to achieving her goal of visiting Paris.

But when this trip had been presented to them as a way of spreading good cheer, she about tripped over her own feet getting to the sign-up table. Katherine laughed at her that day and said, "Seems like this is the most coveted mission trip Oberlin has to offer."

Anna had glanced behind her. Numerous others got in line to sign up for the trip. Mary and Ida were in line also. "The opportunity to see other parts of this world means more to me than anything," she'd told Katherine.

"I hope I get to take the trip with you. I'm going to sign up too." Katherine's eyes lit with excitement.

"It would be so grand, wouldn't it?"

"As you know," Mrs. Johnston continued while standing in front of the tables that held the promise of adventure for Anna, "you were asked to pick three of the seven missions we have to offer this year so that we could place you in another mission if your first choice was unavailable. The selections have been made." She stepped closer to the tables and extended a hand toward the folders. "You will find your name on the list in the manila folder on one of the six tables behind me."

One of the students raised her hand, and Mrs. Johnston nodded in her direction. "But there were seven missions. Why do we only have six tables?"

"Good question." Mrs. Johnston held up the manila folder in her hand. "In here we have the names of the students who have been assigned to the European mission trip. There are only two slots for the women and there will be two slots for the men."

Mrs. Johnston opened the folder and glanced at the paper

inside, then back to the group before her. "There are three names on this list, but as I stated, only two women will be allowed on this mission trip. The coordinators could not decide between these three worthy candidates, due to the fact that each of them maintained the same high score in their language class." She looked out at the anxious women, took a deep breath, then exhaled. "When I call your name, please come forward."

Suzie McFarland stepped forward in expectation.

"Katherine Smalls."

Anna smiled and clapped for her friend while inwardly praying, *Please . . . please . . . please.*

"Mary Church."

Suzie folded her arms across her chest. Anna clapped. Two of her friends had been selected for the European mission. Her heart was cracking at the thought that she would not be able to live out her dream. But she was determined to be happy for her friends. What a great opportunity this was for them.

"And Anna Cooper."

Mary and Katherine hugged each other and jumped for joy once Anna's name was called. Anna could hardly believe it. Was this happening for *her*? As she started walking to the front of the room to join her friends, Suzie stuck a hand out and stood in her way.

"Wait one minute. How could two Colored girls be chosen for this mission over White women?" Suzie glanced around the room, searching for those who thought like she did. "The administrators must have made a mistake." She pleaded with Mrs. Johnston, saying, "You can't let this happen. I belong on that trip."

Anna walked around her to stand with Mary and Katherine. Mrs. Johnston told Suzie, "There's no mistake. As I already stated, the students for this mission trip were chosen based on the highest marks in language class."

Suzie huffed. "There's no way Anna and Mary have higher marks than me." Suzie shifted an evil eye in their direction. But Suzie didn't cast a glance Katherine's way, as if she could find no fault with the selection of a White woman for this trip.

"I'm afraid they do, dear." Mrs. Johnston sighed, her patience seeming to run thin at Suzie's antics.

Why this girl was so hateful to them, Anna didn't understand. She, Mary, and Ida worked hard to make their grades. They didn't step on other people's toes and tried their very best to get along with the students at this school. But some of them made the go-along-to-get-along method unbearable.

Suzie sucked air through her teeth and stomped her foot. "That's not fair. I'm going to talk with President Fairchild. Something has to be done about all of the riffraff taking away opportunities from good White folks." She stalked out of the room as if she was on a mission to right all the wrongs White people had suffered since slavery ended. Since they were no longer able to sell off children from their mothers or degrade human beings for existing in spaces White folks didn't want them to be in.

Mrs. Johnston came over to them. The expression on her face told them she didn't approve of Suzie's actions, but she didn't say it out loud so that others could hear and possibly come to understand that poor treatment of human beings due to the color of their skin was hateful and unacceptable. Anna longed for the day when the principal of the Ladies'

Department would put other students on notice that their horrid behavior toward Colored people would not be accepted.

Anna liked Mrs. Johnston. The woman had been nothing but kind to her whenever she entered Ladies Hall. She was a silent ally for Colored folks. But sometimes silent allies seemed more like endorsers of all that was so wrong in this country.

"Ladies," Mrs. Johnston began, "this was the most coveted mission trip of the year. Unfortunately, only two of you can attend, but don't worry. Each of you has been picked for another mission as well. So decide amongst yourselves if this is the trip of your heart or if you're willing to go on a different trip."

Mrs. Johnston walked away from them to attend to the other ladies in the room. "Come on down and discover your assignments." There were about forty women in the room. Each one rushed to the front and began reviewing the list of names inside each folder. Some squealed with delight, while others bemoaned the difficult assignment they would have to endure.

Anna's stomach churned as she pictured herself having to walk over to those tables and groan as well. "What were the organizers thinking? How are we ever to choose between the three of us?"

"This is difficult. We all deserve to go," Katherine said.

"And it's London, Belgium, and Paris." Mary's eyes danced with imagination for other lands.

"I've dreamed about a trip like this, but never in my wildest imagination could I ever figure out how to pay for it." Anna bit her lower lip.

"What are we supposed to do, pull straws to determine which of us will go?" Katherine asked.

Anna shook her head. "No, let's not do that. I always end up with the short end of the stick anyway."

Anna's eyes filled with disappointment as she declared that she always ended up with the short end of the stick. Mary was drowned with compassion, which left her searching deep inside for what was right and what was most important to her.

Ever since President Garfield had died, Mary had carried this aching feeling that she needed to do something. The trip to London sounded wonderful, but was it her heart's desire?

"What we need to do is figure out which of us wants this trip the most and eliminate the third person in that manner," Katherine suggested. "To be honest, I had already picked two other missions before deciding to sign up for this one."

Anna said, "This was my first choice. If I'm being honest, there's no other mission I want as much as this one."

"I plan to study abroad when I graduate, so I was interested in this trip for that reason. But it wasn't my first choice," Mary told them.

Lifting a finger, Katherine asked, "Was it second or third?"

Mary grinned, knowing exactly where this was going. "Actually, it was my second choice."

Katherine jabbed a finger in her direction. Her lips turned down. "Then I guess I'm out. I'll go see which one of the other mission trips I've been assigned to."

"Mary!" Ida called out.

Mary swung around as Ida held up a piece of paper and squealed, "We've both been assigned to the voter registration drive with the Readjuster Party!"

There it was. Mary's heart's desire was to do something of import for her race of people. Europe had always been second to her heart's desire.

Mary stretched out a hand, stopping Katherine from moving to the tables. "As I already told you, I plan to study abroad when I graduate. I don't need to do all that traveling this summer."

Katherine's eyes grew wide. "Are you sure?"

Mary nodded. "Anna wants this, and I think she should have it."

But Anna held up a hand. "Hold on—you don't feel sorry for me, do you? I don't need charity."

"No, silly." Mary glanced from Anna to Katherine. "Going to Europe is not as important to me as the voter registration mission. Mr. Danly asked me to help with it a couple of years ago, and I begged off. But I've had a change of heart on the matter."

Anna hugged her and whispered in her ear, "Thanks, friend."

CHAPTER 30

Mr. Danly stood before them as the wagons were being fitted with enough hay to help their bottoms endure the bumpy ride from Oberlin to Danville, Virginia. "I'm proud of you all. And I want to thank you for joining us in this fight. But I must warn you: We're traveling to enemy territory. The Democrats in Danville are angry over the Readjuster Party being in control in their town, and they blame Colored men and poor Whites for this."

Mary and Ida glanced at each other. The most dangerous situation either of them had faced was traveling without a chaperone from school to their home states. Six students and two professors were on this mission trip. Mary, Ida, and Suzie were the only ladies. Mary had no idea why Suzie had been assigned to this mission. She didn't even like Colored people.

Two of the male students were White and one was Black. Mary nudged Ida when Timothy approached the group. He had asked Mary out during their freshman year but had been sweet on Ida since sophomore year. She wouldn't give him the time of day, and Mary didn't understand it.

"Stop nudging me. I couldn't care less that Timothy is joining us."

"That's mean, Ida. Why do you treat him so terribly when all he wants is a chance to court you?" Mary whispered.

"He wants to court my father's money, that's what he wants," Ida whispered back, while cutting her eyes in Timothy's direction.

"Why do you say such things? He's a respectable suitor."

Ida rolled her eyes. "He prefers women who are more like you and Anna. I'm too plain and dark for him."

Mary held her hand to her mouth. "That is a terrible thing to say about yourself. You're not plain and you're only a shade or two darker than I am."

"It's a terrible thing to know."

The silence between Ida and Mary was louder than anything they'd ever spoken to each other. The sad truth was that their community seemed to be color struck, favoring lighter skin over dark, even though they knew how lighter skin was inherited. Which in Mary's estimation was nothing to be rewarded. But the world they lived in had somehow perceived White as better—therefore, the lighter the better in the Black community.

"Okay, everyone, we're ready to go." Mr. Danly gestured to the first wagon. "The ladies can get in there and the men will ride in the other. Professor Stockton and I will guide the horses," Mr. Danly told them.

They each picked up their bags and loaded them into the wagons. A blanket had been placed on top of the hay so they wouldn't get poked the whole way of their journey. Suzie got in first and took her time deciding which side of the wagon she wanted to sit on.

"This is crazy. Why do we even have to do this?" Suzie plopped her bottom down on the right side of the wagon.

Mr. Danly extended his hand and helped Mary and Ida into the wagon. They both sat on the left side, as far away from Suzie as they could get. Mary tied her bonnet tight around her neck. "It's going to be a hot day. I hope this bonnet keeps the sun at bay," she said to Ida.

"We shouldn't even be doing a trip like this in the summertime. Doesn't even make sense." Suzie yanked open her parasol and huffed as the wagon pitched forward.

As the sun beat down on Mary's back, she opened her parasol and Ida did likewise. "It's going to take a few days to get there, so we might as well relax and enjoy the journey."

"I brought a book to read," Ida said.

"I stuffed some yarn in my bag for knitting. I'm terrible at it, but it'll help pass the time."

"You two make me sick," Suzie hissed. "Of course you're happy to be in this godforsaken wagon. We're going off to help your people."

Mary blew out hot, disgruntled air. Suzie . . . always Suzie. Mary was past tired of this girl. She wet her lips, getting ready to put the girl in her place, until Ida nudged her. Remembering her etiquette classes, Mary closed her mouth.

"What? Why are you staring at me?"

Mary cocked her head to the side. She continued staring at Suzie as she asked, "What have we done to make you hate us so?"

"I don't hate you. Your people don't belong here, that's all."

Ida lifted onto her knees, hands to her hips. "Where do we belong, then? Tell us that." The wagon wheel rode over a bump in the road, and she landed back on her bottom.

Suzie flicked a dismissive hand at them. "Y'all wanted to be free. Okay, you're free. Now go back where you came from and stop taking what belongs to the good White folks of this nation."

"Where did my people come from?" Mary's face burned with anger. "If you know which region of Africa my ancestors were stolen from, I'd love to hear it. Especially since their enslavers left no clues . . . no records . . . nothing for us to find our way back. But you smugly say, 'Go back to where you came from,' without the slightest realization of how that privilege was stripped away from my people."

Ida wagged a finger in Suzie's face. "My mother was born in America. My grandmother and my great-grandmother . . . and even my great-great-grandmother was born in America."

Mary added, "So deal with the fact that we now belong here in America, like you."

Suzie's lips twisted. "You'll never be like me. White people founded this country; Black people were brought here to work."

Ida put a hand to her heart and audibly groaned at the insult.

Mary breathed in the warmth of the sun. The wagon jumped as they rode over another rough patch. She turned steely eyes on Suzie. "You've taken history classes at Oberlin same as the rest of us."

Suzie's eyes rolled heavenward. "So?"

"Your ancestors murdered the Indigenous people of this land. They stole this land. Then they stole my ancestors from Africa in order to get free labor. *Sooo* . . . you have correctly stated that we are not like you. We would never spill so much innocent blood to get the things we wanted out of life. We care too much for humanity to be so wicked."

Suzie harrumphed and scooted farther away from them. For the rest of the ride, she didn't say a word to them, and that was completely fine with Mary.

"I simply cannot believe I'm getting ready to board a ship headed for London. Please pinch me so I can wake up." Anna held out her arm to Katherine.

"After I pinch you, I'm going to need a pinch as well. Never in my life did I ever imagine doing anything like this." Katherine pulled Anna into a hug. "Thank you for dreaming big. I never would have put my name on that form if you hadn't."

The ship they would be sailing on was docked in New York. It was a British-built passenger steamship, with steel hulls that made it faster than the wooden sailing ships that passengers used to sail to places around the world. Even though this ship had a steam engine, it also had the sail backup, which provided stability during rough seas. They could propel the ship if the engine failed.

"Come on, let's go." Katherine grabbed Anna's arm and rushed her to the ship's entrance. Their benefactor for the voyage, one of Oberlin's alumni, had purchased first-class tickets for each of them.

Katherine handed her ticket to the man standing at the front of the boat. "Welcome aboard," he said to her after taking her ticket.

Anna smiled, as gleeful as Katherine was when he welcomed her aboard. However, after the man took her ticket, he gave her the once-over. His lips curved into a frown.

"Is there a problem?" Katherine spoke up.

Anna was thankful for her friend's interference, as she was struggling to regain her composure in light of the noticeable difference in the way she and Katherine were being treated.

"We cannot put you in first class. It's against our protocol."

"Why not?" Anna pointed at the ticket. "I'm in first class."

Matter-of-factly, he told her, "We have to keep our first-class passengers separate from our Negro passengers. It's the law."

The elation she'd felt a few moments ago when they first laid eyes on the massive steamship was replaced by a deep, penetrating sorrow. As if the Jim Crow law of the land had spit into an open wound and left her infected with its foul stench.

Katherine glanced back at Anna. "Maybe we should wait for the others. Professor Lewis would know how to handle this."

Professor Lewis had traveled abroad numerous times. Hope sprang up in Anna's heart. Yes, they needed to let Professor Lewis handle this matter.

"I apologize, ma'am." He directed his apology to Katherine. "I've already taken your ticket, so you must move along to your area." He glanced down at Anna's ticket once more. "I can board you, but not in first class."

Elongating her neck, projecting as much dignity as she could muster, Anna asked, "What accommodations do you have for me?"

"We can put you in the steerage section, at the lower level of the boat. I can also guarantee you a bunk down there."

This was Anna's first trip by ship, so she wasn't familiar with the steerage section, but that would have to do. She was going to London. She was seeing other lands. She could make this work. "Thank you for your kindness," she said even though she didn't see much kindness in stripping someone of a first-class ticket that had been bought and paid for.

Anna and Katherine gathered their things. Anna kept her eyes cast down toward her bags and the wooden plank floor as they went inside the boat to find their sleeping quarters. She couldn't bring herself to face Katherine after what she'd endured at the hand of the ticket taker.

"This is so unfair," Katherine complained as they followed the porter. "I should be in the steerage section with you."

Anna shook her head. "I won't allow you to do that. Enjoy this voyage. That's your right and privilege."

When they reached the stairwell, another porter approached with a brisk nod and motioned for Katherine to follow him down a long corridor, its walls adorned with ornate wood paneling and sconces that flickered with the dim glow of gaslight. The polished floor gleamed beneath their feet, and the hush of refinement followed them down the hall.

But Anna was led in the opposite direction, down a narrow flight of creaking wooden stairs, the air turning stale and putrid with each step. The room she entered was crowded and chaotic, lit by a few dangling lanterns that cast long, restless shadows on the walls. People milled around a cluster of scarred wooden tables in the center of the room, their voices low and wary.

Mothers clutched their children to their skirts, eyes darting from face to face as if danger could come from any corner. No one lingered near the edges of the room, where bunks had been built into the walls—narrow, three-tiered beds stacked tightly together like coffins prepared for sea.

"Hey, watch where you're steppin'!" a man barked at another, his voice cracking like a whip.

"Then move your feet. I have the same right to walk as you." They collided as they jostled for space.

The porter barely acknowledged the scuffle. "You can take that one." He showed her to a top bunk as they passed midway through the room.

Anna let her eyes drift upward, grateful not to be placed in one of the bottom bunks. They were too exposed, too reachable, too vulnerable. She clutched her luggage bag close and began to climb.

Below, the argument escalated. The man who'd been stepped on lunged forward, fists flying, striking the other with a sickening thud. Gasps rippled through the room, but most people turned away, eyes fixed on their own troubles, their own survival.

Anna hauled herself onto the upper bunk, her heart thudding as hard as the blows below. This was no place for comfort. It was savage and unyielding. A place for degenerates, not a schoolgirl on her way to London.

A woman ran over and pushed the man off her husband. She screamed, "Look what you did to his beautiful face!" She reached down to pull the man up.

Anna clenched her legs and prayed she wouldn't have to use the bathroom. Not now, not here. She couldn't face pushing her way through the press of bodies again. Better to stay in her bunk, invisible, forgotten. A few hours of rest, that was all she asked.

She shifted, trying to find comfort, but the mattress bit back. Straw, dry and sharp as needles, poked through the thin fabric, tickling and stabbing her skin. Each jab made her ache for the soft bed at Mr. Wilson Bruce Evans's house. For the small room that belonged to her, if only for a little while.

The noise around her swelled, voices rising like waves against the hull . . . arguing, coughing, crying. She pressed her hands over her ears, but it did no good. So many people. So much fear. The air itself felt crowded.

Then came the sound. The heavy clank and scrape of the hatch closing. A finality that made her stomach twist. The air thickened, stale and wet, pressing down on her chest. Somewhere, a baby wailed. The ship lurched, and she clutched the side of the bunk, swallowing hard.

At first the shouting scared her most. But then . . . the suffocating dark, the air gone dead around her, this was worse. Much worse.

Anna leaned over her bunk and hurled the contents of her stomach onto the wood planks below. She was thankful no one had been passing by at the time, or that person might have climbed up to her bunk and bashed her head in.

When the waves finally settled and the boat stopped rocking, Anna laid her head down on the dirty makeshift mattress. *Rest . . . get some rest.* Her eyes drooped as she fell into a deep, much-needed sleep, then something tugged.

Her luggage bag was beneath her head, safe and secure . . . but it was moving. Her eyes popped open. She screamed and screamed and screamed as a man with rotted teeth climbed up the side of her bunk, tugging at her bag. "Stop! Stop! Go away!"

"Hey, what're you doing up there?" The man on the bottom bunk jumped up and snatched the would-be thief down, his big fist pounding the man's face before he scurried off. "You okay up there?" her bunkmate asked as he got back in his bed.

Anna shook all over. She clung to her bag. No, she was not okay. "Th-thank you." Her eyes went wild, scanning the room, expecting danger at every turn. *London, you're going to London*, she reminded herself. *This will all be worth it once you step on foreign soil.*

Even with all the chanting about London, the next morning, Anna was cold inside. Fear trickled down her spine as her eyes darted from one side of steerage to the other. She left the steering area to find a bathroom, holding her bag closely to her chest. There was a long line. Anna leaned her back against the wall, breathing in the smells emanating from the bathroom.

As bad as the smells out here were, they didn't bother her as much as the space she was sharing with strangers. As she moved up the line, Anna thought of ways she could stay in the hall area and not go back down those dreaded stairs so early in the day.

While mulling over ways she could stow away in the crevices of this ship, she heard her name being called far off. "Anna . . . Anna!"

Katherine was running up the corridor. Anna waved to her.

"Thank God I found you." She gave Anna the once-over. "And you still have my luggage." Katherine took her by the arm. "You must come with me at once."

Anna's brows scrunched. Confusion played tricks on her

mind. Was Katherine accusing her of stealing? She walked away from the line and spoke in a whisper. "I don't have your luggage bag."

They moved farther away from the people lined up at the bathroom, and Katherine shushed her. "I know you don't, but Professor Lewis came up with an idea that can get you out of the steerage area."

"Yes! Yes! Yes!" Anna cheered. "Let me hear it."

As she entered the first-class area, Anna's eyes widened with joy. She noted the difference from the god-awful place she had been thrown into. Compared to the steerage area, first class was like a floating palace with velvet-upholstered seating in the social area, crystal chandeliers, fine paintings, and plush carpeting. She was in heaven.

"For the rest of the trip, you'll be my maid. That way you will be allowed to share the room with me. Professor Lewis already informed the porter that I've been handicapped by not having my maid with me."

"I'm your . . . maid?" Anna's voice took on a hollow, small tone as she gulped back the bitter taste of humiliation rising in her throat.

"Pretend," Katherine whispered. "This was the only way we could get you out of steerage."

Anna's pulse fluttered. *Pretend.* The word steadied her enough that she could breathe again. *Pretend I'm less than I am, in order to survive.* Wasn't that what this whole journey had been?

"Okay then, ma'am. Where should I put your luggage?" For the moment Anna was willing to play along. Anything to get her away from that awful place they'd put her in.

Katherine led Anna to the room they'd be sharing. The cabins were arranged around the social area. There were single cabins and shared ones, but there were absolutely no bunks littering the social area.

As Anna walked inside their cabin and put her bag down next to her bed, she took note of the mattress stuffed with cotton, the clean white walls with a colorful painting on the back wall. In this room she could rest and enjoy traveling to London.

But the fact that she could only enter this room as a maid, not a highly educated college student on her way to London to address an assembly, dampened Anna's spirit. When would the country of her birth recognize her strengths and not consider her skin color a weakness that outweighed all else?

Katherine sat on the twin bed across from hers. She crossed her legs and pulled out a notepad. "I'm going to work on my speech. I think I want to talk about the progress and ingenuity in America."

That was a good idea. Maybe working on her speech would take her mind off the awful way she'd been treated thus far on a trip she had dreamed about for so many years. Anna pulled some paper out of her bag, studied the words she'd already written, and then jotted other things on the page.

"What will your speech be about?" Katherine lifted her head from the paper she was writing.

Anna popped her head up. "Unity." She then went back to writing. In her estimation everyone loved the idea of unity. The topic wouldn't get anyone riled up, and she could go back to her seat after her speech without much fanfare.

"Isn't this room lovely?" Katherine beamed, her voice

light and full of wonder as she spun in a circle. Her eyes sparkled with the joy of things to come. "There's a whole world out there, Anna. And we're about to explore it."

Anna sat stiffly on the edge of her narrow bed, hands tightly clasping the paper in her lap. She tried to mirror Katherine's delight, to let herself be swept up in the promise of adventure and freedom. But her heart pounded with a different rhythm . . . one not of excitement but of ache. She wanted to scream . . . to shout . . . to be seen for more than what the world had told her she was.

How could she, a former slave girl with no wealth, no pedigree, no voice, ever make a sound loud enough to matter? How could she rise above the silence she'd been forced to live in all of her life?

CHAPTER 31

Danville, Virginia, bore the stench of industry and sin in equal measure. Once a sleepy trading post, it had swollen into a bustling town, fat with tobacco money and choked by smoke from the mills. Railroads screamed through its heart, drawing in not only honest laborers but also gamblers with twitchy fingers, men soaked in liquor, and women who sold what virtue they had left. The streets pulsed with both promise and peril.

Yet amid the clamor and corruption, a new political wind had begun to stir. The Readjuster Party—a curious coalition of Black freedmen and a few renegade Whites—had managed, to the shock of many, to wrest control of the city council. Most of those seated on the council's benches still wore pale faces, but the power behind them now had darker skin. For the first time in Danville's memory, Black men had a say in how the city was governed.

Mr. Danly, a stout man with fire in his belly, believed the moment was ripe. "If we can get more of our Colored brethren to the polls"—Danly's voice boomed like thunder rolling across the hills—"we might sweep the filth from these streets. We'll put decent men in office and drive out the devil's tomfoolery that's plagued this town for too long."

Hope, cautious but growing, stirred in Danville's alleyways and parlor rooms as surely as mischief still crept in with the evening fog.

Mr. Danly set up a table right outside the marketplace where most Black folks purchased their groceries. "Come over here, gentlemen. It's time to get registered so you can cast your vote," he yelled out to them.

The men seemed plumb worn out. Timothy leaned close to Ida and said, "They've had a hard day's work over at that tobacco factory."

"What do you know of it?" Ida snarled as she took a step back, moving away from Timothy.

"One of the workers told me all about it."

Ida leaned closer to Mary as they stood behind the table, waiting to hand out registration forms. Mary whispered to her, "Stop being so mean."

With tight lips, Ida said, "He should leave me alone."

"I'm already registered," one of the men told them while walking into the market. He gave them an encouraging smile.

"You girls work the table. I'm going to talk to the men inside the market," Mr. Danly told them.

Mary and Ida passed out registration forms to a few of the men who came over to their table, while Suzie stood back and complained. "This is such a waste of a summer break."

Mary glanced back at Suzie. "Why'd you come if you weren't going to work?"

Unfolding her arms, Suzie admitted, "My marks in

literature class are poor. My professor is allowing me to do a paper based on a mission trip. A tragedy I got saddled with this one."

Mary breathed in deeply, then exhaled. "Well, if you have to write about this mission trip, shouldn't you experience what it's like to help someone who might be trying to gain a better life for himself and his family?"

"I didn't think about it like that." Suzie approached the table and picked up the registration forms. As a few men passed by them, she said, "Would you like to register to vote?"

The man stopped at the table. "What difference will it make if I register? I'll still be over at the tobacco plant. Still be getting these low wages."

Suzie shrugged and handed a registration form to another man. While Ida was explaining the form to someone else, Mary told the man, "You'll have a say in your government. They might even pass laws for higher wages."

He took the form, but he didn't fill it out. "I'll think about it," he mumbled and then went into the market.

As he walked away from their table, a group of White men gathered in front of the market. A White man with a red face and blond hair lifted a rifle and yelled, "Y'all not taking over our government. This ends today."

Mary glanced up the road and saw more White men marching forward, their faces set on doing the devil's business. Ida backed away from the table and said, "What's going on here?"

Mr. Danly, Professor Stockton, Timothy, and the other men from Oberlin who'd gone inside the market came out and approached the men. Mr. Danly said, "H-hold on a minute.

We're not doing anything illegal. We're merely registering men to vote. If you have men who need to get registered, we can help with that too."

"It won't matter," one of the White men yelled back. "It's more of them than there is of us in this town."

"Yeah," another man yelled. "If we let them register, they'll outvote us and we'll never get our town back."

Mary tried to wrap her mind around the absurd position these White men stood on. How was this their town if more Colored folks lived here than White folks? Seemed they would understand the town would naturally have a majority rule.

The man who'd taken the registration form but hadn't decided whether or not to sign it came back to the table. Filled it out and lifted it to the heavens. "You won't steal what belongs to me and my family. I'm casting my vote in the next election for sure."

He slammed the paper back down on the table and then pushed his way through the crowd. As more White men arrived, the yelling and screaming got louder. Black men and White men balled their fists and an all-out brawl broke out in the street in front of the market.

"You don't have a right to vote!" a White man yelled as he jabbed a smaller Black man in the nose.

"You don't have a right to stop me," the Black man said as he swung a left hook to the side of the White man's face.

Mary clamped her hands over her ears as the sounds of anger and vitriol penetrated her soul. "Stop! Stop! Stop!" she yelled, but no one was listening. The street was filled with fists and slurs, and then the first shot rang through the crowd.

Ida screamed. Suzie screamed. Mr. Danly ran over to them. "Everybody, back to the wagon."

More shots rang out. Mary and Ida followed Mr. Danly and the others. The men helped them load into the back of the wagon.

"Where's Suzie?" Mr. Danly asked.

Mary's eyes went wide with panic as she jolted upright. She shielded her brow with a trembling hand, squinting hard against the sun and dust. Her gaze scanned the chaos until it locked onto a single figure frozen in place like a statue.

"There," she cried, voice cracking. "She's still behind the table!"

Suzie hadn't moved. Still clutching her hand against her chest, she stood rooted while the world around her crumbled. Bullets cracked through the air, sharp and unrelenting.

Without hesitation, without so much as a backward glance, Mr. Danly leapt from the wagon bed and charged back down the road, his boots thudding against the earth. Gunfire flared down by the market, but he didn't slow. He reached Suzie and seized her by the arm, shaking her out of whatever spell had gripped her. "Run!" he shouted.

She stumbled, then obeyed, legs pumping beneath her skirts as they sprinted for the waiting wagons.

They were nearly there.

Then another barrage of shots rang out—closer this time.

Mr. Danly gasped, lurched forward, and fell hard, knocking Suzie off her feet. She cried out as they hit the dirt, his weight pressing her down. He didn't move.

"Help!" Suzie screamed.

“What happened? Why are they lying there?” Ida asked.

Mary wrapped her arms around her chest, rocking from side to side. “I—I don’t know.”

Professor Stockton ran down the road toward them. “He’s been shot,” he yelled up to them. “Men, come help me.”

Timothy and the two White students rushed over to where Mr. Danly lay. They lifted him off Suzie, who was now screaming in a trancelike state. The men came to the wagon with Mr. Danly’s limp body.

Mary’s gaze fell back on Suzie, who seemed incapable of finding her way to them.

Suzie needed help. If Mary went after Suzie, would the same fate Mr. Danly was now suffering befall her? As Mary was deciding whether to help her lost classmate, a Black man fell to the ground clutching his chest. He was about ten feet from where Suzie stood, dazed and confused.

A group of about ten men, all whaling on each other, inched closer to them. The Oberlin students placed Mr. Danly in the back of the second wagon. Mary steepled her hands to heaven, then jumped down and took off in Suzie’s direction.

Ida yelled, “No, it’s not safe!”

“I can’t leave her there.” Within seconds Mary had her hands on Suzie, pulling her forward. “Snap out of it. We’ve got to get out of here.”

“Sh-shot . . . sh-sh-shot . . . M-Mr. D-Danly.”

Suzie sounded as if a bucket of ice water had been poured on her and she’d been chilled to the bone. When they reached the wagon, Professor Stockton said, “He’s dead. Oh my dear Lord, he’s dead.”

Suzie climbed into the wagon while a dust of emotions

swirled around Mary. She caught sight of Mr. Danly's shoes as he lay on his back; memories of the man who desired to do good in this world flashed before her. "*Our mission is a worthy endeavor*," he'd said.

His pants were black and the shirt he'd worn that day was white, but it now had splotches of blood and dirt on the front. His eyes were closed and his body was . . . still. Not even a finger moved. A loud guttural moan escaped Professor Stockon's lips, and the others yelled as if in pain as they clung to Mr. Danly's body.

Mary spun in place, heart pounding, mind reeling. Around her, the noise of the riot had shifted, moved farther down the street, but the residue remained with them. It was lying in the wagon before her. The fight was in Mr. Danly's still-warm body. It breathed through every sob, every bloodstain, every scream still echoing from the direction of the market.

Was this what progress cost?

Was this the price?

Tears came fast, unbidden, blurring her vision. Had it even mattered . . . his speech, his courage, his goodness? Would Colored people ever gain the rights they had bled for if men filled with hate could charge through on a peaceful day, guns drawn and eyes ablaze with rage?

Mr. Danly had been a kind man. A gentle man. He listened when others talked over them. He stood for something when others ignored their plight. And now he was gone.

She watched as the men climbed down from his wagon, men with blood on their hands. That kind of blood would soak into the soul. It would never be wiped clean.

Too many good men had died. President Garfield.

Charles. Mr. Danly. Snatched from a world that barely had time to notice their sacrifices. And yet hate—loud, unrepentant, tireless—marched on.

Then it came. Another crack of a gun. Mary jerked her head toward the marketplace.

Another Black man collapsed in the street.

And still, hate lived on.

Professor Stockton manned the wagon with Mr. Danly stretched out in the back. Mary, Ida, Suzie, Timothy, and a White male student all sat in the wagon while the other White male student from Oberlin drove them away from the melee.

Tears flowed like waterfalls. Mary, Ida, and Suzie were inconsolable. The men also shed tears, but they tried to console the girls with pats on the back and shoulders to lean on.

On the second day of their travel back to Oberlin, Suzie pushed her legs against her chest and wrapped her arms around them. A tear drifted down her cheek. "Why was this mission so important? Why was Mr. Danly willing to die for it?"

Mr. Danly wouldn't be dead if he hadn't gone back to get Suzie, who'd stood frozen behind that table when the fighting and shooting broke out. Processing that fact would likely be one of the hardest things Suzie would ever have to do. So for now she chose to question Mr. Danly's judgment in putting together such a mission trip in the first place.

But Mary would not let this tragedy be laid at Mr. Danly's feet. Wiping the wetness from her face, Mary told Suzie, "He did it because he believes the rights of a Colored man matter as much as any other man's."

"But why?" Suzie moaned. Sorrow gripped her and wouldn't let go as she rocked back and forth, like she was on a seesaw tilting from one side of an emotion to the other. One minute she was throwing insults, blaming the Black men in town for getting those good White folks riled up enough to come to that market. The next she was crying and blubbering about how evil the world was.

Timothy said, "I, for one, will never forget what a great man Mr. Danly was. He fought for what was right, no matter the cost."

They rode in silence the rest of the journey, with each person holding on to their thoughts and feelings about the cost of equality in a nation that would not so easily give it to those who needed it like they needed air to breathe.

CHAPTER 32

The boat docked in Liverpool and Anna's group took a wagon into London. Anna's eyes glistened with the joy of discovering a new way of life. A place with castles and manors, but also a place with smog and pollution.

She coughed as her body adjusted to the new environment. "I can barely see in front of me. Why is the air quality so poor here?"

"With the massive increase in factories and industries, smog and pollution have come as well," Professor Lewis told them.

Katherine and another student covered their mouths and coughed. "I remember reading about it in class, but I didn't expect it to be so thick."

Professor Lewis said, "We have a treat for you all." He paid for tickets so all five of them could ride on the Metropolitan Railway. London was the first city to build an underground railway system. It had opened in 1863, and the world envied London's innovation.

Anna's cheeks warmed with awe and wonderment as

they went underground to ride in wooden boxes propelled by steam locomotives that pushed the trains through the tunnels. When the ride was over, hydraulic lifts ascended them from the platform level to street level. It was simply the most amazing thing Anna had ever experienced. "Thank you, Professor Lewis. That was fun."

Katherine and the others thanked Professor Lewis as well, and then they found a horseman with a wagon to take them to their resting place for the evening.

Anna quickly learned that London was a city of extremes, with wealthy aristocrats and royalty living in well-kept castles and manors while the peasantry lived in overcrowded and unsanitary slums.

The smog thickened once again as the horses trotted down the muddy road. "This air is choking me." Anna coughed again and again.

"Once we're farther down the road, the smog should lift a bit. We're riding near one of the bigger factories at the moment," the horseman told them.

Just as he had said, the smog lifted tremendously as they rode by a palace. Anna had seen plenty of big homes and manors in America. But never in her life had she borne witness to a castle. Her hand went to her heart. A small squeal escaped her lips as the horseman said, "This is Kensington Palace."

He flapped the reins so the horse continued moving forward as he explained, "Queen Victoria grew up in this castle. Her daughter, Princess Louise, lives there now with her husband, who recently ended his term as governor general of Canada."

The reddish-brick building was massive. Anna couldn't imagine what it would be like to live in such a place. Or to be treated like a princess.

The lush greenery and the hedged-to-perfection bushes were simply marvelous in Anna's sight. If she didn't live another day, she'd seen a piece of London that mere books had not done justice. Even breathing in the smog-filled air, she decided there was no place else she'd rather be at that moment.

Later that evening they picked up the perishables that they would be giving away and then traveled to the slums of London to deliver bags of rice, canned goods, and cheer. That was when Anna saw for herself that the stark contrast between the wealthy and the poor was not solely an American situation. But the poverty in London was worse than anything she had lived out in America.

Thick fog left residents in coughing fits; the dirty, muddy, manure-filled streets left a stench in the overpopulated area of town that was filled with sickness and disease.

"Thank you kindly, my lady," a little boy said as Anna handed him a few cans of beans.

The boy's hands were caked with grime like he'd been playing in the mud from the roadway. His clothes bore days-old stains. Smudges of dirt covered his face as if he were getting ready to put on one of those disgraceful minstrel shows.

Another child rushed over to Anna, but his mother steered him away. She let the boy accept food supplies from Katherine and then went back down the street. The behavior was a bit odd, but she kept working and smiling as she handed out food that would hopefully help the families stretch what they had until their next pay came in.

When the wagon was almost empty, Anna grabbed the last of the rice and attempted to hand it to a little girl who was so thin, Anna feared she had missed more meals than her body could stand. Instead of being grateful for the sustenance, the girl folded her arms in front of her growling belly and called Anna a slur she'd heard countless times on American soil.

Anna handed the bag of rice to Katherine. A tear drifted down her face as she climbed back into the wagon and waited for the others.

How could this be? She was in London, a place she'd dreamed of going. A place she imagined would be better than her homeland. She sighed deeply and waited for her peers. As they rode to the parish where they would be staying for the night, the slur from the little girl rang in her ears over and over.

"Are you nervous about giving your speech tomorrow?" Katherine asked as the horses trudged through the muddy streets of London and the wagon wheels rolled with thick cakes of mud falling off every so often.

"No." Anna glanced back down the street as they continued to move forward. "I thought things would be different here." She didn't expect to find White supremacy so far from home. And yet here it was, showing itself in those who called her slurs and steered their children away from her.

Katherine rested a hand on Anna's arm. That small gesture brought Anna comfort.

After their group had left the mission site, the thing that stuck in Anna's mind was the reality that there were poor people everywhere. And they were worse off than poor Black folks in America. But poor White folks still believed they were better than even the wealthiest Colored man. Black people were the lap dogs for the world, being treated as the lowest mongrel in the pack. When would that change? What could she do to ensure her people were seen for who they truly were—resilient overcomers who had proven their ability to adapt in any environment?

Anna stewed on her discontent overnight. By the time they made it to the event hall where she and Katherine would give their speeches, she no longer wanted to unify; she wanted to clarify. After Katherine delivered her speech and received applause, Anna stood and walked to the podium.

She had her notes in her hand as she stared out at all the White faces in the crowd, those who'd clapped and applauded for Katherine but now peered at her with questioning eyes. "I can see on your faces that you're wondering what qualifies me to stand before you."

Her hands gripped both sides of the podium. "Let's address this issue up front." She hesitated a moment, leaning closer to the podium. "There is a Negro problem in America and apparently in other lands as well. But I will only speak on America since that is also my land.

"I stand before you as a reminder that people of color are human. We bleed as you do. We have dreams and hopes as you do. Even as a Black woman, I dream and I hope. Where I come from, Black women face both a woman problem and a race problem, yet we remain unacknowledged in both sectors.

"I was born into slavery, but I still entered this world with undisputed dignity. I have grown and learned and educated myself, all with the knowledge that my hopes and dreams for tomorrow are not only for me, but I bring the entire Black race with me."

The room was silent as the people stared. But Anna was inspired to go on, as they appeared to be listening with open ears and open hearts. "Only the Black woman can say when and where she enters, in the quiet, undisputed dignity of her womanhood, without violence and without suing or special patronage, then and there the whole Negro race enters with her.

"We're not saying Blacks are more special than another race, but we are human beings. And as humans we deserve the same rights as others. So the Negro problem in America can be solved once we turn away from the lies that have been perpetuated by those who desire to see us in chains. Once we understand that Colored folks are not these subhuman caricatures that people who want to dehumanize portray us as, that will be the day when freedom comes to America."

Anna kept speaking her truth in hopes that her words would be so loud they'd travel all the way back to America and ring in the ears of those who would *other* her people and demean them simply because of the color of their skin.

In Paris Anna didn't feel the sting of rejection she'd experienced on the ship or in London. Many Black Americans found a degree of freedom and acceptance in Paris that was not afforded to them in America. Parisian society had not been subjected to the rigid system of racial segregation and discrimination that was present in the American South.

Anna took note of Black people who looked like her, walking the streets with scarves flowing in the air. Freedom from oppression lined their smiles. She exhaled in the city and allowed herself to just be.

In 1883 Paris was experiencing a period of peace, economic prosperity, and cultural growth under the Third French Republic. The city was undergoing significant modernization and expansion, even beyond the grand boulevards and parks established by Haussmann's earlier renovations, and Anna and Katherine wanted to see it all. They only had five days in Paris before going back to Liverpool to board the ship back to America. So when Professor Lewis allowed them to explore the city, off they went, arm in arm, skipping down the street.

Their first stop was Le Procope. They were told it was the oldest café in Paris. It was a meeting place for enlightened philosophers like Voltaire, Rousseau, and Diderot. This café was bustling and boisterous, and Anna and Katherine enjoyed it immensely.

When they were seated, Anna right away began practicing her French. "*Je prendrai une tasse de café*," she said to the waiter girl.

The waiter girl responded, "*Oui oui, madame, le café arrive tout de suite.*"

Anna understood each word. "Yes, yes, madam, the coffee is coming right away."

Katherine only wanted eggs, so she said, "*Je ne prendrai que des œufs, s'il vous plait.*"

The girl left with their orders. Anna leaned closer to Katherine and whispered, "I wish there was a place in the States where I could order coffee like that."

"*Oui oui*, we are putting our language lessons to good use here," Katherine agreed.

The girl returned with their orders. Anna drank her coffee and Katherine ate her eggs. A lively conversation broke out behind them. Two philosophers had differing opinions on civil liberties and the role of the church. The girls were elated that they understood most of the conversation.

"We can learn more about languages here than in our stuffy old classrooms." Anna leaned back and continued eavesdropping on the fascinating conversation.

After breakfast they took a carriage ride to see sights like the Louvre Museum, Notre-Dame Cathedral, and Sainte-Chapelle. Anna was dazzled by the architecture, but she would not venture inside any of the magnificent structures. Even though Blacks were received in Paris in a more open fashion than in America, jitters overtook her. Someone might be offended by her presence. She didn't want to spoil the allure of Paris, so she stayed in the carriage and found herself peeking out at a world she could not fully possess.

CHAPTER 33

September 1883, Senior Year

With her luggage in hand, Mary climbed the stone steps of Ladies Hall, each footfall a quiet declaration. The autumn air clung to her skin—warm, humid, tinged with the scent of earth and fading blooms. She paused at the top, inhaling deeply, then slowly exhaled, letting the weight of the season settle in her chest.

The summer of her junior year had left scars and gifts in equal measure, both heartbreaking and awakening. She still saw it when she closed her eyes: Mr. Danly running into the chaos, into the sharp snap of gunfire and smoke, to save a girl frozen in fear. He hadn't paused to protect himself. He hadn't waited for peace. In watching him, Mary had come to understand that peace, real peace, often required confrontation.

The articles she wrote for *The Oberlin Review* on the color line had not been as effective as she had hoped. At the end of the day, not adding her name to them had been a mistake. Change came with disruption, not silence and anonymity.

Sometimes one had to run straight into the fire, even if it was hot. Others might not make it out otherwise.

She placed her hand on the door, remembering how she used to love this dormitory. She had let the sting of prejudice push her out, let whispered slights and treacherous schemes exile her from a space she once claimed with pride. No more.

Today, she wasn't stepping away. She was stepping back in with eyes opened and a steady heart.

Mary opened the door. From this day forward, she would walk into the fire when needed and, in so doing, become the kind of woman other Colored girls could point to and say, "If she can stand, so can I."

She would hold her head up, take the bullets while fighting against oppression in hopes that her fight would make it possible for others like her to thrive in schools and businesses all around this country. One day her people would sit in boardrooms. They'd own businesses that other races would shop at. Mary was convinced that if she could prove that she was equal to her classmates, they would see others in her race as equals too. It started here. First she would conquer Ladies Hall and then the whole system that tried to deny her equality.

"Mary, you're back." One of the students who'd lived in Ladies Hall during her freshman year gave her a hug as she entered the gathering room.

Mary set her bags down and hugged the friendly ally. "Yes, I'm back and I'm thrilled to live amongst you all once again."

Mrs. Johnston rushed over to her. "This is such a blessed day. It made my heart glad to see you walk through those doors."

"Mine as well." Mary picked up her bags. Shook her

shoulders as if shaking off the past. "Let me go unpack and I'll join you all in the gathering room later this evening."

Mary planned to make the most of her senior year. Her only regret was that Ida had decided to stay at the boarding-house her father had picked for her. Mary now had a room to herself but still shared the community bathroom with a group of women who took too long handling their business.

"I certainly didn't miss this aspect of dormitory living," Mary told one of the girls who stood in line with her.

"I've been here two years and I'm always number ten or eleven in line and always late to my first class," the girl said.

At that moment Mary was number ten and the girl was number eleven. "You might want to get up a little earlier each morning. That's what I used to do when I lived here a few years ago."

The girl yawned. "I'm always so sleepy. I wish there was a rooster outside my window that could wake me up in the morning."

Mary's head fell back as she laughed. Then the girl at the front of the line banged on the bathroom door and yelled, "Hey, princess, there's a line out here."

The girl next to Mary said, "Every day someone has to bang on the door to get the line moving."

"So what you're telling me is, nothing has changed." The bathroom door opened. One girl stepped out and another went in. Mary smiled. This process didn't annoy her today. Today, she was happy to be back.

Later that day the Aeolian Literary Society would meet to vote in a new president. Janet graduated last year, leaving the vacancy.

No Black woman had ever led as president of Aeolian. In

Mary's estimation it was time to elevate the thinking of the ladies in her literary group. She'd put her name on the ballot for president, feeling that she was just as qualified, if not more qualified than anyone else who might want the post.

With butterflies dancing in her stomach, she went to the dining hall to eat her lunch. Then, as she headed back to her room since her afternoon class had been canceled, Mrs. Johnston yelled out, "Mail call!"

A smile crept across Mary's face—she was back home at Ladies Hall. As the girls rushed to the stairwell, Mary stood next to the fireplace in the gathering room, watching as they eagerly grabbed their mail and then took a seat in the gathering room or ran upstairs to open their letters in private.

Mrs. Johnston's hand shot up with a piece of mail. "Mary Church."

Mary's brows scrunched as she squinted her eyes. She had written to her mother in New York and her father in Memphis, letting them know she had arrived safely back on campus. In all her years away at boarding school or college, they had never written back this fast.

She took the envelope from Mrs. Johnston, noting that the missive had been addressed to Oberlin College, not the Ladies Hall. Then the name of the sender came into full view, and her eyeballs nearly fell out of her head, she stared so hard.

Mary ran upstairs to her room and closed the door. She pressed the envelope to her chest as she sat at her desk and extracted a letter opener. Robert Terrell, the gentleman she'd met on the train right before her sophomore year, was the name on the envelope.

Although he'd crossed her mind on numerous occasions,

she'd assumed he'd forgotten her and gone on with his life. She sliced open the envelope, pulled the paper out, and read the missive.

My dearest Mary,

I hope you won't find me presumptuous. But I have not been able to think of anyone other than you since we met. I'm sending this letter in hopes that it reaches you and that you might find it in your heart to write back.

If you would like to hear from me again, please write to the address I provided on the envelope. If you prefer I reach out to your parents before writing to you again, please let me know and I will do it posthaste. My intentions are pure, and I would be forever grateful if you would allow me the chance to show you.

Yours intentionally,
Robert Heberton Terrell

She flipped the envelope back over and noted that his return address was indeed Cambridge, Massachusetts. A Harvard man. Mary crushed the letter to her chest as she pictured the dashing Mr. Terrell, with his thick mustache and piercing brown eyes.

But as she began daydreaming about becoming pen pals with this man of valor and imagining his name combined with hers—Mary Church Terrell—her mind got stuck between her parents announcing their divorce and her declaration not to even think about marriage until she was sure it would last until they parted in death. She put the letter back in the envelope. She would give Mr. Terrell's request some thought.

A knock on her door caused Mary to jump. She put the envelope back on the desk before another knock came. "What are you doing in there?"

The voice was easy to recognize. Mary opened the door and Ida pulled on her shirtsleeve. "Come on, we've got to go."

"Why are you in such a hurry?"

"They're ready to announce the president of our literary group."

Those butterflies fluttered around again. Mary put a hand on her stomach. "I don't know. What if they didn't choose me?"

Ida stepped back and put a hand on her hip. "Britain finally passed a law enabling women to buy, own, and sell property, so what makes you jittery about this election?"

"That was in Britain. The women in America are still in bondage."

Ignoring Mary's moment of doubt, Ida said, "You have won two elections already, my friend."

When Mary didn't respond, Ida added, "Don't be consumed with worry now. Progress is happening all around the world." She reached out her hand to Mary. "And today we will see progress for the Negro. Come on, Mary, I can feel it. You are about to make history at this school."

Mary thought back to the inauguration ball and the day her eyes beheld the *Statue of America*. Progress wouldn't come only for America . . . It would come for the Negro as well. "Yes, let's go."

They entered the assembly room, where others were waiting for the announcement of the presidents for the Aeolian Literary Society and the Ladies Literary Society. Mary, Ida, and Anna took seats in the second row, trying to appear calm.

As if this election held no extra weight. It was just another natural occurrence at Oberlin.

The fact that Anna held Mary's left hand as Ida held her right was the only clue that this election mattered to the only three Black women who were set to become the first trio of Black women graduates with a four-year degree from Oberlin.

Mrs. Johnston stood in the front of the room. She held two pieces of paper. Gazing out at them, she said, "The president of the Ladies Literary Society will be . . . Katherine Smalls."

Claps and congratulations went around the room. No one was surprised. This was Katherine's senior year, and she had been voted in as president three of the four years she'd been here.

Mrs. Johnston opened the other paper, and a smile creased the sides of her lips. "And this year's president of the Aeolian Literary Society is . . . Mary Church."

Anna and Ida hugged her. Ida whispered in her ear, "What did I tell you . . . progress."

Mary pressed her hands to her face, laughter bubbling up before she could stop it. The applause thundered in her ears, but her thoughts had already leapt ahead. She wasn't jumping and shouting as she had when she became vice president. This was the natural progression of things. What she should've expected due to the work she had put in. Her becoming president was simply a matter of her peers selecting the best candidate for the job.

As progress continued to roll in for them, Mary imagined that one day a Negro woman would be able to run for the presidency of the United States of America. And who knew, maybe one day this country would recognize the equality of Colored folks and actually elect one.

CHAPTER 34

October 1883

Anna and Ida walked to Oberlin together one cold October morning, discussing their future plans. "I've applied to Wilberforce University. I'll either teach there or at St. Augustine's in my hometown after graduation." Anna cringed at the thought of going home again. But she needed employment. Fact of the matter was, if things didn't work out with Wilberforce, she would have to go back to Raleigh until she could formulate another plan.

"I've applied to Alabama Agricultural and Mechanical College. My father wants me to come back home after college, but I want to work for as many years as I can before I get married," Ida said.

Anna was all too familiar with the laws that forced women to stop working after marriage. "One day when we women get to vote, we're going to vote down that law."

"I feel like it's coming soon. Take England for example. Their women now have the right to buy and sell property."

They were outside of Oberlin. Anna stopped walking. "You mean White women. Black women are not treated any better in England than they are in America."

"Sounds like you didn't enjoy your trip."

Anna rolled her eyes. Threw her hands up. "Come on, let's get to class. I don't want to talk or think about that place."

Even though her days in Paris were the only part of Anna's trip she could say anything positive about, she came home inspired in spite of the hardship . . . but in a different way than she ever expected. Anna was writing in hopes of turning her musings into a book one of these days.

She had no idea how she would get this project published or if anyone would want to publish it. But she had a great deal to say. Anna had spent her whole life being quiet, keeping her head down, and staying out of other people's way.

She had grown since being at Oberlin, become stronger. The speech she gave in London with so many White faces looking on and trying to figure out if they could get behind the truth she spoke was only the beginning. She was now determined to make this world hear her.

When Anna left her last class and went home for the day, she had no time to relax. She sat at her desk and began putting her thoughts on paper just as she'd been doing ever since she arrived back in America.

She was writing for Black women in the South specifically. That was the place she knew. She'd seen firsthand the significant role Black women played in shaping their own destinies and contributing to the nation's history. Anna argued that Black women's experiences and perspectives were crucial for understanding and addressing the challenges faced in the Black community.

The Negro problem in America would never be fixed until the Black woman was uplifted to her rightful place. Accordingly, Anna wrote about educated Black women being the key to uplifting the whole race.

Anna worked on her book late into the night. Each page she finished sparked the next thought. And then it hit her. If she had to sum up the book she was working on, she could do it in two words: *justice* and *equality*.

Those were the things that mattered to her, and they were also the things Black people in America received so little of. But the day would come when all men and women would acknowledge the resilience of Black people.

Anna would always advocate for opportunities for all Americans regardless of race or gender. But her goal with this project would be to uplift Black women in America. She wanted them to know how unique and special they were.

As Anna saw it, the cause of freedom was the very birthright of humanity.

October 14, 1883

"I hear you're working on a book," Mary said when she ran into Anna during the Sunday evening prayer meeting at Ladies Hall.

"I am, Madam President." Anna curtsied in front of Mary.

"Don't 'madam president' me. The Aeolian Literary Society is one thing, but a whole book is a true accomplishment."

"Thank you. I thought it would be simple to write my thoughts out and create a book, but it's been challenging lately."

The two took their seats in the assembly hall as they waited for the prayer meeting to start. "What's the book about?"

Anna's chin lifted ever so slightly as she answered, "Justice and equality."

"Amen to that, sister. Do you have a title?"

"I'm not sure. I've been mulling over a few, but nothing has stuck yet."

Mrs. Johnston called the prayer meeting to order, and they bowed their heads. After prayer, the ladies discussed other matters of importance. Mary had been pondering something that she thought might be beneficial for the ladies at Oberlin. She stood and raised her hand.

"Yes, Mary," Mrs. Johnston said, acknowledging her.

"I've been thinking about Mr. Danly a lot lately. He had a heart for helping those who couldn't help themselves. I would love for us to form a Young Ladies Missionary Society in his honor."

Anna and Ida stood and clapped for her. "That's an excellent idea," they said. Others stood and clapped as well.

Mrs. Johnston's eyes lit with interest. "What a blessed suggestion. With all the people standing right now, I'm assuming that you're all in favor. Is that correct?"

"Yes, yes!" came the ladies' shouts.

Mrs. Johnston turned back to Mary. "What would be the benefits to such a program?"

"For one, it would teach the ladies leadership skills and help them with communication since we would meet with other missionary groups to do good works in communities that might find themselves in need."

"I'll need a constitution drawn up so I can present it to my leadership." Mrs. Johnston gave Mary a pointed stare. "I'm assuming you will help write our bylaws?"

"Yes, of course," Mary said, still standing.

Peering out at the crowd, the principal asked, "Can I get anyone else to help with this important assignment?"

Suzie had been seated in the back of the room. She stood, her hands clasped in front of her. "Since this is in honor of Mr. Danly, I would like to help in any way I can."

"Perfect," Mrs. Johnston said as she continued to survey the room. "Anyone else?"

Another girl raised her hand. "I'd like to help."

"We have our committee. Thank you, ladies. I'll expect your constitution on my desk by the end of the week."

Mary wasn't happy about being on another committee with Suzie, but she could stomach it for one week as long as they were able to put together the bylaws for a sustainable society group that was about more than literary debates and teas. This one would also be about lending a helping hand.

The three of them researched what other missionary groups were doing, then set meeting times. They discussed events and programs the new group would conduct and, above all else, the mission. Mary suggested their motto should be

"Lending a Helping Hand." Her committee members wholeheartedly agreed, and the bylaws were complete. Now they needed to elect leaders.

This was Mary's last year as an undergraduate at Oberlin. She had been involved in several different organizations, including her church, the Aeolian Literary Society, and *The Oberlin Review.* But she hadn't started any of those organizations. The Young Ladies Missionary Society would have her fingerprints on it. The leadership would have to acknowledge that she, a woman of color, had done something substantial before leaving Oberlin.

That was the way Mary thought of it, but when the votes were cast and Mrs. Johnston was named president of the Young Ladies Missionary Society and Suzie named the vice president, without even the recorder position going to Mary, she recognized that her peers would not allow her to shine even in an organization that she herself had started and written the bylaws for.

This was nothing new for Mary. In all her days at Oberlin, she had excelled in front of them even while the sneaky little ghouls who did the devil's work tried to lower her station. Despite their schemes and hateful behavior, Mary continued to show kindness.

The Young Ladies Missionary Society quickly made connections with other groups of similar interests. Mary and thirty-five other members rode to Wellington to attend a ladies' missionary meeting with Mrs. Johnston.

Despite the crispness in the November air, the wagon ride was pleasant and the road conditions were excellent. The Wellington group had a tasty lunch prepared for them upon arrival. Mrs. Johnston asked Mary to help her place the cups on the tables.

Mary did as requested, moving from one table to the next, placing a saucer and a teacup at each place setting. When she reached the table Suzie was sitting at with a few of her friends, one of the girls snickered as Mary approached, then said, "They finally have her doing work her people are more suited for."

The girl to the left of Suzie said, "Mary would make a great server. I should ask my parents to hire her at our home after graduation."

Mary slammed the cup in front of the girl. Through gritted teeth, as she leaned close enough to whisper her insults, Mary said, "You have an imagined ideal of my station in life. You and I both know that your parents can't afford to hire anyone to do the cleaning. I'm sure you'll be doing it for free."

The girl's face reddened. She stood and puffed out her chest. "How dare you. My parents are fine, upstanding members of our community. Not divorcees, like your degenerate parents."

"Be that as it may, my father doesn't clean his own toilet." With that last jab Mary lifted her chin and walked away.

But the girl to the right of Suzie wasn't done with her. "You think you're so much, don't you, Mary Church? Always aiming higher than your betters. That's why we voted for Suzie as vice president of this missionary group. And that's why Suzie beat you in all those debates."

Mary swung back around, fire in her eyes. Suzie had put these girls up to this horrid behavior, she was sure of it. But Suzie told her friends, "Mary doesn't need to debate anymore. She is the president of Aeolian. Why should she concern herself with such things?"

Was Suzie taunting her? Were she and her friends setting Mary up for more humiliation on the debate stage? Mary hadn't debated since the end of her freshman year. She had served as recorder, historian, vice president, and now president of Aeolian. Securing those positions should have been enough to prove her intellect and show that she was as qualified as her peers. But the fact that she had been cheated out of those debates still stung. She walked back over to the table.

It was in bad form to boast and went against all the etiquette classes she'd taken. But nothing could stop her from the path she was about to take. They'd denied her and belittled her for the last time. "As president of my literary group, I say who debates and who does not. And I will be on that debate stage for the next one. I expect that you will be there as well." She glared at Suzie, then walked away from that hateful table.

If debating was what it would take to prove to these people that she was as good as any of them, then she would stand on that debate stage again and let the chips fall where they may. But this time, Mary was determined they would fall in her favor.

CHAPTER 35

"I have never been angrier in my life. They're not getting away with it this time," Mary told Anna as the two of them were studying in the library.

"What are you going to do about it?" Anna asked.

Mary closed her philosophy book and leaned back in her chair. "I'm going to show them who they're dealing with. I'm so tired of people thinking that Colored folks are inferior when I could best any of those girls."

"Your scores are higher than Suzie's and any of her friends. Those girls aren't serious about learning. They're just here to find husbands."

"Exactly," Mary declared. "While we're here with the weight of our people to concern ourselves with."

Anna leaned forward, then glanced around the library. "What's your plan?"

Exhaling, Mary said, "I put myself on the list for the next debate. If Suzie wants to prove she's so much better, then she will sign up to debate me as I told her."

Anna's lips tightened. She fell back against her chair. "Are you sure you want to do this? Those girls take pleasure in voting against you."

"It's mostly the ones in your literary society. You and Katherine are the only nice girls in that group."

"We have a few others," Anna said as she closed her book.

"Well then, hopefully they'll vote for me this time. Even *The Oberlin Review* reported that I was cheated out of at least one of those debates."

They both stood, gathered their belongings, and left the library. Worry creased the corners of Anna's eyes. "Are you sure you want to bother with this debate? You've proven yourself over and over at this school. Why subject yourself to the whims of our classmates?"

Mary gaped at Anna. "You don't believe I can best her, do you?"

Anna waved that notion off. "I've already witnessed a debate where you bested Suzie. All I'm saying is, these systems are not set up for us to win."

"But win we must. We owe this to those who come behind us."

"This is important to you, isn't it?"

Mary's throat tightened. "If I can't beat Suzie, maybe I'm not meant to take on anything bigger than this college. Maybe I should go home to Memphis after graduation. Host parties, raise money, do the polite work, and leave the real fights to someone braver."

The words scraped her throat raw. *God, why did I say that out loud?* Heat pricked behind her eyes. If she couldn't win this debate, how could she ever stand on a stage that mattered, where people's lives, not trophies, were on the line?

She confessed to Anna, "I don't know what I've been doing wrong."

Anna held on to her books with one hand. The other rubbed her chin as she appeared to be in earnest thought. "You've been giving the judges what you think they want."

Mary wasn't understanding what Anna was trying to tell her. "I researched and wrote the best speeches or rebuttals I could give for those debates."

"Look around, Mary." Anna lifted her arm and let it sweep across the distance. "You're a Colored woman who has moved excellently in a White world, but if you want respect for who you are, you'll need to dig deeper."

When Mary was younger, she never cared about fitting into a White world. Her skin was so fair that she could have passed for White if she so chose. But she was proud that she was Colored and that even while being Colored, her father had amassed great wealth. It wasn't until she discovered that her ancestors had been slaves—and that they had been treated like they were less than human—that what others thought when they saw her mattered.

Through growth in age and experience, she now cared about what the dominant group thought of her entire race. In her twenty years of living, she had met many Colored folks of excellent character. She was grieved that others could not see the reality of this truth she held.

Anna jabbed a finger at the left side of Mary's chest. "Pull your message from the depths of your heart and smother them with what matters to you."

The discussion with Anna lit a fire under Mary. She walked around campus, meditating on Anna's words. What mattered to her? The plight of Colored people mattered. The way her people were perceived by others mattered.

She strolled the campus for what seemed like hours, her steps aimless, her thoughts anything but. Eventually her wandering carried her to the front steps of Ladies Hall—the one place where she'd experienced both good and bad, hope and sorrow. As she opened the door and stood in the gathering room, the staircase leading to the dormitory before her, Mary imagined herself running down those stairs for this or that event. The activities at Ladies Hall kept her busy.

Her hand trailed the banister as she made her way to her room, thoughts swirling. *Dig deep. What's in your heart?* A thousand questions swam through her head before she entered her dorm room. She fell on her bed and grabbed the box of cookies her mother had sent.

Bite after bite, as the chocolate filled her mouth, Mary contemplated her next move. What would she . . . what could she ever do to convince these girls that she and others in her race weren't born for servitude?

Slamming her fist against the cushion of her mattress, she stood and paced the floor. How could she fight against the weight of this world when she couldn't even best one girl? How could she challenge Jim Crow, face the fury of lynch mobs, demand justice for her people, when her heart was so tangled in doubt?

Her father had sent her to Oberlin to learn how to fight, not with fists but with intellect, with dignity, with faith. But what if she couldn't? What if she never learned how to rise above the ridicule, never found her voice, never became the fighter her father believed she could be?

Mid-bite of her next chocolate chip cookie, Mary caught sight of her journal. She'd been writing her thoughts, accomplishments, and heartbreak in this book since freshman year. She'd never taken the time to review the words she'd put on those pages. With a few months remaining in the last year of her undergraduate studies, maybe it was time.

Even as she sat down and opened her journal, Suzie's cruel words echoed throughout the room, doing damage like shattered glass under her bare feet. Cutting deep and leaving scars.

"I told Mrs. Johnston that you people would dirty up this place."

Mary flipped pages in her journal and came to the place where she'd written about Mrs. Johnston calling her to the front of the room and thanking her for her efforts to get Ladies Hall renovated.

"Why does your literary society keep pitting you against your betters?"

The tenth, twentieth, and thirtieth pages of her journal were filled with one win after the next, until she'd won the election for president of her literary society. No other woman at Oberlin, White or Colored, had held as many offices, put in as much work as she had.

"We voted for Peter so Oberlin wouldn't have the stain of a nothing Colored girl representing us."

Yes, she had been denied the class poet position for her sophomore year, but she'd delivered numerous speeches as she represented her school. Her literary group and Oberlin authorities trusted her as an orator—her journal notes proved that fact.

"Colored girls sit in the back."

Colored girls belonged wherever their talent and God-given ability took them, and it wasn't in anyone's back seat or backroom table. Her sit-in had proven that. But Mary wasn't done teaching lessons to these privileged girls.

She wasn't letting the lies strangle her into submission. Strength like the wings of an eagle renewed her as she closed the journal. Poring through her journal had also reminded her of the one thing she missed out on during her years at Oberlin. They'd denied her the opportunity to recite one of her poems. But they had no say over what she chose to do for this next debate.

Mary pulled out paper and her writing instrument. But as she attempted to put pen to paper, she was wracked with a coughing fit.

She ran to her dresser and pulled out a cloth to wipe her nose. "Not again."

Mary and several other girls at Ladies Hall had fallen ill a few times during the year. No one had been able to figure out the cause, but the last time she'd felt like this, she'd been in bed for a week.

She took her cloth to bed with her as another lingering cough assaulted her body. Pulling the covers over her body, she tried to concentrate on the debate, but sleep . . . sleep was what she needed.

The cough, runny nose, and headache kept Mary in bed for two days. On the third morning she got up and stood in line to use the bathroom.

A scream penetrated the hallway. A girl ran out of the bathroom, yelling, "Mold . . . There's mold in our bathroom!"

Getting out of the line, Mary went downstairs to use the bathroom, only to discover that there was also a mold problem in the kitchen and dining room. "This shouldn't be happening, especially with all the renovations that have been done," Mary said to one of the students.

Mrs. Johnston stood in the middle of the gathering room, holding up a hand as murmuring and complaints went around the room. "Everyone, remain calm. We're going to fix this problem."

"No wonder so many of us have been ill lately. The hall is infested with mold," one of the girls said.

"I've gone to the doctor twice for a tonic, and nothing has helped me."

A steady throbbing beat against Mary's skull. All she wanted to do was lie back down. After using the bathroom, she went back to her room, stuffed cloth under her door, and cracked her window open.

Thick with confusion, her head bounced in her hands. Not a single line of her argument had yet found its way to the page, and the debate was only three days off. Why had she opened her mouth? Why had she demanded a debate? For the first time since arriving at Oberlin, had she taken on more than she could conquer?

CHAPTER 36

The brown skirt her mother had sewn for her when she left Raleigh for Oberlin College smelled faintly of lye soap. Anna smoothed it over her knees as the train lurched forward. The white blouse Mary had given her itched at the collar, but she wore it anyway. Mary had said it gave the image of a teacher.

Outside the window the countryside slid past in shades of late-winter brown. Xenia, Ohio. Wilberforce University. The words pulsed like a heartbeat in her mind.

A teaching position.

She pressed her shawl to her chest, trying to steady herself. Senior year wasn't over yet, and already she was supposed to think of the future. Freedom had given her choices, but choices could feel heavier than chains.

She pulled out the letter her mother had written a few weeks ago. She'd read it so many times, the paper was worn.

My dearest Anna,

I pray all is going well for you. I can hardly believe that time has moved so fast and you are about to graduate from that northern school.

I spoke with the administrator at St. Augustine's and there is a teaching position waiting on you the moment you graduate. Isn't that wonderful? They didn't forget about you. Everyone at St. Augustine's is so proud of you, and so am I.

Write me back and let me know what to tell them. Will you arrive home directly after graduation, or will you be delayed?

Your loving mother

Anna folded the letter and put it back in her purse. Her mother had healed from the illness she'd dealt with during Anna's freshman year. In no uncertain terms, Mama wanted her to come back home after graduation. Now she had gone so far as to ensure that Anna had employment. But Raleigh was not where she wanted to reside.

Anna didn't want to break her mother's heart, but she didn't want to stifle her own growth either. She would have to respond soon. So much was on the line with her interview today. If she was offered a position, would her mother understand? Could Anna be happy at Wilberforce?

When she stepped off the train, the air smelled of damp earth and woodsmoke. The campus rose ahead, green hills rolling toward a wide T-shaped building of pale wood. The cottages scattered around seemed harmless now, sunlight glinting off their whitewashed walls. But she knew better.

Tawawa Springs.

Her throat tightened. They said abolitionists once brought runaway slaves here to rest before their journey to freedom. This place had served the Underground Railroad well. But others—men like her mother's former master—brought their own kind of suffering.

Southern slave owners discovered this beautiful gem and began bringing their slave mistresses and the mulatto children born through those women to this place.

As she walked past the nine cottages, making her way to the main building, echoes from the past spoke of the women who'd endured what had once been called pleasure houses. As if pain could ever be pleasure.

"There was no pleasure here for me. No one heard my cries or grieved my shame."

"The man who owned me brought me and my children to this place. We entertained his whims and no one said a word."

"I escaped my abuser with the help of a kind abolitionist. My children and I lived free and I retrieved my dignity."

The whispers in the wind spoke of her mother's shame. Words she'd never been able to utter. The cruelty that Anna's family had endured was not theirs alone. Many Colored women suffered at the hands of lustful slave owners. The stories of the women who'd endured this place drifted up from the soil and clung to her like cobwebs. Anna's fingers trembled as she adjusted her shawl and wrapped herself in them. Swaying with the trees, breathing in the air of redemption.

The ambience here was different now that Tawawa Springs was no more. The wind moved through the trees with a cleansing rustle, like lyrical notes rising. She let herself sway with its cadence, breathing in change.

This was a new day.

Ahead, the great building loomed, its white columns

catching the sun. Wilberforce. Named for the man who'd fought to end the trade that had birthed her. The irony twisted and settled somewhere deep, but so did gratitude. From pleasure house to college. From the daughter of a former slave mistress to teacher's candidate.

Heart pounding, Anna climbed the steps. The door opened, and a small brown-skinned woman with silver hair smiled warmly. "Mrs. Cooper?"

"Yes," Anna managed, her voice steadier than she felt.

"We've been expecting you. This way, please."

They walked through long halls polished by a century of footsteps. Music floated their way, young voices blending in harmony.

"Where is that coming from?" Anna asked.

"The Wilberforce concert company," the woman said proudly. "They're rehearsing before their tour."

Anna smiled. She'd once dreamed of teaching music, but mathematics had claimed her mind the way melody claimed her heart. Still, the sound lifted her spirit. The vocalists reminded her of the Jubilee Singers from Fisk University. They traveled the country performing in order to earn money for their college. This concert company most likely did the same.

They reached the office door. "President Mitchell is waiting."

Anna drew a breath deep enough to carry her mother's love and her own hope to the place she was destined to be.

She stepped inside.

"Mr. Mitchell." She offered him her hand. "It's an honor to meet you."

"Likewise," he said, his grip firm, his manner polished with years of authority. "Please, Mrs. Cooper, have a seat."

Anna folded her gloved hands in her lap, willing them to be still. The air in the office smelled faintly of pipe smoke and old books, the kind of room where decisions about futures were made, most often the futures of men. She kept her gaze steady, though a familiar unease fluttered at the edge of her composure. Would he see her for what she was capable of or merely for what she had been?

Shuffling a few papers on his desk, President Mitchell said, "I've received several impressive recommendations for you."

Her heart gave a small leap. *They spoke well of me.* Mrs. Johnston, her professors, even her former employer—all of them had lent their good names to hers. "I am deeply grateful, sir. Their kindness humbles me."

President Mitchell set the papers aside and leaned forward, elbows on the desk. "You're here for the mathematics position, which I see you are well qualified for."

The faint pause before *qualified* tightened her spine. She waited. One learned to wait in such rooms.

"But," he continued, "we have other needs here at Wilberforce."

Other needs. The words pricked at her composure. Not mathematics, then? Had another, perhaps a man, already been chosen? Her pulse beat louder than the clock ticking somewhere behind him.

"Sir?" she managed. "Other needs?"

He nodded, steepling his fingers. "I've been here but a short while, yet I've had time enough to review our curriculum. It is, I regret to say, deficient in the study of foreign languages. Other universities are advancing, and we must not lag behind."

Anna's posture straightened before she could stop herself. Languages. Greek and Latin . . . worlds that had always opened to her like doors others did not wish her to enter. "I see," she said carefully. "I'm fluent and have some small experience teaching both."

Mr. Mitchell's eyes brightened. "We know you can teach, Mrs. Cooper. What I wish to know is, can you build? Can you devise a course of study and train others to teach as you do?"

She blinked, sure she had misheard. "You wish me to instruct . . . other teachers?" Her voice faltered despite her best effort. *He cannot mean it.*

"Not only instruct," he said, and for the first time, a genuine smile curved his lips. "We would like you to head the Department of Modern Languages and Science."

The words settled in the air like a benediction. Head the department. For a moment she could not speak; her throat tightened with something perilously close to tears. He was still talking . . . something about innovation, about progress, but all she could hear was the thrilling truth: *He sees me.*

Later, as she made her way back to the train station, the world seemed somehow lighter beneath her feet. The wind lifted her veil, the cinders along the track glinted in the sun. President Mitchell had looked beyond convention, beyond expectation. He had seen her mind, her worth, her possibility.

Anna Julia Cooper, the first woman to head a modern language and science department for an institute of higher learning. She would write to her mother. Surely she would understand the reason Anna could not return home now.

Mama would never ask Anna to leave this place, not now, not when she had finally been seen.

CHAPTER 37

Mrs. Johnston brought in the maintenance team, and they washed down the walls. The mold was gone and her head had stopped fighting against her, so Mary was up late into the night, writing and then crumpling the paper. She wrote more and then crumpled the paper again. Nothing was coming out right. "*Pull it from your heart*," Anna had said.

As Mary began to write again, she remembered Frederick Douglass saying to her, "*If there's no struggle, there is no progress.*"

Progress—that's what she longed for, cried out for in the depths of her soul. Her people had come so far, had bled and clawed and prayed their way through generations of hardship, carving out victories where none were offered. But progress . . . oh, progress came slow and soft, like a hesitant whisper, when it came to Colored folks. And far too often it didn't only stall, it recoiled, snatching back what little ground had been gained and trampling the dreams that had dared to take root.

She ached for more—for dignity, for safety, for a chance to rise and stay risen. She needed her people to live in this world as the full living, breathing human beings they were. To stand tall. To taste success not as a miracle but as a right. Even if they had to scrape and fight for every inch of it.

Was that so much to ask? How could she get others to understand what was in her heart if the words kept coming out wrong? Then an idea struck and she started writing again.

Sweat dripped from Mary's forehead as she stepped into the assembly room. It was the second week of January, still cold outside, but a raging inferno blazed within her and would not let go. She had lived a privileged life, but it was not without wounds and scars. It was not without care for her fellow man and woman.

If she lost this debate, the diploma would still be hers. Honors from Oberlin College would still bear her name. The speeches she'd given, the essays she'd written, the long nights of study—all of it would stand. But none of that mattered today. Today wasn't about Mary Church at all.

Today was about the aching weight pressing down on her chest. The burden of being one of the first, of being seen, of being expected to be perfect. It was about the nameless little Black boys and Black girls who hadn't yet been born, who didn't yet know the sting of being called less, but would. And when that day came, what would they see when they discovered her accomplishments?

They had to see a person who stood firm. Someone who fought not merely to win but to prove something vital—that they were more than the names spat at them in the streets. More than the low expectations scribbled beside their names. More than the slurs whispered in corners when they passed. Her people were not built for shame or silence. No, they were built for brilliance, carved from the resilience of generations that refused to break.

She needed to show them that. She needed them to believe that if she could rise, then so could they. Even if her voice shook, even if her hands quivered behind the podium, she had to become the proof—their belief in themselves might begin with her.

"I'm rooting for you, Mary," Katherine whispered to her. Even though Katherine was president of the Ladies Literary Society and would be going up against Mary today, she was always on the side of right, and Mary loved her for that.

She only wished that Janet hadn't graduated last year; then surely she would've had two White votes she could count on.

Anna and Ida had taken front row seats, and they smiled at her as she stood behind the podium. Mary exhaled. It was now or never. Either her peers would accept the truth of her words or they would reject it. Either way, she wasn't backing down or running from their contempt ever again.

They had denied her the class poet position at the Sophomore Exhibition and the Junior Exhibition, choosing others who were far less qualified. Today, they would hear what she had to say. After Mrs. Johnston called the meeting to order, she took her seat at a table in the front of the room where Suzie was seated.

It was time for Mary to present her argument, and she was going to do it in the form of a poem. She cleared her throat, releasing the anxiety that tried to lodge there. And then gave them what they had denied her for all these years:

I may be a Colored woman in a White world,
But I am not blind to the insults hurled.
This is a fight you cannot win,
For the blood in the earth speaks of
    your sin.

We've cooked their bread, we've warmed
    their beds,
With hymns still dancing in our heads.
And though the chain is cast away,
The yoke remains in a crueler way.

But hush now, child, don't lift your gaze—
The law's no friend in these new days.
They say we're free, but hang us on trees,
No vote, no voice, no one to speak for me.

Yet still we hum our mother's song,
Where right was right, and wrong stayed
    wrong,
And dream beneath the good ol' oak tree
Of days our children might see equality.

So let them scorn us, and about us they
    do lie;

Our roots run deep, our heads are
held high.
They tell their children the color of skin is
the difference;
We tell our children to rise and shine with
excellence and eloquence.

They say we're equal now—but colored
lines remain in soil and law,
We scream, "I, too, am America," as we
claw and claw and claw.
Nonetheless, we're sent to slaughter, while
green eyes look the other way,
Yet still we fill our children's hearts with
that sweet, blessed hope of . . .
someday.

Mary lingered behind the podium a moment after she finished. Her heart thudded in her chest, not from fear, but from the weight of what she had laid bare. She scanned the room, seeing the faces of classmates who had cheered her on and others who had never wanted her to stand there in the first place. Her voice, steady but full of fire, broke the silence.

"I just gave you a poem," she said, her eyes holding theirs. "What, pray tell, will you do with it?"

Sniffles, as if from the shedding of tears, could be heard around the room. Mary walked away from the podium, and the room erupted in cheers. She sat on the right side of Mrs. Johnston as Suzie stood and walked to the front.

Holding her breath, Mary waited for Suzie to accuse

Colored folks of being out of their depth, of not being where they belonged . . . of taking from White folks what rightfully belonged to them. But the sniffles she'd borne witness to did not just come from the attendees.

Mary glanced at Suzie and noted that the girl stood before the whole assembly in tears.

Mrs. Johnston handed her a handkerchief, and Suzie wiped her face, then set her eyes on the crowd and began, "I'm a daughter of the South. I grew up in a place where Whites didn't mix with Coloreds." She slid a strand of hair behind her ear. "My daddy told me that Colored folks weren't even human."

Suzie shrugged and wiped her face again. "When I came to Oberlin, there was no way I could accept that any of the Colored students could be smarter than me. That simply couldn't happen."

She sighed deeply. "But I stand here today having been introduced to men like Mr. Danly and President Fairchild and many others on this campus who think differently than the way I was raised."

As more tears streamed down her face, Suzie turned to Mary. "Y-you *are* smarter than me. And I have been jealous of you since the day your father escorted you to President Garfield's inaugural ball. I couldn't fathom how a Colored girl could be held in such high esteem when all I'd ever been taught was that Colored people were not superior to White people."

A lump rose so thick in Mary's throat, she could hardly breathe. Tears welled up fast, blurring everything in front of her until the room became a wash of light and shadow. She swiped at her eyes with the back of her hand, but the tears kept coming. Her chin quivered, her breath hitched, and for a moment, she wasn't sure if she could hold herself together.

Tears like a river ran down Suzie's face as well, but she continued. "I don't want to be your enemy anymore. I have a feeling that you'll do great things for your people one day. And"—Suzie put a hand to her chest—"th-this Southern girl will be cheering you on."

With that Suzie took her seat next to Mrs. Johnston. Mary leaned forward and held out her hand to Suzie. As their hands locked, they lifted them high as a symbol of unity. And Mary couldn't stop the tears from flowing.

When the votes were cast, the clear winner of the debate was Mary. But not only her, for if every person in that room took heed to what she and Suzie said, they would become winners in this fight for equality. The ones who believed would no longer be able to sit in silence. That, at least, was Mary's greatest prayer.

CHAPTER 38

The night before graduation, Mary was in her room packing her things. Her father would be arriving soon, and she was going back to Memphis for a few months to rest. The administration had tried several times to rid them of the mold, but it kept coming back. Mary's and several other girls' health had suffered due to the issue.

Her body was not fully recovered, so she had decided to go home before entering into her profession. Her plan was to heal and then seek out a university to teach at in the winter.

Her father was not fully supportive of her plan, but Mary had carved out a path for herself, and only she would determine where it would lead. Mary was expecting her mother any minute, so when the knock came at her door, she threw it open, prepared to receive a hug and kiss on her cheek.

But instead of her mother, Mrs. Johnston stood at her door. "I hope I'm not disturbing you."

"No, not at all. I'm packing so I'll be prepared to leave after the commencement ceremony tomorrow." She stepped to the side and allowed Mrs. Johnston to enter the room.

Mrs. Johnston gestured to the chair behind Mary's desk. "Do you mind if I sit here?"

"Please." Mary sat on the edge of her bed, her feet tapping against the floor.

"Don't worry, I'm not going to hold you up for long. I wanted to come and see you before you leave us." Mrs. Johnston's smile was bittersweet. "It has been a joy having you at Ladies Hall."

Mary nodded. "I have enjoyed my time here."

"All of your days here haven't been pleasant, and for that I am truly sorry." Mrs. Johnston glanced away as if trying to hide her shame. "When you first arrived, I thought you'd get along great with all the girls. Then our newer White students refused to eat with our Colored students, and a few of the girls gave you such a hard time."

"None of that was your fault, Mrs. Johnston. Please don't blame yourself."

"I struggled with how to help you. Lord knows I wanted to do more."

They sat there in silence a moment. Mary wanted to encourage her principal, but there had been times when she'd wished Mrs. Johnston had done more to stop the hateful behavior. But Mary had survived, so there were no regrets.

"I had hoped that you would have been named president or vice president of the Young Ladies Missionary Society since the group was your idea in the first place. I pray you don't hate me for not speaking up about the unfairness of that situation."

Mary could honestly say that she was leaving school without malice against anyone. Suzie's apology had soothed her soul. She lifted a hand. "I'm not bothered by what happened with that group. I'm not sure how or when, but I plan to organize other groups that will help my people gain equality. I see the work I've done at Oberlin as my proving ground. But there is so much more to do."

The smile Mrs. Johnston held now was not bitter, only sweet. "I have no doubt you will do exactly that." She stood. "Anyway, I came to your room to say thank you again for the work you put in to have this dorm renovated. And I wanted you to be the first to know that the mold issue has become too much, so we will be tearing down Ladies Hall and building a new dormitory for our ladies."

Mary put a hand to her heart. "Oh no!" She let her eyes dance around her room. Yes, students had become ill of late, but she never imagined a time when she would walk the Oberlin campus and not see Ladies Hall. "This news is so distressing. I've come to love Ladies Hall and will hate to see it go."

Mrs. Johnston's lip quivered as she lifted her head. "Ladies Hall will remain in our hearts. We shall never forget the beauty we created here."

Nor the pain, Mary thought but did not say those words out loud. For in truth, Ladies Hall had been all things to her—a place of peace, growth, pain, and triumph—and she would miss this place that had become like home to her.

"Can you believe this day is finally here?" Anna asked as they prepared to take their seats for the commencement ceremony.

Mary waved at her father, who was seated with his new wife. She then waved at her mother and brother, who were seated a few rows above her father. She nudged Ida when she spotted her parents in seats not far from the stage. “I see your dad.” Mary pointed.

Ida waved at her parents, then told Anna and Mary, “I hope they won’t try to change my mind about teaching at Alabama Agricultural and Mechanical College.”

“I’m taking a break for a few months, but I’ll be teaching by winter, I can promise you that. And my father will have to accept the way I choose to live my life,” Mary said.

Anna smiled at her friends, but inwardly, she wished she had someone to fight with about her choice to teach at Wilberforce University instead of going back home to Raleigh. Someone to tell her she was being foolish, or brave, or both. Someone who cared enough to argue.

Her brother, Rufus, was on tour with his musical group, and her mother couldn’t afford to make the trip. Anna glanced to the left where Mr. and Mrs. Evans were seated in the third row. She waved at them. Someone was here for her. That was enough.

Her head was being lifted as well as her station in life today. She would celebrate it with the classmates she had come to know and love. It was telling that when they all started out, there were sixty-five men and only fifteen women registered in the Classical Gentlemen’s Course, but today, as they stood in First Church preparing to take their seats, there were only twenty-seven men and fourteen women in the graduating class. A smirk crossed Anna’s face as the proof that women could handle any challenge put before them shined bright today.

Anna was thankful that she’d come to Oberlin. She’d

grown here, become more confident, and now she was ready to take on the world. She'd start her world domination with her position at Wilberforce University.

Anna also planned to continue working on her book. One day she would find a publisher for her thoughts on being a voice from the South. Her book would be sold to readers who wanted to understand the power that education had to lift Black women from a low station all the way to the highest heights. Knowledge opened doors, and Anna would spread the knowledge she had with as many as would listen.

The music started. It was time for the graduates to march down the aisle. Mary hugged Anna and Ida. "I've got to go. See you after the ceremony."

Anna glowed with pride as she watched her friend rush over to the stage where she would be sitting with the faculty. Ida pulled on her sleeve. "Come on, let's line up."

Touching her stomach to steady her nerves, Anna followed Ida. *You're doing this . . . You're redefining what it means to be a Colored woman in America . . . Keep going.* And since no family was here to tell her, she told herself, "I'm proud of you."

Once everyone was seated, President Fairchild welcomed all in attendance. "And now we will have words from our valedictorian, Miss Mary Church."

Several of the graduating class jumped out of their seats and yelled, "Yay! All right, Mary!" President Fairchild pressed a finger to his lips, then stretched his hands out and lowered them.

"Graduates, please take your seats. We want to make sure our valedictorian has enough time to deliver her speech."

They sat back down, but how could he expect them to be quiet? Mary was the first Colored woman ever to receive the title of valedictorian from a college with both White and Black students. Anna prayed she wouldn't be the last.

Mary walked to the podium. The title of her speech was written in their program booklets: "The Mission of Tyranny."

"My fellow graduates, faculty, family, and friends, thank you for celebrating this day with us," she began, then proceeded to set the auditorium ablaze with her speech:

"What I have learned during my time at Oberlin is that this fight for equality is won one step at a time, with one person at a time. With each of us doing our part to build a more perfect union where we live and grow together. Men and women, Black and White.

"From evil can come good, as from the darkness of night the light of the sun. And so tyranny, though it has crushed many a heart, blighted many a life, has a mission well defined, and has played no insignificant part in the progress of nations. Tyranny has revealed the nature of the human heart. It has shown man as a fiend, and pictured him with an inspiration almost divine. Tyranny has another work which has wrought well for the world. Look back over the history of the ages, and whence has come the inspiration of those who have lifted themselves from the level of the brute to the dignity of manhood? Has it not come from the oppressor's chains? Tyranny's mission is to teach. It has proclaimed in clarion tones, which have echoed and re-echoed through all the battles, 'Man must be free.'"

Anna found herself with a mouth full of smiles as her friend Mary did not shy away from the cry of freedom that their people were desperate for. The chains were loosed, but they also required freedom to live their lives.

The thing that most surprised Anna was that not one ounce of jealousy found its way to her heart. She was happy for Mary and celebrated her accomplishments. This had been Mary's desire from the time she discovered she had been born into a world that enslaved her ancestors: to stand before the dominant group, not as their peer, but as their victor.

After a few other speeches came the conferring of degrees, and then a great shout of victory went up as the students each walked down from the stage with a diploma in hand.

Mary, Anna, and Ida huddled together with jumps and shouts. They hugged each other and made promises to stay in touch.

"I promise," each of them said.

Mary took Anna's hands in hers and stared into her eyes. "You are nobody's second-class citizen, Anna Julia Cooper. Today you have stepped into a whole new world. Don't you let anyone tell you different. You hear me?"

Mary was only twenty years old, and the youngest graduate of their entire class, but she proved to have wisdom beyond her years.

"I hear you."

The three hugged again, then shouted, "We did it!"

CHAPTER 39

Twenty-Five Years Later

Mary Church, now Mary Church Terrell, Anna Julia Cooper, and Ida Gibbs, now Ida Gibbs Hunt, were invited guests for the dedication of the newest Oberlin building: Finney Chapel. They were also celebrating Oberlin's seventy-fifth anniversary. Even though they had been disappointed in the ways in which Oberlin had embraced segregation at the turn of the century, something the three of them fought against, they still were honored to celebrate with their alma mater.

Finney Chapel had a Romanesque architectural style with oak pews that seated nearly two thousand people. This building had excellent acoustics, making it the perfect place to host musical performances and celebratory gatherings.

"So good to see you," Mary said as she hugged Ida and Anna.

"I'm glad to be here, but I almost didn't make it. We've only been back in the States for a week," Ida told them.

After college, Ida taught English at Alabama Agricultural and Mechanical College. She also taught at Florida A&M University and M Street High School, a prestigious African American college preparatory school in Washington, D.C. But when she married William Henry Hunt in 1904, she was forced to quit her teaching position. She now traveled with her diplomat husband to different countries as he received assignments. Thus far, they had lived in Liberia and France.

"Look at you," Ida said to Anna. "We are so honored to be in your presence being that you are the first Colored woman to be named principal of a high school."

Anna curtsied. "Principal Cooper at your service." Anna had taught Latin, math, and science before becoming principal at M Street.

"I could have been principal somewhere if they hadn't forced me to quit after getting married," Ida remarked bitterly.

"Don't you worry, women will have the right to vote soon. And one of the first things we'll do is demand an end to that disgraceful law," Mary told them.

"I'm sure you and your buddy Susan B. Anthony will make sure of that," Ida said.

Mary had indeed become acquainted with Susan B. Anthony and Lucy Stone. To date, she was the only woman of color who'd been allowed to speak at the National American Woman Suffrage Association conference. Her speech was not simply about the plight of women but about the double plight of also being a woman of color.

"Don't forget, I too was forced to quit teaching at M Street when I married my husband." Mary's Harvard man had come calling once she graduated college, and by 1891 she had fallen for his charms and married him. Robert Heberton Terrell was a force. By 1901 he had been appointed to serve as justice of the peace in Washington, D.C. Mary was proud to be his wife, but until civil rights for Blacks was upheld in the South, she hesitated to call it progress.

"That didn't stop you. Civil rights has always been your calling, and you are blazing trails," Anna said with admiration in her voice. "And I hear that W. E. B. Du Bois contacted you personally about this new organization he's starting."

Mary smiled. "Du Bois has asked myself and Ida B. Wells to become members of the National Association for the Advancement of Colored People. But he's still pulling that together. We're not scheduled to meet until sometime next year."

Mary had become a vocal leader in the fight for women's and civil rights. In 1892 she, Anna, and several other Black women formed the Colored Women's League to uplift the issues Black women faced in America. By 1898 they joined forces with another organization with similar goals, forming the first secular national organization dedicated to the livelihood of African American women. The National Association of Colored Women's Club motto was "Lifting as We Climb," and Mary became its first president.

Mary put a hand to her heart. "Oh my dear Lord, I haven't seen Dean Johnston in almost a decade."

Ida and Anna both swung around as the white-haired woman approached them while holding on to the arm of another woman. They each took turns giving their former principal a hug.

"Well, I'll be, Mrs. Johnston, retirement shines on you. You aren't letting grass grow under your feet," Ida said.

Mrs. Johnston was now seventy-one years old. She'd recently been out of the country and was now writing a novel. "You ladies have blazed trails of your own, and I feel blessed to have been principal of the Ladies' Department when you all were students." She squeezed each of their cheeks. "My, have I enjoyed seeing each of you blossom."

"We're not finished yet," Mary told her. "But we've enjoyed hearing about your growth as well. Becoming the first female faculty member is no small feat."

"And on that note, allow me to introduce you to Dean Mary Forbes. She is the new dean of women." Mrs. Johnston pulled the woman whom she had been arm in arm with forward.

They shook hands, but then Anna said, "I thought Elizabeth Lord took over as dean when you retired."

Mrs. Johnston nodded. "She did. But she has since left the position."

They all took their seats as the program got underway. President Fairchild had resigned back in 1898 and then passed away in 1902. Henry Churchill King was now presiding as president of Oberlin College, and with a booming voice he welcomed the guests to the dedication.

After a song selection, William C. Cochran, Charles Finney's oldest grandchild, delivered the memorial address. Mary was pleased with his speech since he reminded all those in attendance that Charles Finney, the former president of Oberlin College, fought to have Black students educated at Oberlin the same as White students, not pushed aside into their own dorms and classrooms that had become inferior to the other classrooms.

After the dedication, Anna and Katherine Smalls found each other and hugged like long-lost friends. Katherine was now a civil rights attorney and aided them in the fight for equality. Mary often spoke with her when in need of legal advice on a cause that was being pursued by her organization, the National Association of Colored Women's Club.

"You cut your hair," Mary noted after Katherine and Anna ended their embrace.

Katherine ran her hand through her hair. "It took too long to get ready each morning. I decided I didn't need long hair as much as I needed to be on time for court cases."

"There is still much work to be done, so we thank you for being in the fight with us." Anna pulled her close in a one-armed hug.

"Mary Church, is that you?"

Mary tensed as she faced the woman who'd tried to stifle her growth at Oberlin. She stood in front of her with spectacles and a wide grin. "Suzie McFarland?"

"It's Washington now." Suzie pulled Mary into an embrace that caused her to stumble as she tried to recover her wits. "I wanted to thank you. I was there for your speech at the National American Woman Suffrage Association convention. After that, I joined the fight. One day soon we women will have the vote."

Mary was astonished by the woman who stood before her. It just went to show you couldn't judge people by their youthful folly. "It's a worthy fight, Suzie. One we will win."

Mary, Anna, and Ida stepped out of Finney Chapel into the golden hush of early evening, the last strains of music and conversation echoing behind them. Their shoes clicked softly against the brick path as they made their way a block down Professor Street, the warm light of gas lamps beginning to glow along the walk. When they reached the corner where Talcott Hall now stood, they paused.

But their eyes didn't rest on the building before them. Instead, their minds drifted to the past . . . to the towering silhouette of Ladies Hall that once loomed on this ground. It had been a stern, stone-faced structure, its windows tall and narrow, its halls always slightly too cold, its rules even colder. A fire had devoured it years ago, reducing its bricks and beams to char and smoke, but the memories refused to burn away. Laughter in shared rooms, tears shed under the dark of night, whispered dreams of the future—all still lingered in the air like ghosts.

"This, ladies, was where it all began." A tear trickled down Anna's face. "I don't know where I'd be if I hadn't come to Oberlin."

They hadn't stopped after graduating with a four-year "men's degree" in 1884. Mary and Anna came back to Oberlin and graduated with master's degrees in 1888. Not long afterward, Ida received her master's degree from Oberlin in 1892.

They made memories in those halls—deep, complicated memories etched into the creaking floorboards and worn stairwells. Their time at this school had been about more than textbooks or classmates. It was within the solid brick walls of Ladies Hall that they had learned how to fight.

This was where they first found their voices, trembling at first, then rising strong and bold against the current of a world that doubted their worth. They had studied, debated, wept from exhaustion, and stood arm in arm when the world tried to shrink them.

Now, each one had carried what they'd gained into a wider world. Into classrooms, stages all around the world, and picket lines, fighting for that elusive, stubborn thing called equality. Their platforms had grown, their reach extending far beyond anything they'd once imagined.

But it had all begun here. In the chapel where they once knelt in prayer. In the dormitory rooms where secrets were shared and ambitions confessed in whispers. In Ladies Hall, their first battleground and their truest home.

EPILOGUE

Mary Church Terrell didn't move as briskly as she had when she was traveling back and forth to Europe, studying the languages, being honored with a luncheon by the Duchess of Warwick. Or when she was invited to tea in the House of Parliament by Lady Astor.

Her travels abroad had been special, but she was an older woman of eighty-six and no longer desired the rigorous travel going abroad would require. Oh, sure, airplanes were flying in the sky these days, but Mary wasn't so sure she'd trust an iron bird to take her all the way to Europe.

So much had changed in the world since they had entered the twentieth century. Her bathroom was more convenient and a place to relax rather than get in and rush out. The telephone that now hung on her wall and rang frequently with requests for speaking engagements caused Mary to chuckle.

It rang now as if thinking on it woke it into action. Mary picked up her cane and made her way to the twentieth-century instrument, thinking that her ride might be calling for directions.

But to her delight it was Janet Swift, her old college friend. Back then she had been Janet Huntington McKelvey. The two women had remained friends for nearly seventy years now. As recently as 1946, she and Janet had worked together to repeal the discriminatory policies of the American Association of University Women, which stated that Colored women could not join.

When Janet discovered the policy, she immediately called Mary and asked her to apply. Mary, always thinking of what each battle she took on would mean for the next generation, applied to the organization. After three years of fighting this unjust policy, Mary was admitted, and now other Colored women could join if they so chose.

"What are you up to on this beautiful summer day?" Janet asked.

"I'm waiting on my ride. I'm going to Thompson Restaurant for lunch."

"The one in Washington, D.C.?" Janet asked.

"Of course. It's the only one I know of."

"Isn't that restaurant segregated?"

Mary laughed into the phone. "Why do you think I'm going? I might be old, but I'm still a rabble-rouser."

Janet laughed with her. "Old friend, I wish I had the energy that God gave you. If I did, I'd come over there and join you for lunch so I could see the glares on those old stuffed-shirt customers' faces."

A lawyer friend had recently informed Mary of local integration laws in the District of Columbia dating back to the 1870s that required restaurant proprietors "to serve any respectable, well-behaved person regardless of color, or face a thousand-dollar fine and forfeiture of their license."

Mary was the leader and spokesperson for the Coordinating Committee for the Enforcement of the District of Columbia Anti-Discrimination Laws, which was the reason her lawyer friend reached out to her. "I never knew that law was on the books," Mary told him, then leaned forward with a gleeful smile. "Let's make them honor it."

After Mary's phone conversation with Janet, her ride arrived and she, Arthur F. Elmer, Clark F. King, and Essie Thompson entered Thompson Restaurant and attempted to be seated.

"We don't serve your kind," the waiter said.

Without missing a beat, Mary told the proprietor, "I hope you have a thousand dollars to spare."

"What's that supposed to mean?" He practically snarled at her.

"I'll give you one more chance," she said. "According to laws set forth in the District of Columbia, you cannot refuse service to us based simply on color."

The man angrily waved them toward the door. "Get out of here."

After they left Thompson Restaurant, they immediately filed a lawsuit. It took three years, but they received a favorable decision from the Supreme Court. During their wait, Mary and others boycotted, picketed, and held sit-ins. Finally on June 8, 1953, the courts ruled that segregated eating places in Washington, D.C., were unconstitutional.

Mary was tireless in her fight for justice all the way until the day she died on July 24, 1954. And the people remembered her sacrifice. Her body lay in state at the National Association of Colored Women's Club in Washington, D.C., an organization she co-founded. Thousands came to pay their respects to a woman who became a civil rights leader, suffragist, and educator.

Members of the NAACP, an organization she was a founding member of; members of Delta Sigma Theta, whose formation she assisted in by contributing her prestige and writing the Delta Oath, which expressed the fundamental morals and values of the organization; and members of numerous other organizations Mary either founded or left her fingerprints on, in one manner or another, came to pay respect.

Anna Julia Cooper and Ida Gibbs Hunt came also. The three women had remained friends and worked on numerous projects through the years. Anna and Ida each had a long list of accomplishments. Even in the lowest of times, life had been good to them. Anna received her PhD and had a long career in education. And Anna's book, *A Voice from the South*, was published in 1892. It was considered to be the first book of essays on Black feminism in the country.

Although Ida was forced to stop teaching after she married, she fought tirelessly for civil rights and women's rights through essays, speeches, and her work with W. E . B. Du Bois on the Pan African Conference.

The lives, times, and exploits of these women showcased excellence that crossed color lines as they gave everything they had for all-consuming causes. And though the work for equality is not finished . . . they left the blueprint.

AUTHOR'S NOTE

It was the honor of a lifetime to be able to bring Mary Church Terrell, Anna Julia Cooper, and Ida Gibbs Hunt to life in my novel *The Ladies Hall*. I spent month after month researching these women and getting to know them. I then decided that since Mary and Ida both came from similar backgrounds, I would use only one of them as a main character. Therefore, in this novel you receive points of view from Mary and Anna. I pray you understand that Ida's accomplishments were no less important, but for the sake of the story, I did not provide her viewpoint but tried to show through her actions what was important to her. I hope I did justice to the lives they lived out loud and with pride.

This book primarily covers their time in college and introduces you to the philosophy that guided Oberlin College. That philosophy, to teach Black and White students as equals and allow them to learn together, was upheld for a little over fifty years. From 1880 to 1884, the years Mary, Anna, and Ida attended Oberlin College, Black students were allowed to attend classes and live in the same dormitories as White students. But as the founders and those who were like-minded passed away and others who did not believe as the founders took their place, Black students were forced out of dormitories and lunch areas where White students could no longer stand seeing Black students treated as equals.

Although Mary Jane Patterson is documented as the first Black woman to earn a degree at Oberlin, Mary Church Terrell, Anna Julia Cooper, and Ida Gibbs Hunt were the first Black women not only to receive bachelor's degrees from Oberlin but to return and receive their master's degrees as well. Mary was later awarded an honorary doctorate degree from Oberlin. Anna went back to school later in life for her doctorate and received it from a school in Paris when she was sixty-four!

For the purposes of understanding this novel, I would like the reader to know that almost every scene in this book was crafted based on research. So when I show Mary working on a petition for Ladies Hall, this is actually what she did. When I write about the students voting against her during debates or for class poet, this is actually what they did, and these events were documented in the Oberlin archives. Some scenes were written into the novel that actually occurred several years after the three women had graduated from Oberlin, but they struck me as important in my research phase, so I added them to the novel. I will make mention of a few instances within this author's note.

OBERLIN

The Ladies Hall features two main characters, Mary Church Terrell and Anna Julia Cooper. Oberlin itself became my third main character. I wanted to introduce my readers to not just the school but the whole abolitionist town.

Founded as the Oberlin Collegiate Institute in 1833, the school eventually changed its name to Oberlin College (1850). In 1835 Oberlin became one of the first colleges in the United States to admit African Americans, and in 1837 the college admitted the first women. Because of its progressive outlook on education, many like-minded families moved to Oberlin, including many abolitionists.

I mention Oberlin as one of the towns runaway slaves passed through by way of the Underground Railroad. I also mention the Oberlin-Wellington Rescue, an event that occurred in 1858. Please note that Mr. Wilson Bruce Evans was truly a member of this rescue team, and it was my pleasure to introduce him to you. I provided the address of the home he and his wife lived in during that time. If you ever take a trip to Oberlin, Ohio, and I hope you do, this home is open for tours.

Were it not for space restrictions, I could say so much more about this beautiful area and this time in history when abolitionists, both White and Black, stood up for what they believed was right and fought against an oppressive system that would hold humans in bondage. I have provided links in the References section so you can read more about Oberlin.

LADIES HALL

The first Ladies Hall was constructed in the 1830s and was later replaced by a larger brick structure (Second Ladies Hall) in 1865. This is the dormitory that Mary Church Terrell lived in during her freshman and senior years of college. She did have a roommate by the name of Ida during her freshman year, but in my research I discovered that this student was not Ida Gibbs Hunt. In an effort not to confuse the reader with two Idas, I simply made Ida Gibbs her roommate.

The second Ladies Hall burned down in 1886, leading to the construction of Talcott Hall, a stone building still in use today. It now serves as a co-ed dorm with the historic significance of housing women students and hosting their literary societies in the nineteenth century.

MARY CHURCH TERRELL

Mary Church Terrell was a wife, mother, educator, author, and activist in the civil rights and women's rights movements. Her interest in women's rights began at Oberlin, but I would venture to say that her interest in human rights as a whole began after a family friend from Memphis was lynched. I re-created this story in my novel because it was pivotal to her thought process on lynching and civil rights. However, for historical accuracy, I must state that this incident did not occur while she was enrolled at Oberlin. She was already married and suffered a miscarriage around the same time as the lynching.

I use the name Charles for the family friend. His real name was Thomas Moss. Ida B. Wells began her anti-lynching campaign due to his death and Mary joined her in this endeavor. The actual lynching occurred in 1892. Since Mary's brother was also named Thomas, I decided to give her friend a different name.

Terrell believed that Black Americans could uplift the race through education, hard work, and active participation in the community. I tried to display these beliefs within this novel. I pray you felt it, even as the fight for equality has had to rear its head again during our lifetime. I wanted to display these women of excellence in such a way that you would see their struggles but also their triumphs and their allies. This fight for equality is won as we all rise together.

Terrell was a member of many organizations during her lifetime. However, she was a founding member of the National Association of Colored Women's Club (NACWC) and the National Association for the Advancement of Colored People (NAACP). She served as president of the NACWC.

Though Black women were not allowed membership in the National American Woman Suffrage Association (NAWSA), Mary was one of the only Black women allowed to speak at their conventions on numerous occasions. When she spoke, she reminded them that Black women faced a double burden in this country: their gender and their race.

Mary and her lifelong friend Janet Swift worked together to integrate the American Association of University Women (AAUW). Mary also cofounded the College Alumnae Club (whose name later changed to National Association of University Women). This organization was created for college-educated Black women.

Terrell wrote the book *A Colored Woman in a White World* in 1940 along with numerous papers and essays. She also wrote under at least one pen name: Euphemia Kirk. Terrell could have led a life of leisure due to her father's wealth and her husband's standing as a judge, but she chose to get up every morning and fight for equality so you and I could one day hold the careers of our choosing and not be relegated to lowly positions that White supremacists consider Black jobs.

There are two scenes in the novel I'd like to address. In

the prologue Mary discovers that her family had been enslaved, and she resolves to show her White classmates that she is their equal. That scene was developed from her own words in records I discovered in the Oberlin archives. I would venture to say that she not only accomplished her vow but exceeded it by becoming valedictorian of her class. Mary took her education seriously.

This novel also includes a scene about the Danville Massacre. This was an actual event that occurred at a Danville, Virginia, market on November 3, 1883, where four African Americans and one White man were killed. However, there is no evidence that Mary and Ida participated in enrolling Black men for the vote before the massacre took place. Since this event occurred during the time they were in school and since Oberlin was known to be involved in events such as this, I decided to incorporate this event for historical context. It is my hope that as we read about this situation, we all will come to realize that hate is never the answer.

Mary was an honorary member of the Delta Sigma Theta Sorority. She served as an advisor and helped pull together the group's bylaws. As I show in the last chapter of this book, Mary's accomplishments were so well known and appreciated that when she died, her body lay in state at the National Association of Colored Women's Club (NACW) headquarters. Thousands of mourners paid their respects.

THE FIRE THAT DESTROYED THE CHURCHES' HOME IN MEMPHIS

The city of Memphis did indeed host a demonstration of fire equipment on the street where Robert Church's home was.

His home was burned down as an act of revenge by the mayor of Memphis. However, the incident occurred many years after Mary graduated from Oberlin. When I discovered this fact in my research, I decided to move up the timeline to allow readers to see for themselves the evils that hatred causes.

ANNA JULIA COOPER

Education helped Anna Julia Cooper beat the odds. She was enslaved until she was about six years old. Her family didn't have money, yet she was able to attend school and later college at Oberlin after the death of her husband.

Anna was an educator, author, and civil rights and women's rights activist. Her book *A Voice from the South* is what many people point to when associating Anna with Black feminism. In her lifetime she gave many speeches and her words appear in the U.S. Passport booklet: "The cause of freedom is not the cause of a race or a sect, a party or a class—it is the cause of humankind, the very birthright of humanity." I included those words at the end of chapter 24 of this novel to honor her.

For the sake of the book's flow, I show Anna arriving at the school a few weeks after Mary has begun her freshman year at college. However, Anna actually arrived at Oberlin at the beginning of Mary's sophomore year. Due to Anna's stellar work history and the classes she had already mastered, the administration at Oberlin bumped her up to a sophomore, and that is the reason Anna was able to graduate at the same time as Mary and Ida, even though she arrived after them. I needed to bring the two women together sooner rather than later, so my easiest solution was to have them both begin as freshmen. At the same time, I didn't want to take away from

Anna this great accomplishment of being able to skip an entire grade level, so I'm providing this information to you here. Hopefully this adjustment didn't cause any confusion for you.

Anna Julia Cooper excelled in her career, becoming a teacher and then the principal of M Street Preparatory School in Washington, D.C. Later she also became president of Frelinghuysen University.

The fact that Anna went back to school later in life for her PhD inspired me to register at Queen University in Charlotte, North Carolina, for their low-residency MFA program. After researching Anna Cooper, I realized that age is just a number, and as long as we have dreams left to conquer, we should keep moving toward them. So thanks to Anna, I'm headed back to school in 2026.

In 1900 Anna made her first trip to Europe to participate in the First Pan-African Conference in London. After that, she visited Scotland and England. She went to Paris for the World Exposition. Anna also went to Oberammergau, Germany, to see the Passion Play, then on to Italy, visiting Rome, Naples, Venice, Pompeii, Mount Vesuvius, and Florence. Her travels were so extensive and impressive for a formerly enslaved woman with no husband or family money that I had to bring a bit of them into the story.

No, Anna did not travel to London and Paris during her time as a student at Oberlin, but the fact that she made not only those voyages but so many others was something I needed to highlight, so my bit of fiction is that I moved up the timeline. I wanted the reader to see her in other lands and know that she'd experienced these wonderful adventures. And now you know that her travels were much more extensive.

Anna was a member of the National Association of Colored Women's Club. She was also an Alpha Kappa Alpha Sorority member.

Schools have been named after this remarkable woman. There is also an Anna Julia Cooper Professor of Women's Studies at Spelman College.

Anna Julia Cooper lived to be 105 years old. At that point she had lived a great deal of her life in Washington, D.C. However, North Carolina did not forget its daughter. Her memorial was held in a chapel on the campus of St. Augustine's College in Raleigh, North Carolina, where she taught her first lesson. She was buried next to her husband at the City Cemetery of Raleigh.

FREDERICK DOUGLASS AND HIS ESSAY "THE COLOR LINE"

I was delighted to write about Frederick Douglass and to add bits of his essay to this novel. The fact of the matter is, the research indicates that Mary met Frederick Douglass at President Garfield's inauguration. I would have included the scene of Mary at the inauguration even if she hadn't met Frederick Douglass there, because that was some real Black girl magic. I mean, how many of us have ever been invited to an event such as that?

But imagine my surprise while reading through issue after issue of the 1879–1884 *Oberlin Review* when I came across anonymous articles asking if there was a color line at Oberlin. These issues were printed in *The Oberlin Review* after the 1881 essay "The Color Line" by Frederick Douglass was printed in *The North American Review*.

Well, my writer's mind started thinking. What if the anonymous writer was Mary (she was writing for *The Oberlin Review* at the time those articles on the color line appeared)? And what if after reading Frederick Douglass's essay the summer of 1881, she became inspired to challenge her school? Now, there is no proof that Mary Church Terrell did anything other than write her society articles while at Oberlin. But she was the one person at Oberlin during those days who had access to Frederick Douglass (through her father), so I created the scenario where Mary was the writer of those articles. But whether she wrote them or another Black student did, the fact remains that the students didn't remain quiet about the treatment they received at the school. They spoke out, and I believe it was Frederick Douglass's essay "The Color Line" that gave them the strength to do so. This is the reason I included bits of his essay on the part 1, 2, 3, and 4 pages of the book. I hope it helps bring understanding not only to what Black people went through in the nineteenth century, but also to what we still deal with today.

REFERENCES

Cooper, Anna Julia. *A Voice from the South.* Xenia, OH: Aldine Printing House, 1892.

Douglass, Frederick. "The Color Line." *North American Review* (1881).

Howard University Archives Department. Howard University, Washington, DC.

Oberlin College Archives Department. Oberlin College, Oberlin, OH.

The Oberlin Review. Oberlin, OH, 1879–1884.

Parker, Alison M. *Unceasing Militant: The Life of Mary Church Terrell.* Chapel Hill: University of North Carolina Press, 2020.

The Portable Anna Julia Cooper. Edited by Shirley Moody-Turner. New York: Penguin Classics, 2017.

Terrell, Mary Church. *A Colored Woman in a White World.* Washington, DC: Ransdell, 1940.

WEBSITES

BlackPast. "Hunt, Ida Alexander Gibbs (1862–1957)." Accessed February 2, 2026. https://blackpast.org/african-american-history/hunt-ida-alexander-gibbs-1862-1957/

Howard University Digital Commons. "Anna Julia Cooper." Accessed February 2, 2026. https://dh.howard.edu/do/search/?q=Anna%20Julia%20Cooper&start=0&context=4339039&facet=

National Museum of African American History and Culture. "Anna Julia Cooper: Educator, Writer, and Intellectual." Accessed February 2, 2026. https://nmaahc.si.edu/explore/stories/anna-julia-cooper-educator-writer-and-intellectual

National Women's History Museum. "Mary Church Terrell." Accessed February 2, 2026. https://www.womenshistory.org/education-resources/biographies/mary-church-terrell

Oberlin College. "A Stroll Through Oberlin History." Accessed February 2, 2026. https://www.oberlin.edu/blogs/stroll-through-oberlin-history

Oberlin College. "Rust Methodist Episcopal Church." Accessed February 2, 2026. https://www2.oberlin.edu/external/EOG/AfAmChurches/Rust.htm

Oberlin College Library. *Mary Church Terrell Project*. Accessed February 2, 2026. https://terrell.oberlincollegelibrary.org/scalar/mct/index

Oberlin Heritage Center. "The Oberlin–Wellington Rescue of 1858." Accessed February 2, 2026. https://oberlinheritagecenter.org/the-oberlin-wellington-rescue-1858/

The Oberlin Review. "Oberlin Monuments Honor Abolitionist Movement, African American Legacy." Accessed February 2, 2026. https://oberlinreview.org/30203/arts/oberlin-monuments-honor-abolitionist-movement-african-american-legacy/

Smithsonian Institution. "Anna Julia Cooper Collection." Accessed February 2, 2026. https://cdm15963.contentdm.oclc.org/digital/collection/p15963coll9/id/30465/rec/134

YouTube. "Anna Julia Cooper." Video. Accessed February 2, 2026. https://www.youtube.com/watch?v=zv3rZjOofP0

ACKNOWLEDGMENTS

I'm always amazed when I come to the end of a book and am at the point where I need to acknowledge the people who helped bring this book to life. I'm amazed because with each book I begin, I think, *How am I ever going to finish this?* What you are able to read in a few days, sometimes hours, I labor over for more than a year, until one day I look at the finished product and finally breathe a sigh of relief as it is shaped into what it was meant to be all along.

And now I get to thank the people who helped make *The Ladies Hall* possible. First and forevermore, I must thank God for giving me this gift of writing and the desire to keep putting words on the page.

I am so thankful for my agent, Emily Sylvan Kim, and my editor at HarperCollins / Thomas Nelson, Laura Wheeler, who both saw something in this book that I wanted to write and helped me make it everything it is today. I also need to thank all the amazing people at my publishing house from editing to marketing, publicity, and sales. People like Nekasha, Margaret, Taylor, Colleen, and LaTasha. You all make my job so much easier by being advocates for my books, and I appreciate it.

This year I worked with a new line editor, Julee Schwarzburg. Oh my goodness, you are amazing. Thank you so much for having such an eagle eye.

This story would not have come to life without all of the information I received from the Oberlin College archives. Ken Grossi, the college archivist, was so patient with me, taking time to answer question after question and pointing me in the right direction. There are impactful scenes in this book that never would have occurred without all of the information Oberlin College preserved for someone like me, who would come sniffing around almost a hundred and fifty years later. Thank you!

I am also thankful that each copy of *The Oberlin Review* has been preserved hundreds of years later. I will admit that I wasn't so thankful while spending a month poring over each issue, looking for that nugget to include in the book. My time was not wasted. *The Oberlin Review* played a big part in my understanding of what equality meant to the students.

I would also like to thank Denise K. Williams, the current president of the National Association of Colored Women's Clubs. Mary Church Terrell was one of the founders of this organization and served as president for many years. I reached out to Denise to inform her about *The Ladies Hall*, and she was just as excited as I am. We will be partnering on a few events to continue to lift as we climb. We're doing it, Mary—your motto lives on, even after all these years.

I have to thank my family and friends who are always cheering for me. My husband, David Pierce, has a vision of my books being turned into movies, and nothing is going to stop him from believing that we will see the manifestation of that dream. I am so blessed to have someone who believes in my books like that.

Finally, I always have to thank my readers. You all are the true blessing in my life. Without your support I could not continue to do what I love so much. I pray you enjoy *The Ladies Hall*. I wrote it for *you*!

DISCUSSION QUESTIONS

1. What were your overall impressions of *The Ladies Hall*? Did anything surprise you about the experiences of Black women at Oberlin during the 1880s?
2. Before reading the book, what did you know about Mary Church Terrell, Anna Julia Cooper, or Ida Gibbs Hunt? How did the novel deepen or change your understanding of them?
3. What role does friendship and community among the women in Ladies Hall play in helping them survive the challenges they face?
4. Which scene or moment in the book impacted you the most and why?
5. Oberlin had a reputation for being progressive. How does the story reveal the limits of that progressivism?
6. What forms of discrimination did Mary, Anna, and Ida face, and which do you think were the most damaging?

7. How does the novel show the importance of education as a tool for empowerment and social change?
8. How did Mary Church Terrell's perspective evolve—from expecting powerful men like her father or President Garfield to change things to realizing she must fight for equality herself?
9. What parallels do you see between the discrimination Mary and Anna faced in the nineteenth century and issues that exist today?
10. What lessons about perseverance, courage, and leadership can modern readers take from this story?
11. Why do you think some white students at Oberlin began resisting the idea of Black students being educated as their equals? What does this reveal about the tensions of the time?
12. How might the women's experiences at Oberlin have shaped their later work as educators, activists, and leaders?

ABOUT THE AUTHOR

Photo by Sean Evans Photography

Vanessa Miller is a celebrated *USA TODAY* bestselling and award-winning author whose prolific body of work spans over fifty titles that explore deep themes of redemption, resilience, and faith—often spotlighting strong Black women during pivotal moments of history.

Vanessa also wears the hats of playwright, motivational speaker, and retreat host—channeling her storytelling gift across multiple creative platforms. She lives in North Carolina with her husband and family.

Connect with her online at vanessamiller.com
Facebook: @vanessamiller01
Instagram: @authorvanessamiller
X: @vanessamiller01

FOR MORE FROM VANESSA MILLER, DON'T MISS THE *USA TODAY* BESTSELLER *THE FILLING STATION*

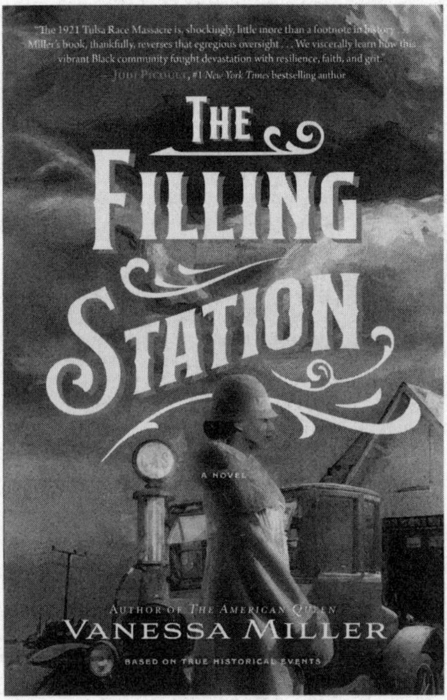

"The 1921 Tulsa Race Massacre is, shockingly, little more than a footnote in history . . . Miller's book, thankfully, reverses that egregious oversight . . . We viscerally learn how this vibrant Black community fought devastation with resilience, faith, and grit."

—Jodi Picoult, #1 *New York Times* bestselling author

AVAILABLE IN PRINT, E-BOOK, AND AUDIO

LOOKING FOR MORE GREAT READS? LOOK NO FURTHER!

THOMAS NELSON

Since 1798

Visit us online to learn more:
thomasnelsonfiction.com

Or scan the below code and sign up to receive email updates on new releases, giveaways, book deals, and more:

TikTok

@thomasnelsonfiction

From the Publisher

GREAT BOOKS

ARE EVEN BETTER WHEN THEY'RE SHARED!

Help other readers find this one

- Post a review at your favorite online bookseller
- Post a picture on a social media account and share why you enjoyed it
- Send a note to a friend who would also love it—or better yet, give them a copy

Thanks for reading!